MEGHAN MARCH

Copyright © 2016 by Meghan March LLC

ISBN:: 978-1-943796-81-6

All rights reserved.

Editor: Pam Berehulke, Bulletproof Editing
www.bulletproofediting.com

Cover design: @ Emma Hart
www.emmahart.org

Photo: © anetta
www.shutterstock.com

Interior Design: Stacey Blake, Champagne Formats
www.champagneformats.com

No part of this book may be reproduced or transmitted in any form or by any means, electronic or mechanical, including photocopying, recording, or by any information storage and retrieval system without the written permission of the author, except for the use of brief quotations in a review.

This book is a work of fiction. Names, characters, places, and incidents are either products of the author's imagination or are used fictitiously. Any resemblance to actual persons, living or dead, events, or locales is entirely coincidental. The author acknowledges the trademarked status and trademark owners of various products referenced in this work of fiction, which have been used without permission. The publication/use of these trademarks is not authorized, associated with, or sponsored by the trademark owners.

Visit my website at www.meghanmarch.com.

About this Book

He's so arrogant.

She's so self-righteous.

I can't stand him.

I want her.

He's a distraction I don't need.

She'll say yes eventually because I'm not giving up.

Justine Porter is stuck between a rock and a stripper pole. She lost her law school scholarship, which means she has two choices to keep her life on track: strip for her tuition or tutor the most distractingly sexy guy in her class—the one she's been turning down for two years straight. It should be an easy choice, but tutoring Ryker Grant could derail her plans to graduate with honors faster than two-for-one night at the Déjà Vu. Then again, topless has never really been her color.

She could take the easy road, just this once . . . but the deal has enough loopholes to trip anyone up.

Who knew they taught bad judgment in law school?

Chapter 1

Justine

"Becca saw Ryker at the gym last night and he was wearing these shorts, and let's just say she said his dick print looked massive. Cock-a-licious, to quote her properly."

I drop my overstuffed chicken burrito on the metal pie plate, and the tortilla splits down the side. *Perfect*. When I snap my attention to my best friend, Merica's face is the picture of innocence. The devil dancing in her gray eyes is the only thing that gives away her dirty thoughts.

"Really? Are you trying to kill my appetite on purpose?" Because I'm not interested in anything that has to do with Ryker Grant, or his penis. *No, really, I'm not.*

Merica's blond brows wing up toward her hairline in a *what could you possibly mean* expression. She gestures to me with her fork. "Look, if a sexy-as-hell guy had been hitting on me for two years, I'd be pretty damn interested now that I have some inside info about what he's packing."

The last thing I want to hear about is one of our mutual friends staring at the crotch area of Ryker Grant's shorts at the gym, trying to gauge the size of his package by the imprint it leaves. *Who made up the term* dick print *anyway?*

"Not. Interested." I enunciate each word clearly as I stare down at my burrito.

I'm in law school to study, kick ass, and graduate with honors. For ten years, I've been pushing toward this goal. Which means I don't have time for distractions, and Ryker Grant would be the biggest distraction of all. While he might be tall, sexy, and mouth-wateringly gorgeous, he's also got a lock on the crown for the kingdom of Entitled Douche Bag.

I reach down to retrieve my busted burrito, but pause before wrapping my fingers around it. Before today, I would have said nothing could put me off the chicken, rice, beans, pico, and avocado goodness before me, but I would have been wrong. Now I can't look at it without phallic thoughts running through my head.

Hearing about Ryker Grant's dick print has officially thrown me off my game. On top of being a Grade-A jerk, he's stupid hot. As in, the kind of hot that makes smart girls stupid. Which is why I've been turning him down since our first week of law school.

No time for distractions.

It's not like Ryker has been crying into his beer over my rejections. He's been seen with plenty of girls in our law school class in the early hours of the morning at the bars along Red River Avenue. I absolutely and unequivocally refuse to admit that I might have watched him out of the corner of my eye on the rare occasions I let Merica drag me out for a night.

"I'm just saying that even I'd consider taking a ride on that stallion if I didn't already have my own stud. Come on,

Jus. It might be good for you to de-stress a little." She leans closer, pressing both elbows on the metal table between us. "Plus, you've got to confirm the dick-print rumors for womankind."

Wanting to do anything I can to stop this conversation before I get some kind of terrible idea in my head, I wrap my hands around the burrito and lift it to my lips. Or at least, I try. Stalling out midair, all I can picture is this supposedly massive dick Ryker is packing in his shorts heading for my mouth.

And . . . nope. *Operation: Stuff My Face to End Conversation* fails. I can't be thinking thoughts like that. I've got finals coming up, and then it's off to my legal aid job for the summer to make an actual difference in people's lives.

That's what matters—making a difference. That's why I'm studying more hours each week than most people put in at a full-time job. *I'm not here to fantasize about the hottest guy I've ever met.*

I drop the burrito on my plate again and consider it a total loss. I can't be wrapping my lips around anything that makes me think of Ryker Grant's penis. Bad. Plan.

I reach for a brown paper napkin to wipe my hands, determined to get my mind back on track. Crumpling the napkin into a ball, I meet my friend's laughing gaze.

"Stop. Seriously. You know I'm not going there. Never gonna happen."

"But you want to. You can deny it all you want, but we both know the struggle to not think about his equipment is real."

I toss the balled-up napkin at her head, and Merica bats it away one-handed as she shovels more of her burrito bowl into her mouth. You'd never know from her napkin-defense skills that she's one of the most uncoordinated people I've ever met.

First day of law school orientation as we were filing into the amphitheater-style auditorium, she tripped going *up* the stairs. Somehow her flailing hands reached me first and we both crashed to the floor in front of three hundred people. My cheeks burned with embarrassment, but Merica popped right back up and took a bow. Her positivity is infectious, and we've been best friends ever since.

She drops her fork and pushes the bowl away. "Come on, you know you want to. He can be your reward for kicking ass on finals!"

I rub a hand across my face. "My reward for kicking ass on finals will be getting the grades I need to keep my scholarship. That's all that matters right now—not Ryker's supposedly massive dick."

My scholarship is riding on my GPA staying above a 3.75, and without it, I won't be able to finish school. The sale of Gramps's small house left me enough to cover most of my living expenses and buy books. That's what he told me to do with it, because this was his dream for me too. He wanted me to make a difference, just like the legal aid lawyer who helped him fight for custody of me when my deadbeat parents tried to suck me deeper into their cons. So here I am, and I'm going to make this dream come true for both of us.

"You know my only other choice is to ask Kristy Horner about Ryker, and I'm not doing it. She takes up two parking spots in the garage with her BMW, even when she sees you coming and knows there are no other spots left. Do you know how many times I've been late to class because she's a bitch?"

"Kristy being a bitch isn't a new development, but you're still not getting that info from me. Sorry, babe. You're going to have to live with the mystery."

Merica leans back in her chair, releasing an exasperated sigh. "You're impossible. I've been getting the same dick for two years, and I need to live vicariously through my friends to get the variety I'm missing. You need to take one for the team here, hottie."

I choke on the sip of water I'm taking and lower the cup to the table quickly enough to have it sloshing over the sides.

"Really? Take one for the team? Pun much?"

Merica's smile is quick and bright. "You know you want it. How long has it been anyway? I mean, your va-jay-jay is probably waving a distress flag because it thinks you've forgotten about it."

She's not wrong, but I'm also not going there.

"Ryker and me? Never going to happen."

"Famous last words." Merica stands and tosses me a cheesy wink.

Chapter 2

Justine

Two weeks later

"Can I get you another?" The bartender at Ziggy's leans forward as I take up space on a bar stool, playing with my straw and my empty drink.

I scan the room for Merica, wondering how she can possibly take seven years to go to the bathroom, before I jerk my gaze back to his face. His shoulders stretch his tight black T-shirt as he stares at me.

I've been watching him for the last five minutes as he's been reaching, leaning, pouring, and doing other bartender-y things. I know, there are actual verbs for those things, but right now I'm running on a strong mixture of vanilla vodka and root beer, and I used up all my actual smart words on my finals. Which are finally done. *Thank God.*

And now the bartender is staring at me, waiting for an answer.

Crap. I have to respond. Get with it, Justine. Do I really need another drink? What would it hurt? I'm celebrating, after all. Second year of law school, in the books.

"Sure. One more. That'd be good." My words don't sound slurred, thankfully. *Winning.*

"Root beer and vanilla vodka, right?"

He remembers my drink?

I nod, ignoring the fact that I probably look like a bobblehead. "That's right. Thanks."

"I haven't seen you around much," he says as he turns to grab the liquor and then reaches for the soda gun. "You here by yourself or with friends?"

"Friends." I clear my throat as if to dislodge the words. "We're celebrating our last finals being over."

I scan the packed barroom again for Merica, but don't see her blond head through the crowd of students. I'm a failure when it comes to flirting and making small talk, and I can always count on her to rescue me from my own awkwardness.

The bartender slides the glass across the bar on a cocktail napkin. "This one's on me then. Congratulations on knocking out your exams."

Wait, what?

Fumbling for the cash I shoved into my pocket, I fish out a few bills. "You really don't need to do that."

He holds up a hand. "I insist. You deserve it." His lips curve up into the kind of smile that would ensure he wouldn't have to leave the bar alone any night of the week. Messy blond hair falls over his forehead and curls around his ears.

I open my mouth to thank him for the gesture when an arm slides around my shoulder and a bill is slapped down on the bar in front of me.

"I got this one. It's a rare day when my girl goes anywhere but the library or class. You sure you don't want something more festive, baby? This deserves its own celebration."

Heat burns across my cheeks as the bartender narrows his eyes on Ryker's possessive touch. The bartender lifts his chin at Ryker.

"Grant. Where's your flavor of the week?"

I want to thank the bartender for not automatically assuming I'm Ryker Grant's flavor of the week, but Ryker pulls me closer into his side. Now it's not just my cheeks heating, but every point of contact between us. *Bad Justine. This is why I avoid him. Stupid hot*, I remind myself.

"You should watch how you talk about women, Caruthers. They don't like to be called flavor of the week."

I'm surprised Ryker knows the bartender, but then again, I'm sure he spends way more time here than I do.

"They probably prefer to be treated better than you treat them," Caruthers says, pushing Ryker's money back across the bar. "Her drink is on the house. I don't want your money."

As I duck out from under Ryker's arm, I block out how amazing he smells under those layers of entitlement. *So freaking good.* It's just because I'm drunk. That's the only reason. I need to find Merica and get out of here before I do something stupid.

I grab my drink and step away from the danger zone surrounding Ryker.

"I'll just get out of here so you guys can whip 'em out and measure them." Forcing myself not to drop my gaze to Ryker's crotch to gauge the truthfulness of the dick-print rumor for myself, I drop a ten on the bar. My pride won't let either of them buy me a drink.

"I need to get back to my friends," I toss out as I walk away, impressed at how steady I am on the heels Merica forced me to wear with my short black skirt and borrowed black low-cut top. Not my normal outfit choice at all, but how often do you get to celebrate finishing your second year of law school?

Cocky about how well I'm doing on my balance, I sip my drink—and catch a toe on the lip of the stairs. My entire body pitches forward and a vision of the drink flying everywhere as I land on my face flashes before my eyes. *At least Merica won't judge.*

Before even a drop spills over the side, an arm wraps around me and a hand plucks the drink from my grip.

"Are you in such a hurry to get away from me that you'd rather cause a scene?"

Ryker. His deep voice and scent of *all man* mixed with *off-limits for a good reason* identify him immediately. He maneuvers us over to an empty booth as my heart hammers, and I plop down onto the maroon vinyl cushion.

Wrapping both hands around the edge of the table, I suck in a breath. Obviously, I don't need any more to drink, but I unclench one hand to reach for my cocktail anyway and chug a few gulps to steady my nerves. It's not until I put the glass down that I notice the crumpled ten on the table next to it.

"You okay?"

My gaze darts up to his brilliantly blue eyes as he towers over me. "What is that for?"

"You shouldn't be buying your own drinks." He says it like this is some obvious piece of information of which I should be well aware.

"I'm not letting you buy them." Needing to extricate

myself from this situation, I scoot out to the edge of the booth and stand.

But Ryker doesn't step back like I expect him to, and my boobs press against his chest as soon as I'm vertical.

My nipples peak with interest at the contact. *Traitors.* I have to force myself not to lean into him. *He's solid. Hard. Man.* I freeze for a beat, hoping he'll step back, but he doesn't.

"Excuse me." My words are a hushed whisper. I need to step back. Move. Something. I have to stop touching him.

Ryker's gaze drops to my cleavage, and I can't breathe. Can't think. Can't do anything but stare at his lowered eyes and wonder if he's feeling what I'm feeling.

It doesn't matter. No distractions allowed.

Several agonizingly long seconds pass before his gaze travels up to meet mine.

"You're not going back to that bartender. Your money is no good with him. He wouldn't even let me pay for the drink. So quit worrying about it."

An odd sense of relief washes over me that Ryker didn't pay for my drink, and I sit back down, desperate to remove all points of contact between us before I do something stupid like press against him harder and let my hands roam.

Why have I gone so long without any physical contact? I will my nipples to stand down. *Bad nipples*. Without any padding in my bra, I'm putting on way too much of a show. *At least I'm not thinking about the dick print anymore.* Crap. I'm eye level with his crotch since he's still standing, so of course my gaze lands right on it.

Oh. Holy. Hell. I can see it. The outline against his jeans. The bulge. Does he not wear underwear? Is it getting *bigger*? Oh my God, is that because of me?

Ryker's chest lifts and lowers with a deep breath, and I snap my eyes up to his.

Mortification sweeps in as Ryker stares down at me, those icy blue eyes blazing with heat. He knows exactly what I was looking at.

"So, what's it going to take, Justine?"

I ignore the question and wrap my hand around my drink. Sucking down the last of it, I buy time to figure out how to get myself out of this situation. *This is why I avoid him.*

Once my glass holds nothing but ice, Ryker plucks it from my grip and sets it on the table.

"What's it going to take?" he asks again.

"Wh—what are you talking about?" My stutter is smoothed by the liquor I've consumed.

"You. What's it going to take for you to say yes to me? You're hell on my ego, but I don't give a shit about that. I want my shot. What's it going to take?"

Oh no. This isn't happening. I cobble together an excuse.

"I can't. I'm busy. I have to keep up my grades."

"School's out, babe. Try again."

I shake my head, which is already fuzzy from more alcohol than I've had in months.

"I'm leaving tomorrow. I've got a job up north for the summer at Legal Aid."

He studies me for a beat as if deciding whether I'm feeding him a line of bull. I must pass, because he nods. "When you come back, we're going out."

Persistence. Ryker has it in spades, and the combination of the alcohol and my body's traitorous reactions are wearing me down. But nothing can change the fact that I don't have time for the distraction. Not now, not next year.

"It's not a good idea. School is my only focus."

He lowers himself down on the bench beside me, and instinctively I slide over to put some space between us. I don't need more contact to melt away the last of my resistance.

"I need to go find my friend. She's probably waiting for me to leave."

"Give me five minutes, and I'll convince you."

That's exactly what I'm afraid of. The words float in my head as I scoot around the U-shaped booth to slide out the other side. With that determined look in his blue eyes and my guard down, there's no telling what he could talk me into in thirty seconds, let alone five minutes.

"I have to go." I keep my tone firm.

Ryker leans back in the booth and crosses both arms over his broad chest. "I think you're scared of me."

Pushing to my feet, I grab the edge of the table to steady myself on Merica's heels. "Excuse me?"

"You're scared. Afraid you might actually want what I want, and that's why you keep shooting me down."

A forced laugh escapes my lips, and something—probably the alcohol—flips my filter to the *off* position. "Are you serious? Come on, we both know that you just haven't given up yet because I'm the only girl who's ever said no to you." I gesture to the empty glass on the table. "I might be a few drinks in, but even I get you're all about the chase. If I said yes, you'd lose interest within days."

"Bullshit."

"Doesn't matter. The answer is still no." And with that I stride away, making an exit that doesn't include me falling on my face. *Win.*

I find Merica at a tall table near the door, and her face is even whiter than her normal Irish-American shade of pale.

"What's wrong? Did something happen?" Taking in the other similarly horrified expressions on the faces around the table, dread curls in my stomach.

Merica turns and grabs me, fingers locking tight around my forearm. "Chad and Chris left the bar and there was an accident. We don't know what happened, except that someone apparently hit them. Rachel just texted to tell me that Chad was in handcuffs and there was an ambulance."

Oh my God. No.

"Chad France? My Chad?" Panic rises in my chest, stealing my breath.

Chad and I have been friends since we were eleven and he taught me how to play marbles in the dirty alley behind Gramps's house. He lived with his grandma because his mom took off, and his dad died in prison for a crime Chad swears to this day he didn't commit. That's why he's here—to become a kick-ass criminal defense attorney.

Merica nods.

"Is he okay? Is he hurt? If Rachel saw him in handcuffs, then he couldn't have been in the ambulance, right?"

"Rachel said he was standing next to the cop car in cuffs. That's all."

She has to be wrong. Maybe Rachel got it wrong. "Did she see it happen? Is she sure it was them?"

"Rachel left here right after they did. Their apartment is on the way to her place. Apparently half of Red River Avenue is closed right now to clean up the accident."

"Oh my God." Handcuffs mean arrest. The most likely

reason being . . . drinking and driving.

We're all thinking the same thing; Merica just says it first. "Chad is fucked if he gets a DUI. He's already got an offer for after graduation with that hotshot defense firm he's been working at, but I bet they'd rescind that before he could say *not guilty*."

"Oh my God," I murmur again, squeezing my eyes shut. Working at the top defense firm in the state has been Chad's goal since before we even started school. *He's going to be devastated.*

Merica looks down at her phone again. "Rachel says they're reopening the road, but Chad's truck looks like it's totaled." She glances over to me. "Wasn't he supposed to help you move your stuff into storage tomorrow?"

"That's the least important thing anyone needs to worry about right now." As much as I'm SOL, I can't be upset that my moving assistance just went out the window because Chad's future at stake is a way bigger deal.

"Maybe Rachel got it wrong. Maybe it wasn't them? And what about Chris? No one has any word on him? This could all be a mix-up." I'm scrambling for some other alternative.

James, a guy in our Evidence class, comes up to the table and holds out his phone. "Did you hear about Chad and Chris? Check out this picture of his truck. Totally crushed. I heard some asshole ran a red light, tagged his bumper, so he spun out and hit a telephone pole, and the person didn't even stop. Unbelievable. That was a sweet ride after he lifted it."

Any hope of Rachel being a typical girl and thinking all pickup trucks look exactly the same disappears. It's definitely Chad's truck.

Sadness and anger shove aside the panic. *Why would he drive drunk? How could he take the chance?*

"I wonder who he's going to call for bail if they throw him in the drunk tank." The speculation comes from James.

"His girlfriend will bail him out." I offer up the information quietly. They've been together since high school, so I know she'll be there for him. But what about after? His job . . . his future . . .

"Why was he even driving?" Merica asks.

James shrugs. "He didn't want to leave his truck in the parking lot overnight. He only had maybe four or five beers. I've seen him drink way more and still act totally sober. That's some shit luck, though. If someone hadn't hit them, I bet they'd be home already."

Shit luck and bad judgment. *Chad, what were you thinking?*

"This sucks all around. Now his entire future could be fucked, and you've got no one to help you move." Merica looks from me to James. "What do you drive?"

"A Harley. Which you'd know if you ever let me take you out."

Merica rolls her eyes. "I have a boyfriend. Not happening. Also, your timing sucks."

Everything about this sucks, and I'm so freaking pissed at Chad. *Why would he take the chance?* We all have too much at stake to take chances like that.

James opens his mouth to reply to Merica, but a familiar voice rumbles from behind me.

"You need help moving?"

I force myself not to turn around when the heat from Ryker's body registers against my back.

I can practically feel the sudden change in the air now

that he is present. It's like the alpha wolf showed up to the discussion.

Always looking out for me, Merica turns her focus on Ryker. "Do you have a truck?"

Oh, hell no. I want to slap a hand over my best friend's mouth, but even that wouldn't pull back the question.

"My old man has a truck we use for deer camp. It's at my parents' house, and they only live a few miles from campus."

It's crazy to hear Ryker refer to his father as his *old man* because he's a state supreme court justice, not just some dad who works a regular nine-to-five. Also, he was my boss for the last four and a half months during my externship at the court.

To this day, I'm shocked Ryker didn't show up in his father's chambers while I was working. Either he didn't know or he considered that venue off-limits—I have no idea which.

Ryker's hand lands on my hip and squeezes before he turns me around to face him. All thoughts of his dad and Chad fall away when those blue eyes pierce me with a direct stare.

"Then you can totally help Justine move tomorrow." Merica's words are bubbly with triumph. No doubt she sees this as a case of life closing a door but opening a window.

"You need my help?" Ryker asks, never breaking eye contact with me.

"If she says no, she's lying," Merica offers unhelpfully.

I have to get out of this conversation before I cave and accept his help. I also need to escape to go call Katie, Chad's girlfriend, and get the scoop on what's happening and see if I can help.

I sidestep Ryker's hold and announce, "I have to pee."

Merica gives me a look that clearly says *are you kidding me?*

I ignore it. "I'll be right back."

Turning, I head for the back of the bar and the restrooms. As I walk, I mentally flip through my list of options for moving help. I come to a screeching halt because, oh wait, that's right, I don't have any other options. Chad was helping me out because he's a good guy and I've known him forever. *And now he's screwed.* My stomach twists with sympathy and disappointment and anger.

I try Katie's phone as I walk through the bar. It goes straight to voice mail four times before I give up. I hope to hell they figure this out. As much as I wish there was something I could do to help, I'm coming up empty.

As I stare into the bathroom mirror, the liquor hits me hard.

I'm drunk. And I need to get home.

Pushing open the bathroom door, I keep my eyes trained on my feet so as not to pitch forward on my now-treacherous heels.

"Oomph." I run into a wall.

Except it's not a wall, because it wraps two hands around my hips. My palms go to his chest, and my apology is halfway out before I realize it's Ryker and he's backing me into the corner of the dark hallway.

"What are you doing?" My back meets the wall and I'm trapped. Where's my fight-or-flight reaction? Where is the panic I should be feeling?

Instead, heat flares in my belly as he places one hand against the wall, next to my head.

"We weren't done with our conversation."

"Sure, we were." My words are steady but my heart pounds so hard in my chest, I'm sure he can feel it.

"You didn't answer my question. You need help, Justine?"

With everything that I am, I want to say no. But some shred of practicality rises up and fuels my words. "Yes."

"Then why are you running away?"

"I'm not running."

He leans closer to whisper in my ear. "Bullshit."

Pulling back just enough for me to see his face, I swallow. "Fine, you win. I wish I didn't need your help." *How's that for honesty?*

A smug smile slides over his face. "Why? You afraid of what it's gonna cost?"

Of course he would put a price on everything. "How much?"

"Not a dime. Just a kiss and a date."

The order throws me off. "I told you, I'm leaving tomorrow—"

"A date next semester. The kiss is payment up front. Right here, right now."

I wish I could say the heat burning low in my belly is anger, but I'd be a liar. As his lips lower toward mine, alarm bells clang in my head. I should stop him. This is by far the worst idea ever.

But my body stays frozen in place, and my lips part as he brushes his across them.

Oh. My. Hell. Ryker Grant is kissing me. My mouth molds to his and my body curls into him.

Oh shit. I'm kissing him back.

Then all the sounds in my head are drowned out by the sheer force of the sensations rocking my body. My nipples pucker hard against his chest, and my hands grip his shirt as though I'm trying not to lose my grip on reality.

His lips take and take, parting mine further until his tongue slips inside and I get my first taste of Ryker.

He tastes even better than he smells.

His hand slides down to cup my ass, and through the thin fabric of the short skirt, I can feel the pads of each finger make contact. He squeezes my cheeks and guides one of my legs to wrap around his hip.

My body sighs at the contact, and it takes me a moment to realize the bulge pressing into me is his erection. And it's just as huge as it looked, except now it's even harder. My clit wakes up from hibernation, and I can't help but rock my hips against him.

All rational thought leaves my brain as a zing of sensation shoots from my clit to my nipples and lights up the pleasure center in my brain. *Oh my God, that feels so good.*

He groans into my mouth, gripping my ass harder, pulling me into him. My panties are soaked, but I keep rocking.

Ryker buries his other hand in my hair, and the change in angle intensifies the friction on my clit.

I'm going to come. I freeze when the realization hits me. *Right here. In a bar. Rubbing against Ryker Grant.* I should feel humiliated, but I can't stop myself from sliding over the edge.

Curling my fingers into his shoulders, I tense as the orgasm bursts through me. My moan is muffled by his mouth because he doesn't slow his kiss. The bathroom door swings open just beyond us, and reality intrudes in the form of chattering drunk girls stumbling back toward the bar. I push off Ryker's chest, desperate to put space between us.

I can't believe that just happened. Thankful for the dark

corner, I know my face is burning red.

"Did you just—"

Slapping a hand over my face, I speak through it. "This never happened. None of it. Please, for the love of anything that's holy, don't ever mention this moment again."

His head drops to my shoulder, and his voice turns husky. "This was hot as fuck. I may not mention it, but there's no way in hell I won't be thinking about it."

"Please let me go."

Thankfully, Ryker steps back, and I hurry out of the corner, heading for the bar.

"Wait, I need your address."

I slow, not turning around as I rattle it off. I have to get out of here before I do something even worse.

"See you at nine," he calls as I hurry away.

Chapter 3

Justine

His mouth on mine.
His hand between my legs.
Wet. Hot. Aching.
I need more. I want more.
Blue eyes burn into mine. "I've been waiting so long to have you under me."

My alarm clock jerks me awake and the dream fades away, but my thudding heart remains, along with my wet panties.

I slap the top of the alarm on my side table to turn it off and yank the covers up over my head. I just had a sex dream. About Ryker Grant. Even the headache lurking in my temple doesn't stop me from wanting to finish the job Dream Ryker started.

I can't face him today. How am I ever going to look him in those icy blue eyes and not remember just how good it felt to be pressed against him?

Stop thinking about it.

I've needed to resist him for two years, and there's no

reason I can't make it through one more day. *No distractions.*

No matter how good that distraction can kiss.

Three hours later, it's clear that I'm not going to need any willpower to resist him, because Ryker is late.

An hour late.

As I sit on the stoop of my apartment building waiting for the promised pickup truck to arrive, all my concerns from earlier this morning are brushed away.

I knew it. I *knew* he was just in it for the chase, and the humiliation that I was right burns hot. Not only did Ryker get a taste of what he claimed to want so badly, but he decided that taste wasn't good enough for seconds.

Douche bag.

Why didn't I trust my instincts? I knew this would happen. So freaking typical. Apparently I should have held out until after he helped me, because now I'm not worth the trouble.

Hurt twines with the humiliation, unleashing slap after slap of regret. I knew better. Bad judgment. That's all it was.

I'm never drinking again—or kissing Ryker Grant.

And now I've got to figure out how to move almost everything I own to my storage unit. My boxes are packed and waiting to go, along with the hand-me-down furniture I bought for a few hundred dollars from a graduating student at the end of last year. The boxes I can haul in my car with a few trips, but the furniture will never fit.

"Why did I think he would actually show?" I ask the question to the empty curb in front of my building.

I'm not sure why I'm speaking out loud, because no one else is here to listen to my idiotic words. I tried both Katie and Chad this morning too. No answers from either of their phones.

What a shit day. I reach for the Pez dispenser beside me on the sidewalk and flip up Cinderella's head to tug out a lemon candy. Pez is my little obsession. Gramps started surprising me with them when I was six or seven, and my collection grew.

Now I pick them out according to my mood. Cinderella should probably remind me that dreams do come true, but today she's only reminding me that Ryker is no Prince Charming.

How could I have fallen for his lines after all this time?

Disgusted with myself, I stand and brush off my butt, ending this little pity party. It's certainly not going to help me move.

And you thought Ryker Grant would really lower himself to help?

The blow to my pride stings more than it should.

The apartment complex's lawn guy parks his beat-up Chevy pickup at the curb in front of my building before hopping out to lower the ramp and roll a lawn mower down it.

An idea strikes. Beggars can't be choosers, and I'm nothing if not resourceful.

"Hey! How would you like to make twenty bucks?" I call out as I head toward him.

Chapter 4

Ryker

I fucked up, and I know it. I'm not a day late and a dollar short. Nope, I'm six hours late and shit out of luck. I pound on the door, but the piece of notebook paper taped to it tells me everything I need to know.

THANKS FOR NOTHING.

She's not inside, and I'd bet the pickup truck out front that Justine Porter doesn't believe in second chances.

The words are written in all caps in black permanent marker. There's no mistaking the angry slashes of the letters. She was pissed when she wrote it, and now she's gone.

Why the hell didn't I get her number at the bar last night? Fucking moron. If I had, I could have called this morning to tell her I was running late.

There was no way in hell I could tell her why, but I guarantee it's not for the reason she thinks. Even if she were here, my vague excuses wouldn't matter to her.

I've never had to work to get a girl, but Justine has

turned me down at every opportunity. I won't lie—I like a challenge—but it's not just the chase I'm after with her. At least, not now.

There was a time when she only fascinated me because of her sexy-as-hell wild dark hair, rockin' body, and her continued shutdowns. But that lasted through orientation and maybe the first week of school—just until I figured out that she was probably the smartest girl I've ever met. It also didn't take long for me to realize that her brains were even sexier than the rest of the package.

And apparently she's too smart to wait for an asshole like me. I deserve it, and yet I'm still disappointed. I shove the Yoda Pez dispenser package back in my pocket. She might think I don't notice anything but her tits and ass, but she's wrong.

I turn away from the apartment and head back to the truck. I've got three and a half months to come up with a new game plan. There's no way in hell I'm giving up on her this easily.

Chapter 5

Justine

Three and a half months later

One more year. One more year and I'll have the diploma I've been working toward for a decade. I just wish Gramps could be here to watch me walk across that stage. He'll be there in spirit, though—I know it.

The summer went by ridiculously fast, but I learned more working at Legal Aid than I did in all the time I've spent in class. I also worked my ass off as a server at the local pub, saving up to help cover my expenses this year, and managed to have a little fun.

Being back on campus just makes me realize how badly I want to be finished with school so I can get back to the real world and start making a difference. I can't save people from eviction sitting in a classroom. I can't help fight for custody of someone's kid while I'm studying in my apartment. So basically, I'm here keeping my grades up while I mark time until graduation.

But I won't take it for granted, because at least I get the

privilege to finish school. Chad not only lost his standing offer at the criminal defense firm, but the school revoked his scholarship. After a month of me texting and calling with no answer, and scouring the Internet for news, he finally e-mailed me to let me know he'd officially dropped out.

Why even bother to finish and rack up the debt when I know I won't be able to get a job to pay it off? Katie was offered a job at a good physical therapy clinic in Arizona, so I'm going with her. Good luck, kid. Go kick law school's ass for both of us.

All my replies after this message went unanswered.

My phone dings with a text from Merica, dragging me out of the depressing thoughts.

MERICA: *Get your ass to the board room. Scholarship meeting starts in 20.*

I'm late getting back in the swing of things because I wanted to work for as long as possible before coming back to campus. Not only because I needed to save the money, but because I felt like I had a purpose. Unfortunately, the Legal Aid office couldn't support another full-time lawyer due to budget cuts, which puts me back to square one in the job hunt.

Hefting my backpack, I head for my car, catching a glimpse of myself in the storefront window. The hour a day I carved out at the gym made a difference. My ass has never looked better, and there's no way Ryker Grant is getting another shot at it.

Nope. Stop. Not thinking about him because he doesn't merit the brain space. Especially because embarrassment still creeps into my veins when I remember that night and how he left me waiting on the curb the next morning. *Asshole.*

I sneak through yellow lights and dodge students on bikes to get to the school on time. Last year's scholarship meeting was a stern lecture about how we had to keep our GPAs at a certain level depending on which scholarship we received.

The room is already packed when I manage to squeeze in the door, but Merica waves from an end seat. Her giant purse takes up the chair next to her, and I'm sure her *don't you even think about asking if you can sit there* look kept plenty of people from trying to take it. I smile and squeeze by a few of the students leaning against the walls.

The dean takes the lectern moments after I sit. The entire board of trustees flanks him on either side—including my former boss and the father of *he who shall not take up any space in my head*. Justice Grant meets my eyes for the briefest moment but doesn't smile before looking away.

What is that about? Justice Grant is one of the nicest people I've ever met—always ready with an easy smile and a kind word. Uneasiness twists my stomach. Does he know what happened between his son and me? The judge was an amazing boss and I thought we parted on great terms, so I don't have any other explanation for his odd behavior.

Actually, the presence of the board of trustees at this meeting is completely different from last year. But the beginning of the dean's speech is exactly the same—a boring rendition of the long proud history of this law school as one of the finest legal academic institutions in the country, and remarks about how grateful he has been to be at the helm through its rise through the ranks. That's where the similarities end.

"And despite our continued rise in the world of academia, we're facing an altogether too common problem shared by many institutions. We are not immune to the downturn in the economy and the financial hardships that have plagued so many schools. This is probably the most disheartening speech I've ever had to deliver during my tenure, but I don't believe in sugarcoating the facts."

He reaches for a glass of water and makes eye contact with Justice Grant. Grant nods in return as if giving the dean a push to deliver the rest of his speech.

What the hell is going on? Because something is definitely wrong.

The dean replaces his water glass on the table next to Grant and stares out into the audience of students and faculty with an apologetic expression.

"What the hell is he dragging his feet for?" Merica mumbles under her breath.

"We faced a difficult choice this summer, and after reviewing all of our options, it has been determined that the merit scholarship program will be suspended indefinitely and immediately."

A collective gasp sweeps through the room, followed by the rising murmur of voices. I overhear dozens of *what in the fuck*s and *no fucking way*s while my stomach drops to my feet. Merica slaps a hand over her mouth to cover her sharp inhale.

I blink repeatedly as if trying to wake myself up from a bad dream. Because this has to be a dream. A really awful, fucking horrible dream. What the dean is saying *can't hap-*

pen. Desperate, I pinch my arm to wake myself up, but all I feel is the sting of my nails digging into my skin.

This isn't a dream. Holy shit. And that's why Justice Grant wasn't smiling. He knew what the dean was going to say. And what's more, he knows I'm here on a full ride.

Merica grabs my arm with her free hand and squeezes.

"We understand the hardship placed on many, but when the choice came down to keeping the law school open for all students and a small fraction losing their merit scholarships, the board of trustees has unanimously voted in favor of the financial health of this institution and the best interest of the greater good. All students with scholarships will receive appointments with the financial aid office to set up alternative financing, if it is required, and if no financial aid is received, you'll be set up on a monthly payment plan for your tuition, which will hopefully make it less burdensome."

"You can't do that!" The man beside me jumps to his feet, and I think every head in the room nods along with his statement. "We'll sue. You've made us promises that we've relied on. You can't do this!"

And this is what happens when you deliver bad news to a room full of law students. The real question: is he right? Can we file a class action against the school to force them to reinstate the scholarships for everyone who has already been awarded them?

The arguments are working through my head, but the dean's next words kill the blooming hope.

"Unfortunately, there is no such recourse available to you. The school has always maintained that it is able to cancel the program at any time and makes no promises. In addition, there are several other legal theories that would prevent the school from being compelled to continue to provide funding, especially for a program that would bankrupt it. We've reviewed the termination of this program with the brightest legal minds in the country, and they all agree. You won't find a class action attorney to take the case because it's going to be a loser."

More shouted comments come from around the room aimed at the dean, and none of them are complimentary. He holds his hand out.

"Please refrain from shouting; it will not change the opinion of the board of trustees, who retains the ultimate say over this matter. Now, if you'll stay seated, we'll have someone come around with the schedule for the financial aid department, and get everyone who needs an appointment in as soon as possible."

Merica's hand is still wrapped around my arm, and my gut twists into knot after knot. *Did the board of trustees decide unanimously? Did Justice Grant agree with this?* It doesn't jibe with the man I thought he was.

The dean looks ill as he swallows the remainder of his water and steps away from the lectern. The man just handed down a judgment that's going to spell the end of more than one legal career before it starts.

Including mine. All the appointments with financial aid in the world won't help me secure a conventional student loan. Why? Because I'm the daughter of two con artists who used my social security number for dozens of loans before I turned eighteen. My credit was trashed before I even had a chance to use it myself. My only way through school has been scholarships, and I've worked my ass off to get them.

How can this happen?

My eyes burn with the threat of tears, but there's no way I'm going to cry in public.

"I need to make an appointment with financial aid before I go beg my stepdad for a loan, just so I have a backup plan. And then after that, we're getting shitfaced." Merica's tone sounds a lot more like she's telling me someone was murdered.

Just our dreams. Hopes. Future plans.

Without an extra sixty grand sitting around to cover my tuition, I'm screwed. Two years of my life, wasted. Any loan I could get would have credit-card-level interest rates, and with my ambition to get a job at Legal Aid . . . there's no way I could afford to live and pay a fraction of the monthly payment.

From behind me comes a hushed conversation. "My old roommate stripped her way through all three years of school. She graduated with no debt."

I peek surreptitiously over my shoulder to see a pretty blonde I remember from classes first year. She wasn't a standout student, just average. She's whispering to a brunette seated beside her.

"At the Vu?"

The blonde nods. "It's better than going into debt for this. I've already got half the tuition my scholarship wasn't going to cover. How bad can it really be? Wearing a wig and a ton of makeup with a stage name, who would ever know? I've still got my job at the library to put on my résumé."

As much as I hate to admit it, what she's saying makes a ton of sense.

The brunette's features take on a determined cast. "Let's go talk to her. Maybe she can get us in?"

When they stand and leave the room without waiting

for the financial aid representative, I'm actually disappointed I can't eavesdrop on the rest of their conversation.

The financial aid rep stops next to Merica with her schedule.

"So, how long do we have to make the first payment without a student loan?" Merica asks.

"Thirty days. Each payment will be due thirty days thereafter for the remainder of the year. The final payment must be made at least seven days prior to graduation in order to walk and receive a diploma."

I do the math in my head and cover my mouth when I choke on a cough at the size of the payments.

"Sign me up for the appointment. I'll cancel if I don't need it."

The rep nods and pencils it into the schedule. When Merica is finished putting the appointment time in her phone, she turns to me. "Ready?"

I'm still not up for forming actual words, so I nod.

I don't have a rich stepdad. Or a pile of cash. Or decent credit. Or a fairy godmother.

As we follow the irate crowd out of the room, Justice Grant lifts a hand toward me. I wish I'd been looking the other direction, because the last thing I want to do is talk to him right now. But I also can't pretend I didn't see him when we just made eye contact.

"Can you give me a second? I'll meet you outside and we can figure out where we're going."

Merica hugs her giant purse closer to her side. "Okay, but hurry. I need tequila, stat. I need to be drunk before I call the stepfather."

"I'll be quick; I promise."

I veer toward Justice Grant and stop a few feet away

from him.

"I'm so sorry that was dropped on you without warning. Your scholarship was a full ride, wasn't it?"

"Yes, sir. It was."

"Have you made an appointment with financial aid?"

I open my mouth to lie because he doesn't need to know the details of my dismal financial circumstances, but the words are caught in my throat and the truth comes out instead.

"I can't get a loan through financial aid. They won't even consider me. My parents screwed up my credit before I turned eighteen, and it hasn't recovered. I have to figure something else out."

"I'm sure if you have someone to cosign for you . . ." He trails off when I shake my head.

"I don't. It's just me. My grandfather passed away at the end of first year. My parents . . . I don't even know where they are, but I guarantee their credit is worse than mine."

His eyebrows arch toward his hairline. "Well hell, Justine. What are you going to do?"

I force a smile onto my face and tell him the truth. "Get drunk. Probably cry. And then either figure something out, or drop out and get a full-time job with my undergrad degree and hope I can save enough to come back and finish in a couple years."

His face falls at my honesty. "I'm so sorry. I know this isn't fair. When they were discussing our options, we knew it was going to cause some students to leave the program, but I never would have expected you to be one of them. You're one of the brightest clerks I've ever had in my chambers, and it would be such a waste of a brilliant mind."

I inject more positivity than I feel into my tone. "I

might not have any other options, but I've already got my books and I've got thirty days to come up with the first payment. Hopefully I can figure out something by then."

"Come talk to me before you make any final decisions. If there's anything I can do to help, even if it's write you a letter of recommendation for another job, I'll do it."

His offer is sincere, and those tears I told him I'd cry later are welling to the surface.

"Thank you, sir. I'll be in touch." I spin and head for the door before they can fall.

What a disaster.

I hope Merica already has a bar picked out because I'm going to spend every last dollar in my wallet on getting drunk. It might not be prudent, but being prudent isn't going to come close to paying my tuition.

Chapter 6

Ryker

"You're going to finish school, and I'm not going to hear another goddamn word to the contrary." My father's voice echoes off the vaulted ceilings of his home office.

"Why is it so fucking important that I finish school? So I can become a judge like you and call in favors? Or so I can count on other people to deal with my mistakes?"

"You watch your mouth when you speak to me."

"Are you in denial, Dad?"

My father's expression turns harsh, and I know I've overstepped. Well, fuck it. I've had enough of the hypocrisy in this house.

"The only thing you need to worry about is graduating with honors and getting a prestigious clerkship."

"What part of *I don't want to be a fucking lawyer or judge* don't you understand?"

"Don't you dare speak to me like that, boy. If you don't want to be a lawyer, fine, but at the very least you'll get your degree and be a *fucking* politician like we decided two years ago."

I cross my arms over my chest, adopting his thunderous expression. "No. I'm done. Dropping out."

"Over my dead body." My father enunciates each word clearly. With the vein bulging in his forehead, I'm a little worried he might keel over where he's standing, making that a possibility.

When I don't respond, he slams his hand on the desk. "You know why you're not going to fucking drop out? Because today a bunch of students got their scholarships yanked, and you're still getting a free ride because I'm on the board of trustees and your free education is a benefit of that position. You can't walk away from that unless you're truly an ungrateful little prick, and I know I didn't raise my son like that."

His words stop me cold. *What the fuck?* I know more than one student getting through law school on a scholarship.

"They pulled everyone's scholarships?"

"Every student in the merit scholarship program."

One particular student comes to mind. The most stubborn girl I've ever met—and the hardest working and smartest.

"Fuck. Really? Can they do that?"

My father inclines his head. "I advised against it, told them to suspend the program for all new applicants and meet the obligations of the current ones by making alternative budget cuts or taking on additional debt, but it wasn't a possibility. There was no way around it."

"That's bullshit." *Justine must be devastated.*

"Yes, and if you're going to walk away from a free law school education when a bunch of your classmates just had the scholarships they earned suspended, then you're not the son I thought I raised."

I scrub a hand over my face. *Nothing like a fucking guilt trip to make me fall in line, Dad.*

"Fine. I'll graduate. But that's all I'm agreeing to."

Chapter 7

Justine

"You can't do it. Seriously. This is insane. I won't let you." Merica is yelling through the phone as I hold it away from my ear. "Stop right there, Justine. You need to think about this."

What she doesn't realize is that I've thought about this over and over again, and it's the only viable alternative I can come up with. Out of desperation, I had a meeting with financial aid this morning, and it revealed exactly what I expected.

"I'm sorry, Ms. Porter, but you're not a candidate for any of our conventional loans unless you have someone who can cosign for you. But here are a few other options you might consider."

Those other options were each more unattractive than the last, and exactly the kind of crippling debt and interest rates I expected.

Cash is king. There's a reason for that saying, and sitting in the parking lot of the Déjà Vu, I see plenty of people coming and going, likely with their wallets stuffed full of it.

I feel like the world's biggest cliché. *What brings a good girl like you here? Oh, I just need to strip my way through law school.* I can almost see the *oh sure* nods I would get. Obviously it's a cliché for a reason, and I'm sure more than one aspiring lawyer has taken this path. The grad from last year's class the girls had been talking about during the meeting obviously had.

So, what's worth more? My sense of modesty or my financial future? It's not like I'm signing up to be a prostitute. I can just strip and take the tips. I don't have to do any . . . extras.

"I'm already here, Mer. I'm just going to go inside and ask for details. I'm not committing to anything."

She's silent for a solid ten seconds before replying. "If you don't call me in half an hour to tell me you're okay, I'm driving over there myself. I don't care if I have to bust down doors and break you out."

I can't help but laugh. "It's a strip club, not a harem. You won't have to break me out. I promise I'll call you as soon as I'm out."

"You better. I swear, if I find a gray hair in the next month, it's all your fault."

"I love you, Mer."

"Love you too, Jus. Be careful."

We hang up, and I survey my surroundings to get my bearings.

The fence around the parking lot provides a certain measure of anonymity to the Deja Vu's clientele, and for that I should probably be grateful. I climb out of my car, and a horrific thought enters my head as I step onto the uneven pavement with shaky legs. *What if I see someone I know?*

No, not possible. *Don't put thoughts like that out into the universe, Jus. You know better. Positive thoughts only.*

I straighten the short black skirt I never returned to Merica after that night at the bar. *The night Ryker Grant kissed the hell out of me and I used his bulge to get myself off in the back hallway of a bar.*

We all know how that story ended.

Digging deep, I find the self-confidence I need to own what I'm doing. It's honest work for honest pay.

I reach the black door and push it open to find a large man in a black shirt standing behind a tall counter just inside the doorway. His expression doesn't change when he sees me.

See? No big deal. I got this.

"Cover for ladies is five dollars tonight," he tells me, stamp held aloft, ready to mark the back of my hand.

Do I tell him why I'm here and ask how I go about applying for a position to work the pole? My other option is paying the cover and slinking around inside, hoping to figure out who I need to talk to.

Practicality wins out. "I'm actually not here to watch. I'm here to apply for a job."

This time his eyes widen a fraction, followed by a once-over. I know what he's seeing, because I put a lot of time and effort in front of my mirror tonight.

Dark hair I curled into "beach waves" after watching a few online tutorials, smoky eyes that I think stayed on the side of sultry rather than raccoon. The push-up bra I'd splurged on boosted my already ample boobs into the tight V-neck of the black tank I paired with my skirt. Black strappy heels, also borrowed from Merica and never returned, completed the look, and made my average-length legs look long and toned.

"You sure?"

"Yes. Could you point me in the direction of the hiring manager?" I'm not sure how formal strip clubs are about the HR hierarchy, but I don't know who else to ask for.

He jerks his head toward the black door across from the counter. A heavy bass beat thumps beyond it, and neon lights peek out from beneath.

"Marv's office is in the back of the club. He's the only manager we got. But I gotta warn ya. He's hired three new girls for the stage this week, and I doubt he's looking for too many more. There's a cocktail waitress position open, though."

A cocktail waitress position won't make anywhere near the kind of cash I need. "Where in the back is his office?"

"Through the doors, across the club to the back left corner. There's a hallway, and his door is the first on the left. Says Manager on the door. You can't miss it."

"Thanks. I appreciate it."

He gives me a short nod, and I head to the door. A healthy *what the fuck am I doing* runs through me.

This is just a means to an end.

Purpose driving my every step, I push open the door, determined to find Marv and get myself a job.

Chapter 8

Ryker

Sitting beside my friend and former frat brother, a stack of ones and two beers between us and two women in tiny G-strings humping brass poles onstage, I feel like I'm back in college.

Except now I'm not entertained by the titty glitter the strippers take pride in smearing all over every man they come in contact with.

I officially feel too old for this shit. But when Brandon called to say he wanted to hit the strip club to celebrate his new promotion, I wasn't going to say no. First, because I'm genuinely happy for the guy, and second, because I don't feel like doing anything else. Not even one whole week into the semester and all I can think about every time I sit down in a class is how much I can't stomach the thought of being a lawyer.

I've officially hit the *zero fucks given* point.

So instead, I'm sitting in a strip club on a Thursday night instead of doing my reading for my classes on Friday. I haven't done the reading for any class yet, so why start now?

"Dayum, you think she's on the menu tonight? She looks a little classy to climb that pole, but if I'm right, I call dibs."

Brandon's gaze leaves the stage and tracks someone moving across the club floor. From my angle, I can't see who he's talking about.

"Where?"

He turns completely around in his chair and nods to the brunette a dozen feet away, head down as though she's intentionally trying not to look at the stage or make eye contact with any of the patrons. Her posture doesn't match any of the strippers working the floor. No way does she work here.

But why does she seem familiar?

She nearly runs into a cocktail waitress in a bra, five-inch heels, and fishnets tucked under booty shorts. The brunette's head pops up and she raises her hands as though to apologize.

That's when I catch a glimpse of her face.

No. Fucking. Way.

"Shit, she's hot as fuck. I'm taking her home tonight." Brandon's voice isn't slurred by the five beers he already put down, which is mildly surprising. I'm the DD tonight, since it's his celebration, but there's no way I'm going to let him make a move on Justine.

"Sorry, bro. I called dibs on her ages ago."

Brandon's eyes widen comically. "Seriously? You know her? Thought you said you hadn't been here since undergrad?"

"She doesn't belong here either, and she sure as shit doesn't work here."

Brandon's smile turns into a lopsided grin. "Maybe she's stripping her way through school. God, that's so fucking hot. I'd throw down enough cash for private dances to pay for at least one class. She's smokin'."

The urge to plant my fist through his face is strong and instinctive, but the echo of his words through my head pulls me back from actually acting on it.

Stripping her way through school.

Shit. She lost her scholarship. Could she be here looking for a job?

Again—*No. Fucking. Way.*

I follow Justine's path until she slips through a doorway and disappears from sight.

Brandon's attention hasn't returned to the stage. It's still on me.

"I'm right, aren't I? The chick you called dibs on is going to start stripping for her tuition."

"Shut the fuck up, and if you ever mention you saw her here to anyone, I'll tell everyone about the transvestite you got head from sophomore year."

Brandon jerks back against his seat. "I didn't know she was a tranny! Those tits looked so fucking real. She barely had an Adam's apple."

"A chick with a dick sucked your cock, and if you want that to stay between us—"

Brandon grabs his beer and knocks back a swig. "Fuck. Fine. But that's the last time you get to pull that card on me. And you're buying me some goddamn Scotch. Get me drunk enough tonight, and I won't even remember if I saw Hillary Clinton working that pole."

"Nasty, dude." But still, I raise my hand to catch the attention of the cocktail waitress. "Get him a double Scotch.

Whatever top shelf you've got."

She smiles flirtatiously at me as she slides one leg between my knees and leans forward. "And what can I get for you, big man?"

"Water."

Her smile falters as she steps back, clearly reading the fact that I'm not down with playing her game. But she's not giving up yet because she lowers her ass to her heels just in front of me, knees spreading wide.

"Are you sure there's nothing? Because I'd be happy to give you a rundown of all the *off menu* items I'm happy to provide."

Just the insinuation that she's willing to fuck me for money is enough to make me want to run down that hallway, grab Justine, and carry her out of here before she has a chance to make whatever bad choices she's considering. She doesn't belong here.

"Water," I repeat, and the cocktail waitress finally stands and returns to the bar.

"Damn, bro. She would've sucked your cock right here if you would've given her a sign."

I flick my gaze toward Brandon. "And that's a challenge how?"

His eyes flash with mischief. "Is that the appeal of little Miss Wannabe Stripper? She's a challenge? Because if she comes to work here, she's not going to be one anymore. If you've been striking out, which must be the case if you're still interested, then maybe it's your key to getting a piece of that sweet ass."

"You're going to drink your Scotch and never fucking mention this again. Understand me?"

Brandon jerks back at the vehemence in my tone. "Got

it, man. Sorry, I was just giving you shit."

Not wanting to taint the night of his celebration, I reach for my wallet and toss a fifty on the table between us. "No harm, no foul. Now, why don't you get that private dance you were wanting? On me. Congrats on the promotion."

The waitress returns with the Scotch, and I pay her before Brandon rises and walks toward the skinny redhead with enormous tits he's been drooling over since we walked in the door. Which frees me up to find out just what the hell Justine was doing.

Tucking my wallet back in my pocket, I head for the hallway.

Chapter 9

Justine

I knock on the door marked Manager, and the only positive thing I can come up with to focus on is the fact that I don't have anything in my stomach to throw up because I couldn't summon up an appetite while I was getting dressed for my . . . interview.

The door jerks open, and I do a double-take when I catch sight of Marv.

Except I know him as Marvin. Gramps's next-door neighbor. The one who would come over and fix leaky sinks and shovel snow off the front walk when Gramps's health started declining. He'd bring over a couple beers, and we'd listen to Gramps tell stories about World War II.

No. Freaking. Way.

His eyes light with the same recognition the moment I step into the room. "Justine? What the hell are you doing here?"

I struggle to find my voice. Do I lie? Do I tell the truth? If I lie, he's going to know I'm lying. So I go with the truth.

"I . . . uh . . . I'm here to see about a job."

Confusion crushes his bushy brows together on his forehead. "You graduated from college. With honors. So I repeat, what the hell are you doing here?"

My mouth opens and closes as I try to find the words to explain how badly things are screwed up right now.

"Sit down, kid. You've got some explaining to do." He nods at the chair across from the desk.

I cross the room and drop into it. "I'm so screwed."

I proceed to spill the entire story of what happened with the scholarship, the details about my parents I wasn't sure Gramps had shared, and my aversion to debt. If I expected sympathy from Marvin, that's not what I would get.

"You're a smart girl, Justine. I refuse to believe this is the best idea you've got."

Fixing a scowl on my face, I glare back at him. "How can you judge me for this? You're the manager of the place!"

"And there are plenty of girls here who don't have the options you do. Not only would I not hire you because my slate of dancers is completely full, but because I respected the hell out of your grandpa, and he's gotta be rolling in his grave right now. I'm not saying there's anything wrong with stripping, because there ain't, but this isn't for you."

"I don't have any other options if I want to stay in school. Don't you understand? There's no job I can get that will pay me enough to cover my tuition."

"And you think this one could?" He shakes his head. "You'd be the new girl. Bottom of the ladder. You'd get the crappiest shifts with the worst tips. There's no guarantees you'd make any more here than anywhere else. It's not like money falls from the sky when these girls strip. This ain't some fancy club in Vegas."

"What about another club?"

Marv leans back in his chair and crosses his arms. "It's gonna be the same no matter where you go. Besides, I know most of the managers, and I promise you that you'll find yourself blackballed if you apply."

What the hell is his problem? "Why would you do that? I need the money."

"Told you, I respected the hell out of your grandpa. He'd have my balls if I let you get sucked into this world. You're a smart girl. Find another way."

I open my mouth to protest one last time, but he shakes his head. "It's good to see you, Justine, but you need to get the hell out of my club." He stands and comes around the side of the desk, reaching out a hand to pull me to my feet. "Someday you'll thank me for this."

Marvin escorts me to the door of his office, gives me a hug, pushes me back out into the hallway, and shuts the door in my face. But not before telling me to keep my ass out of strip clubs until I have a bachelorette party.

I sink against the wall across from his office door and whisper, "What the hell am I going to do now?"

A deep, familiar voice comes out of the darkness. "I want to know what the hell you're doing here to begin with."

No. Freaking. Way.

Chapter 10

Justine

I whirl around in the hallway to face him as my stomach sinks to my feet and the burning heat of mortification fills me.

Ryker stalks toward me, stopping a foot away.

Seriously, Universe? How is this even fair? Of all people . . . why him?

"What the hell are you doing here?" Ryker asks again.

My eyes dart from him to Marvin's office door. It won't take Ryker long to guess why, if he hasn't figured it out already.

"None of your damn business." And it's not. *Nothing about me is any of Ryker's business.*

"That's where we disagree."

Screw him. I don't owe him any explanation. Striding forward, I intend to sidestep him, but he wraps a hand around my wrist. Before I can yank it free, he spins us both and pins me against the wall.

Memories of the back hallway at the bar bombard me, but I shut them down. *I need to get out of here.*

"Let me go." I shove both hands against his chest.

"No. Because someone needs to have a come-to-Jesus talk with you. See, I know for a fact that you lost your scholarship, and I also know you're too fucking smart to think stripping for your tuition is a good idea."

"It's none of your business what I do for my tuition."

"You get up on that stage and I'll carry you out of here myself."

I have to grit my teeth to stop from telling him I couldn't even get a job as a stripper. Before I can think of a suitable reply, Marvin's office door flies open.

"What the hell? You better get the fuck off her, man."

Ryker drops his hold on me instantly and steps back.

Marvin storms closer, looking from me to Ryker and back to me. "You okay? I'll get security to haul his ass out of here."

I shake my head. "I'm fine. It's . . . a misunderstanding. That's all."

Marvin glares at Ryker. "You lay a hand on any woman in this place, and I'll take you apart myself."

"He's fine, Marvin. It's all good. I'm gone."

I don't wait for his response. Call me a coward, but I need this night to be over. *Now.* So I bolt.

Merica's never going to believe any of this . . .

Chapter 11

Justine

Professional Responsibility isn't anyone's idea of a good time, but it's a required class. For some crap reason, it's only offered on Friday afternoons, which means any chance at a three-day weekend is eliminated if you also happen to have a Monday class, which I do. *For now.*

I don't know why I'm holding on to hope and continuing to go to class, but I can't give up. This is where I belong, and I'm not ready to let go. Not yet. I'll keep coming until they throw me out.

I study the seating chart on the PowerPoint slide until I find my assigned seat. This professor is old school and goes strictly alphabetical. I can't stop myself from checking the G's.

Grant, R. Two rows ahead of me on the opposite side of the room.

Of course he's in this class. Why would I expect anything else? I tell myself I'm not going to look in that direction, but obviously I fail. He's leaning back in his chair, fingers laced behind his head in a casual *I don't give a shit* pose.

King of the Douche Bags, I remind myself.

Professor Babcock waits until the time ticks over to one o'clock. She assigned reading in advance, and she wastes no time diving into the first case. With my two-year-old laptop at the ready, a gift with my defunct scholarship, I take verbatim notes as she discusses the general rules of professional responsibility.

She rattles on for twenty minutes before looking down at her copy of the seating chart and calling on a student for the first case.

"Mr. Grant, go ahead with the facts."

My attention, like everyone else's seated behind him, goes to the back of his head, which is now lowered over his closed laptop. I've been in enough classes over the last two years to realize this isn't normal Ryker behavior.

"Sorry, Professor Babcock, I'm going to have to pass today."

Spoiler alert: There is no passing in law school. At least, not in this one.

"Excuse me, Mr. Grant?"

"I said I have to pass. I haven't read the case, so I don't have the facts."

Professor Babcock's tone borders on incredulous. "You haven't read the case." It's not a question.

"No, ma'am."

"And do you have some excuse for why you failed to be prepared for this lecture?"

"Not one that's going to get me any sympathy."

I think every mouth in the class drops open in shock. *What the hell is he doing? Trying to piss her off?*

Babcock bristles behind the lectern. "Feel free to exit

the room right now if you're not interested in participating. You can always take this *required* class again next semester when you're feeling more engaged."

Wow. Just. Wow.

I don't know what the hell has gotten into him, but this is a completely new development.

Ryker wraps a hand around his unopened laptop and grabs his backpack with the other. "Thanks for the tip." He walks out of the silent room, the door slamming behind him.

"Holy shit," Leslie Pope, the girl beside me, whispers. "Did that just happen?"

Holy shit is right. Ryker might not be a 4.0 student, but he's far from stupid, and what he just did qualifies as idiotic.

He was at the strip club last night. Maybe he's still drunk?

The rest of the class passes without any more fireworks, but in the back of our minds, we're all wondering what the hell happened to transform Ryker from regular cocky law student to idiot asshole.

As soon as class is dismissed, gossip runs rampant as most of the students, including Merica and me, head downstairs to the café. *Did you hear about Ryker Grant walking out of Professional Responsibility? Did he do that in any other classes? Is he smoking something? If so, where can I get some?*

The questions run the gamut and it seems no gossip is off-limits. For some strange reason, people keep coming to me for answers, like I have some.

"He's always asking you out," Merica says when I complain about the third person to ask me if I know what's going on with him.

"He *was*. Past tense and over with."

Merica eyes me sharply. "You don't think he was working up to asking you out again when you made a break for it last night?"

When I'd called her on my drive home from the Vu, she'd practically deafened me with how loudly she'd laughed. There had been no sympathy, only relief that I wasn't taking up stripping as a part-time job.

"I have no idea, but I sure wasn't sticking around to find out. Besides, let's not pretend I'm upset about this change of pace."

I pretend that last bit isn't a lie. My pride still stings from being stood up last summer after he kissed me. *All I want is an apology, and then I can move on.*

"Riiight," Merica drawls, sipping on her can of Diet Coke. "I would call bullshit, but you're so far in denial it won't do any good."

I don't dignify her words with a response. We both know she's right.

"But seriously, do you have any idea what the hell that stunt was? His dad is going to be *pissed* when he finds out. Didn't you say that he's got grand plans of Ryker going on to clerk for the Sixth Circuit Court of Appeals? Or even the US Supreme Court? I don't think all the favors in the world are going to help if Ryker decides he's had enough of 'playing at law school.'"

It was common knowledge in Justice Grant's chambers that he had lofty aspirations for his son, and up until today, I would have said that Ryker was falling in line with what his father wanted.

Leslie Pope sidles up between Merica and me. "So you know how Ryker walked out of PR?"

"Mm-hmm," I mumble. Given that I was sitting beside

her when it happened, the question is ridiculous.

"I heard from Kristy Horner that he hasn't taken any notes all week. She's got some history with him, so she notices these things."

We're all aware of Kristy's "history" with Ryker. She's made no secret of the fact that she considers him to be her property. She also doesn't like me a whole lot, because apparently she considers me competition. She should thank me, in my opinion, because I've purposely gone out of my way *not* to be competition. *And I'm definitely no competition now.*

"Really?" Merica prompts her, giving me the side-eye me like no other. "What else did Kristy say?"

Leslie lowers her voice as if someone is going to overhear her. "Apparently he hasn't even opened his laptop in a class yet. It's like he's deliberately trying to fail this semester. Kristy said she's worried about him."

"If Kristy's so worried, maybe she shouldn't be spreading gossip around," Merica says, letting her trademark snarkiness bleed over into her words.

Leslie shrugs. "I'm just telling you what she told me."

"That's pretty big speculation considering we're only a week in. Maybe he's just bored with this first-week-of-class song and dance." Why am I putting out some kind of explanation for this? It's not like I care either way what Ryker is doing or what the gossips are saying, as long as it doesn't include me.

"I heard from Heath Whitehouse, who clerked with him all summer in Justice Bryant's chambers, that he was totally apathetic from day one. It's like someone flipped a switch. He went from being normal Ryker without a care in the world to a real prick."

"Aren't you just full of gossip today?" Merica sips her Diet Coke again and meets my gaze.

"Didn't you have an externship with Ryker's dad last semester?" Leslie asks me.

I nod.

"Did you find out anything about him that could explain this?"

"He didn't come up as a topic of conversation." My tone is dry, and I hope she picks up on the fact that I'm over this conversation.

"Then I guess this remains an unsolved mystery," Leslie says with another shrug. "Anyway, I gotta get going. I'm heading up north with a couple of my undergrad sorority sisters for one last weekend of fun. Talk to you Monday!"

We watch Leslie bounce away, apparently thrilled that she has shared all the gossip in her arsenal, and Merica pushes aside her now empty can of Diet Coke.

"I'm ready to get the hell out of here. You?"

"More than ready." We both gather up our backpacks, and Merica tosses her can in the recycling bin as we walk out of the café.

"Are you coming over tonight for the *New Girl* marathon?"

I debate my options. Sitting at home and thinking about all the things I can't change, or hanging out with my best friend pretending my problems don't exist. Choice number two is the clear winner.

"Absolutely. See you at seven?"

"Perfect. I'm ordering pizza, so come hungry."

"You know I will."

Chapter 12

Justine

An unknown number shows up on my phone, and out of instinct and caution, I let it go to voice mail. Yes, I screen all my calls.

As soon as the voice mail pops up on my notifications, I check it.

Part of me hopes to hear Ryker's familiar deep voice, but I slap that part upside the head. But shockingly, I'm not that far off.

"Justine, I've been thinking a lot about your predicament, and I want to make sure you've found a suitable solution. Feel free to come by my chambers before six tonight if you'd like to discuss it."

He doesn't even say his name, and he doesn't need to. I'd recognize Justice Grant's voice anywhere.

I wonder if he's already heard through the grapevine that Ryker walked out of class. As a member of the board of trustees, I imagine that word travels pretty quickly to his ears when something happens concerning his son.

For a second I feel a flash of pity for Ryker, but it evaporates just as quickly. Because his dad is a trustee, he doesn't have to worry about paying for tuition. And yet he still walked out of class today like the entitled jerk I've called him more than once. Who does that?

Doesn't he realize how good he has it? He drives around in his Camaro, has the latest and greatest MacBook and access to opportunities most students can only dream about, and now he's spending week nights at the strip club, walking out of class, and apparently is willing to throw it away?

I grow more and more pissed as I ride the bus to the commuter lot and finally climb into my car. My Honda Civic may only be five years younger than me, but she still gets me from A to B.

I'm only partially aware of the turns I'm making until the majestic building housing the state supreme court comes into view.

Apparently when this Grant calls, I come running. But how many other people have called me to inquire about my situation? Asked if I've found a solution? Besides Merica, no one else cares whether I drop out of school or not.

My parents, who I assume are still running cons on unsuspecting marks, never gave a crap about me or my future. If Gramps hadn't fought them tooth and nail for custody, they would have dragged me deeper into their mess, and I was too young to realize what was happening.

The fact that Justice Grant cares more about my future than my own blood isn't something I'm going to dwell on. Honestly, though, other than Gramps, Justice Grant is really the only positive male role model I've had.

Despite the silver-spoon life he's given his son, Grant didn't grow up with everything. He started as a lowly law clerk and worked his way up the ranks through sheer force of will. Because of that, I feel like we have something in common.

I wait in line at the metal detector, and once my purse has been scanned, I follow the path my feet know well and make my way to the third floor of the building where Justice Grant's chambers are located. The halls are quiet at five thirty, and the door to Grant's chambers is closed. I try the knob rather than knocking.

As I step into his chambers, I inhale the scent of old law books. There's something comforting about it—like coming home after a long absence. I loved every minute I spent working here last semester, and that's all due to the man standing near the interior door that leads to his office.

His eyes light up when he sees me, and a ready smile stretches across his face. "Justine, so glad you got my message and could carve out some time for me."

I smile instinctively in return, but then falter when I remember I'm here to tell him that my legal career is over before it really started.

The words are bitter on my tongue, and speaking them is so much harder than I could have imagined. Tears burn my eyes, but again, I won't let them fall.

"Of course. And you told me to talk to you before I made any big decisions, so here I am." I square my shoulders and swallow, wishing I didn't have to say what I'm about to say. "I'm going to be leaving school when the first tuition payment is due. I don't have the money, and I'm not going to be able to get it."

His smile dies a quick death. "No. That's not acceptable. You're too bright to throw the last two years away over something like money."

I choke out a pained laugh. "Money's pretty important

in this situation. The school isn't going to let me stay without it. I'm hoping I won't be throwing the last two years away. My goal would be to graduate . . . someday."

"That's not what I meant, but I spoke poorly." He shrugs a shoulder. "Come in and shut the door. We're going to talk. I have an idea I think will help both of us."

Chapter 13

Justine

I ease the thick wooden door of Justice Grant's chambers closed behind me and follow him into his office. He takes a seat behind the wide wooden desk that looks like it should be in a museum rather than in actual use.

"Sit." He gestures to the dark leather high-backed chairs that are slightly smaller and less ornate versions of his.

I lower myself into the seat, and memories of all the times that I've sat in it before swirl through my mind. The first afternoon of my externship, when most student clerks don't actually get to meet their judges right away, and instead are directed by a permanent law clerk. The times when Grant wanted to discuss particularly tricky points of law when I was researching cases to assist with writing his opinions. The last day of my externship, when he said the door was always open if I ever needed him for anything.

I can't imagine that most state supreme court justices would do the same, but I knew from that first day Grant was different, which explained why his externships were so highly sought after. I may have only spent eight hours a week here, but it was enough to make a lasting impression.

He leans back in his chair and studies me for long moments before speaking. "Have you exhausted all your potential options? I hate to ask, because I know you're a bright girl, and if there was a way for anyone to make this work, you would have already figured it out."

"Everything I can think of, and everything I can live with."

He narrows his eyes on me. "Do I want to know what options you considered that you couldn't live with?"

I shake my head. "No, sir."

"Fair enough." He nods. "Well, I might have an option I think you could live with."

My mind has been turning over and trying to latch onto any possibilities, but I keep coming up empty. What could he possibly think of as a solution that I haven't already considered?

"I'm entertaining all options at this point. I don't want to leave school, but I can't stay and have them kick me out for nonpayment of tuition either."

Grant shifts forward and leans his elbows on the desk before lacing his fingers together. "You know my son, Ryker, correct?"

I force myself to stay motionless when my instinctive reaction is to jerk back in my chair. *What does Ryker have to do with this?*

When Grant raises an eyebrow, I realize he's waiting for me to respond.

"Yes, I know him." That's the simplest answer I can give.

"I thought so. Well, he's having a bit of a crisis of faith right now when it comes to law school." His expression darkens and he adds, "This is between us and doesn't leave this room."

I nod, interested in not only what the hell happened to Ryker over the summer to totally change his attitude, but what it could possibly have to do with me and my tuition. "I won't say anything to anyone."

"Good. Ryker doesn't ever need to know we're having this conversation, regardless of what you decide."

Now my interest is well and truly piqued. What *I* decide?

"The details aren't important, but he isn't sure he wants to be a lawyer anymore and has considered withdrawing from school."

So the rumors aren't so far off. "But why? He's already two years in, and it's not like someone yanked his financial support." As soon as I shut my mouth, it occurs to me that my response is a little too candid. But Grant doesn't reprimand me, or do anything but nod.

"That's exactly what I told him. He's lucky enough to have his tuition covered, and after explaining to him what happened to students like you, I believe he realizes just how foolish, shortsighted, and self-indulgent such a choice would be. He's since agreed to finish out the year."

"I'm glad he realized throwing an opportunity like this away would be stupid."

Grant lowers his head for a moment before meeting my eyes. "That's the problem. I think he's still going to throw this opportunity away, but not by dropping out." He leans back in his chair again and crosses his arms as I wait impatiently for what he has to say next. "According to my colleagues at the law school, Ryker is choosing not to do his reading or put forth any effort when it comes to class. He's going to fail out, or at least damage his GPA to the point where he won't be able to get a decent job, and certainly not a high-level clerkship like I had hoped."

So that explains why Ryker's been acting like he doesn't give a shit in class—because apparently he doesn't anymore. But what it doesn't explain is how this has any connection to my situation.

"I don't understand what this has to do with me," I say, my irritation at Ryker's stupid behavior rising.

How could he throw away a free law school degree? I'd kill not to have to worry about tuition right now, and he's acting like an ass instead of appreciating his opportunity. All because he's having some kind of late-stage rage-against-authority issue?

Justice Grant uncrosses his arms and rests them on the desk. "I want you to make sure he keeps his grades up and doesn't ruin his future over this temporary display of rebelliousness."

Wait. What?

Is he serious? He wants me to help keep Ryker from failing out?

"I don't really understand what you're asking me to do, sir." If Ryker wants to fail, there's nothing I can do to change his mind.

"You have three of the four same classes on your schedule, right?"

My eyebrows shoot up. "How do you know that?"

Justice Grant inclines his head with a small smile. "I have my sources." The ease in his expression fades away just as quickly. "What I want you to do is be Ryker's new study buddy. Make sure he's doing his reading, taking notes in class, and prepping outlines for any midterms and his finals."

But how? I want to ask. If the guy doesn't want to study, it's not like I can force him to do it. Besides, being Ryker's best new study buddy would mean that we'd be spending time together, and that's the last thing I want right now. The bruises to my pride haven't healed sufficiently for me to speak to him in a civil manner.

Grant isn't finished. "In exchange for you getting Ryker back to studying and engaging in class, I'll pay your tuition every month. After grades for finals come out, we can talk about second semester."

His words bounce around in my brain, ricocheting off synapses until the meaning truly hits me.

Justice Grant wants to pay me to get Ryker to study. I have to say the words out loud so I know that I'm not misunderstanding what Grant is saying.

Sitting straighter in my chair, I gather myself. "Let me make sure I have this right. You'll pay my tuition every month in exchange for me making sure Ryker does all the reading and is prepared for class, and if he does well on his finals, you're going to cover my entire second semester."

"That wasn't exactly what I said, but I'll work with you. If you can help him sustain his current GPA and not let it drop, then I will pay for your entire second semester's tuition. But I'll take it on good faith that you're not going to bail on him if he needs proper motivation to keep up the good work."

"But what if he doesn't keep his grades up? You know your son is . . ." I search my vocabulary for an adjective I can use in front of Justice Grant. "Stubborn. If he doesn't want to study, there's nothing I can do to change his mind."

"I don't believe that. You can challenge him, study with him, work on your outlines together. Whatever it takes to get him engaged in school again and through to graduation with his grades intact."

"What if I can't? What if he won't cooperate? Then I'm in the same boat I was before, except I've spent more time working toward a degree I won't be able to finish."

"You'll think of something. I'm confident."

Well, that makes one of us.

Am I even considering this? I can't study with Ryker. I can't spend time sitting across a table from him after what happened between us. Not that he's even interested anymore. I might not have a lot, but one thing I still have is pride. But if studying is the only thing I have to do to get my tuition paid . . .

I might not like this idea, but really, what are my other options?

I don't have any; otherwise, I wouldn't be here.

I know I'm considering his proposition when the next words come out of my mouth. "What if there's nothing I can do to convince him?"

"I don't think that's going to be the case."

"But what if I put in my best efforts"—I throw in a term from Contracts class that I know Justice Grant will clearly understand—"and his grades still drop?"

"It's not going to happen. And if it does, we'll discuss it and come to some kind of fair arrangement."

A fair arrangement. "What does that mean?"

Justice Grant fixes his gaze on me. "It means don't borrow trouble, and don't worry about it until we need to. Now, do we have a deal?"

You know the saying, *if it sounds too good to be true?* Well, it's running through my head right now. But what do I have to lose?

I can cling to my hurt, embarrassment, and pride . . . or I can suck it up and walk away with a law degree and no debt. *For the low, low price of helping Ryker Grant.*

Who would I really be hurting? *Myself, if I say no.*

But how in the world am I ever going to get Ryker to study without raising red flags everywhere? And that's when I know I've made my decision.

Justice Grant must sense it too. "What do you say, Justine? Do we have a deal?"

I nod. "I'll do it."

He stands and holds out a hand. I mimic his motion and we shake on it. A moment later, he releases my hand and returns to his desk. He slides open a drawer and removes two stapled documents before crossing back to the chairs and offering one to me.

"To make it official."

"What is this?" I ask as I accept it. When I glance down, the title jumps out at me in bold letters.

Independent Contractor Agreement

I scan it for a moment before realizing that it's a contract to tutor Ryker in exchange for my tuition.

"Always better to have it in writing," he says.

What did I really expect? Of course he would want it in writing. "Do you mind if I read this over?"

"I'd expect no less."

I settle back into the chair and read every single word. I'm definitely no contract expert, but I don't see anything that stands out as alarming.

When I look back up at Justice Grant, he has a kind smile on his face. "Any questions? The terms are all in your favor, Justine."

"No questions, sir. It's fine."

He holds out a pen. "Then all that's left is the execution. Two copies. We each get one."

Of course. Because lawyers love duplicates and triplicates. I reach out and take the heavy silver pen from him.

After we've both scrawled our signatures above our names on the last page of each copy, I look up at him, not quite sure what to say now. So I go with something bland.

"I guess we're official now."

He smiles at me. "We are. Have a good night, Justine. I'll be in touch."

I walk to the door, and my hand shakes when I reach for the knob.

What did I just do?

Justice Grant's familiar voice interrupts my flicker of internal panic. "Now, just so we're clear, neither Ryker nor anyone else ever knows about any of this, you understand?"

Discomfort slithers through me at the secrecy, even though I understand the need for it.

"You have my word, sir."

It's not just my hand shaking when I get back to my car, but the rest of me as well.

What the hell did I just agree to? How am I going to pull this off?

Ryker is used to getting the frigid side of my cold shoulder, and I can't change that overnight. But I also don't have a lot of time to put this into action. Any more stunts like the one he pulled in Professional Responsibility, and he's going to have the professors looking for any reason to dock him when it comes time to grade final exams.

What I want to do is call Merica and beg for advice, but my vow of silence takes that option off the table. For over two years, I've told her basically everything, so I don't know how I'm going to manage this.

On the way back to my apartment, I decide to aid my problem-solving by taking a detour through the Dairy Queen drive-through. The Oreo and Reese's Peanut Butter Cup Blizzard helps me think better. No, really, it does.

To make room in my cupholder, I move the Chewbacca Pez dispenser. I steal spoonfuls at the red lights all the way home, but I'm not any closer to having a solution than I was when I left Justice Grant's chambers. Unfortunately, no amount of ice cream is going to solve this one for me.

It's Friday night and I'm not going to see Ryker again until Monday, which means I have the entire weekend to come up with something.

I can do this.

I have to do this.

My future is riding on it.

Now if I can just block out the memory of that stupid kiss . . .

Chapter 14

Ryker

I stifle a yawn as I slide into an empty seat in Trusts and Estates on Monday morning. I almost didn't come at all, but this class actually entertains me. And unlike Babcock, Turner doesn't care which seats we take, helping my late arrival go unnoticed.

It isn't until I see the Pez dispenser next to me that a wide grin splits my face. Maybe today is looking up after all.

Justine. She's already furiously typing away on the piece-of-shit laptop provided by the school to the scholarship kids. Somehow she's nursed hers all the way into third year, when most people killed theirs within the first or second semester.

I still need to get a straight answer out of her about the strip club, but now isn't the time or place. The lack of stripper titty glitter on her gives me hope that she didn't take the job.

"What'd I miss?" I ask, keeping my voice low.

"Like you care," she shoots back, and my grin widens.

"You can pretend like I don't exist, but we both know you're watching me like a hawk."

"No one can miss that you've decided to become the class jackass."

Her comment stings more than I expect, and my smile fades.

"And what do you care about it?"

"Other than the fact that you're throwing something away that plenty of people would kill to have? Nothing."

"Excuse me, Ms. Porter. Mr. Grant. Is there something you'd like to share with the class?"

And we've officially been noticed by Turner. Justine's cheeks turn red at the professor's attention.

"Sorry, Professor Turner. I've been asking Ms. Porter out at least once a week for the last two years, and she's still shooting me down. You'd think I'd give up, but I just can't let it go."

Justine's face and ears flame even brighter red, and she slaps a hand over her face and lowers her gaze to the keyboard of her laptop.

"And do you think that announcing this is going to help your case any, Mr. Grant?"

"No, sir, but you asked if I had anything to share with the class."

The middle-aged man seems like he would have been cool in his day, and I know it's true when he doesn't bust my balls any further.

"Fair enough, Mr. Grant, but save it for after class. I imagine you're going to have a lot of apologizing to do, and perhaps some groveling."

"Thank you, sir."

Turner moves on to call on the next person on his list

to recite the facts of the case, and I'm glad he didn't bestow that little honor on me.

Justine grabs the Chewbacca Pez dispenser between us and pops a few yellow candies into her mouth. Her face is still bright red, and Turner's right. I should probably apologize for humiliating her, but it's not like anyone in this room doesn't know I've been trying since the beginning of our first year. She's the only one who pretends like it's not happening—at least until that night after finals at the bar.

I haven't been able to get the way her body curled into mine out of my head. I need to remind her how fucking good we could be together. If that kiss was anything to go by, when we get naked, we'll be explosive.

One more chance. That's all I need to convince her that we have a hell of a lot more to explore.

Class grinds on for what seems like an eternity until Turner dismisses us and everyone starts packing up their laptops and casebooks.

I know I've got one shot to get Justine to agree to talk to me—especially after I made my little announcement to the class.

Biding my time, I wait until she's trying to pass behind me, and I stand so she runs directly into my chest. Thrown off-balance, she wobbles, and I wrap both hands around her hips to steady her.

"I got you."

Her eyes narrow and her mouth curls into a scowl. "You did that on purpose."

"Deliberately got in your way so I could get my hands on you again? Damn right, I did."

I see a flash of confusion and then the anger takes precedence again.

But we both know it's the truth. Getting my hands on her is exactly what I want. Her shirt rides up on the sides, and I sweep my fingers along her bare skin. Fuck, she's soft. Which guarantees my dick isn't.

"Let me go."

Instead of a demand, Justine's words sound breathless. I have to remind myself I'm standing in a classroom with a professor up front and students filing in and out. This isn't the time or place for a hard-on.

"I've got some things I need to say to you, and you're going to let me."

Her brown eyes snap up to mine, surprise clear in them. "Why should I?"

"Because you're nothing if not curious, and you want to know what I have to say."

She steps backward, and I let my fingertips trail across her skin before they drop away. Justine adjusts the straps of her backpack on her shoulders and tucks Chewbacca into a side pocket.

"You know you want to hear the rare sound of me apologizing, don't you?"

Justine purses her lips, and all I can think about is the dreams I had all weekend of her staring down at me from a stage while she danced and stripped. My own private show. I'm not going to admit how many times I jacked off to the mental picture. I need the real thing, and I won't have another shot if she won't even give me a chance to talk to her.

I don't know what changes her mind, but she relaxes her posture and relents. "Fine. You've got five minutes. This better be good."

It's not much, but I'll take it. I lead the way out of the classroom, slipping out the side door I used to make my unobtrusive entrance. Or at least, it was unobtrusive until I decided to share my strike-out history with the entire class at Professor Turner's invitation.

Glancing behind me, I'm marginally surprised to see Justine actually following. I head for the third-floor doors to the library, where the private rooms are. This conversation isn't for public consumption.

The first private room on the right is empty, so I push the door open. Justine trails me inside, and I shrug off my backpack and drop it on one of the four chairs.

She closes the door behind her and leans against it, her arms crossed over her chest. I'm guessing she wouldn't stand that way if she realized how it draws attention to her chest. I force my eyes back to her face. I'm not about to fuck this up.

"Wow, you must really plan on groveling if you need privacy," she says, an eyebrow raised in challenge.

"Maybe I just wanted to get you alone."

She rolls her eyes. "And I'm already getting bored."

"You love to bust my balls, don't you?"

"I don't really like to think about your balls, if you want to know the truth."

I try on my charming smile, the one that has dropped panties for years. "I'm calling bullshit on that. You've thought about me at least once."

She pushes off the door and turns halfway to reach for the handle. "And if that's all you wanted to say, then I think we're done here."

"Wait."

I'm shocked when she listens.

Justine rubs her hands over her face, her every move revealing her frustration. "You ask me out for two years, practically blackmail me into a kiss, then you blow me off completely, and now you're all up in my business again. What the hell do you want from me?"

Her confusion punches me in the gut, making me wish I could tell her why I wasn't there the morning I promised to help her move. It wasn't for any reason she thinks.

I stride toward her, pressing one palm against the door beside her head. "I'm not blowing you off, and I haven't stopped thinking about that night."

"Then why—"

I can't give her the explanation she wants, so I try something different.

Lowering my head, I catch the next words out of her mouth on my lips. They're just as soft as I remember, and I drop my other hand to her hip, drawing her against me. Her fingers curl into the fabric of my T-shirt, almost reluctantly, but she's not pushing me away.

I take her mouth, my tongue diving between her lips to taste her again—finally, but the pulsing of my dick against the zipper of my jeans forces me to back off. If I don't, I'll be laying her out on the table behind us, and that's not what this is about. At least, not *all* of what this is about.

With her face flushed and her hair messy from my fingers, Justine shutters her expression. She's rebuilding her walls brick by brick.

That's not going to work for me.

"What's it going to take, Justine?" I remember asking her the same question at the bar.

Her dark eyes fill with confusion. "What's what going to take?" The words come out defensively.

"With you. To get a second chance. I fucked up once, but doesn't everyone deserve another shot?"

Chapter 15

Justine

My heart is hammering as heat burns in my belly and licks out to the rest of my body. How does he do this to me? We're in the library, for Pete's sake, and I'm rubbing against him like . . . like . . . a freaking cat in heat. And now he wants his second chance?

What am I doing? I'm supposed to be figuring out a way to get him to study, not helping myself to another dose of Ryker's too-tempting mouth. This is never going to work. But how can I possibly go back to Justice Grant and tell him I can't take his deal because I can't control myself around his son, and his son *definitely* can't control himself around me? Nope. Not happening.

You're not quitting, Justine. I give myself a mental pep talk as Ryker waits for an answer. *What's it going to take?* I wish I knew, but I don't. And I have to cobble together some sort of coherent response.

This is going to pay your tuition, Justine. You can do this if you just get your shit together.

"You know what I have time for right now?" I hold

up my hand and raise one finger. "Going to class." I raise a second finger. "Studying for class." I raise a third finger. "Working so I can continue to have the privilege to do the aforementioned number one and two."

Ryker's determined expression doesn't change. "You can carve out time for one date. We'll go somewhere nice. I promise you'll have fun."

I drop my hand and ball it into a fist. *A date is not what we need.* What we need—okay, *what I need*—is for Ryker to get his ass in gear and study. *And to be able to push him away when he kisses me.*

"I don't need you to take me somewhere nice. I need to *study*. You want to impress me, try applying yourself. You're not an idiot, so quit acting like it in class."

He crosses his arms, and I wonder how he's going to respond. "So you'll go out with me if we study." He narrows his eyes. "I'll take that."

Seriously? It can't be that easy. Given that I've got an entire year's worth of tuition riding on getting him to crack a book, I'm not going to say no. But that doesn't mean it's easy to get the word *yes* out.

"Okay." My voice sounds rusty as though I wasn't talking thirty seconds ago.

His eyes light up in triumph, so I quickly continue.

"Meet me at Unwired. Seven o'clock. I'll be there until ten. If you want another shot, that's the only one I'm giving you." I have to pretend I'm not doing mental cartwheels over my easy victory because Ryker would know something is up. A sliver of guilt at manipulating him like this flashes through me, but I push it down.

It's for his own good too. I'm not doing anything wrong.

"It's a date," he says, his smirk intact.

I uncross my arms and grab the door handle. "A *study date*," I clarify before I pull the door open and shut it behind me.

Now I just wonder if he'll show up.

Chapter 16

Justine

Unwired isn't the nicest coffee shop around campus, but it's only five minutes away from my apartment. My phone says it's 6:55 p.m., and my stomach is protesting the lack of proper nutrition in my mac-and-cheese bowl. I need to go to the grocery store to stock up, but I've been putting it off as long as I can. Grocery shopping is one of my least favorite tasks.

One bad thing—or great thing—about Unwired is the giant blueberry muffins in their bakery case. They put that crumbly stuff on top. What's that called? Streusel? And they offer free samples to suck you in against your will.

I'm so busy fantasizing about baked goods that I completely miss the whoosh of the door as someone comes in, hood up, and heads toward me with a rangy stride. It's not until that same person sits down across from me in my booth and drops his backpack beside him that I jerk my gaze away from the bakery case. He shakes the hood off and I have to blink twice to make sure I'm not seeing things.

Ryker Grant. In the flesh. *He showed*.

A small thrill of victory rises in my blood. *I can hold up my end of the deal with his dad.*

He holds up his phone, the screen facing me. "I'm on time."

A smile tugs at the corner of my lips. "I'm impressed." I wait for some innuendo about the other things I'd be impressed with, but it doesn't come.

"I'm going to grab a coffee and something to eat," he says. "You want anything?"

He's really taking this somewhat seriously. Again, I'm impressed, and I shake my head in response.

"No? You good?" He looks down at my cup, which is lidless to let the heat of the burning hot water escape. "What the hell are you drinking anyway? Is that tea with no tea bag?"

I reach into my pocket and pull out a yellow-and-white pouch. "Yeah, I was waiting for the water to cool." I peel open the paper and dunk the bag in.

"Did you bring that from home?" The question isn't condescending, just truly curious.

"Does it matter?"

"Don't like their choices here?"

"Maybe I just love Lipton."

"Fair enough. You want anything else? Muffin? Scone? Cookie? Brownie?"

Torture. He's freaking torturing me by reeling off all the things I would want but don't usually let myself buy. And I'm not the kind of girl to let anyone else buy them for me either.

"I'm good, but thanks."

"You gotta let me buy you something, otherwise there's no *date* in *study date*."

I hit him with a serious stare. "That's not how this works. We come. We *study*. We leave."

"If we were doing this my way, you'd definitely be coming. Sure you don't want to change your mind? I promise you won't regret it."

And there's the innuendo. My cheeks heat as he hits me with an arrogant smirk.

I beat back my instinctive reaction to tell him to go to hell, and instead fold my arms on the table and lean forward. We can both play this game. "I'll do plenty of *coming* after I get home. I don't need you for that."

His mouth drops open at my reply, and this time I'm the one smirking, but it doesn't take him long to recover.

"You think about me when you touch yourself, don't you? You can plead the Fifth if you need to."

My face flames hot again. *Okay, so we can't both play this game.* I have to end this conversation. Now.

So I answer his original question. "Double-chocolate-chip cookie. Or a blueberry muffin. Either works."

He chuckles before heading down the aisle to the cash register and the bakery cases to place an order. My heart pounding just a bit too hard from our verbal sparring match, I flip my book open and uncap a highlighter.

Pretend like you're studying. Pretend like you're not going to think about him when you touch yourself tonight.

Ryker's still smiling when he comes back with a small coffee and a white paper bag. He sets both on the table between us before sliding into his seat.

I brace myself for more innuendo, but he says nothing as he pulls out his Trust and Estates casebook and opens it.

Nothing? Seriously? Just when I think I've got Ryker figured out, he throws me off.

He uncaps a highlighter. "All right, let's do this."

His sudden change into all business jolts me into the same mode.

I lay my highlighter down and meet his stare. "Have you done any of the reading for this class this semester?" I'm pretty sure I know the answer, but I want to hear it from him.

There's no hesitation before he answers. "Not a single page."

"Have you done any of the reading for *any* of your classes this semester?"

"No."

Even though I already figured that was the truth, I'm still stunned by his admission. It really, truly seems like he's planning on failing... and why? Because he's throwing some kind of tantrum?

"If you aren't going to do any of the reading, why are you even going to class?"

"Because I promised my dad I wouldn't drop out." His answer fits with the story Justice Grant told me.

"And so failing out is a better solution?"

"I'm not going to fail. It's more of an experiment to see how little effort I can put forth and still pass."

My frustration grows. "And that makes sense, how?"

"What part of this is your business?" Anger leaks into his expression, and his tone takes on a defensive cast.

"The part where you're supposed to be here to study with me and you don't actually plan to study at all."

He picks the casebook up with both hands and drops it on the table with a thud. "I've got my book open, don't I? I'm not going to sit here and stare at you for a couple hours without at least pretending that I'm doing something."

His admission cracks my shell of annoyance, and I push down the heat that blooms at his words. At least, I try.

"I won't get any work done if you sit and stare at me. You're distracting without even trying."

His anger drains away at my unintentional admission, and his panty-dropping smile slides over his face again.

"Glad to hear I'm not the only one distracted as hell."

"Study date," I say, almost more to remind myself than him. When his smile fades away, I want to kick myself for a moment. *That's not why we're here.* "Okay, this is what we're going to do. You missed a hundred or so pages of reading, and that would be a pain in the ass even if it was only one class, but you missed it in four. Have you taken any lecture notes at all?"

He shakes his head, all business again.

"All right, then I'll give you my notes."

His eyebrows go up, because it's a pretty generous offer.

"But—" I continue.

"There's always a catch." He leans back and crosses his arms over his chest. "Go ahead," he says.

"You're going to start reading for all of your classes, and you're going to catch up on the reading for the class that I'm not in—or you're going to find someone who is as nice as I am to take pity on you."

His eyes narrow on me. "Why would you help me out? You've gone out of your way to shut me down for two years."

Shit. I knew this was too easy. *Why didn't I come up with an answer beforehand? I knew he'd start to wonder if I deviated too much from my normal blow-off behavior. Think, Justine. Think.*

"Because I think it's bullshit that you're going to settle for a barely passing grade when we both know you're capable of so much more. This is the easiest year we have. You worked your ass off to get the GPA you have—you can't deny that. Why would you let it all go? Prove that you can finish what you started, and finish strong."

I feel like a coach delivering a locker-room speech at halftime, but my words aren't BS. I really do mean them. I would hate to see anyone throw away an opportunity like this, and given all of us who have lost our scholarships, the fact that he's thinking about throwing away his free ride really pisses me off.

Ryker reaches for the bakery bag between us but keeps his gaze on mine. "I don't think you've said that many words to me at once . . . ever."

"Someone has to point out how shortsighted you're being to waste an opportunity that some people can only dream about."

Again, my words are not only the truth, but ones I strongly believe. With the kind of doors his parents can open for him, Ryker could have a life that I can't even imagine. The more I think about him throwing that away, the angrier it makes me. I open my mouth to say more, but he raises his hand between us.

"I get it. You'll think I'm a totally ungrateful little prick if I don't get my head out of my ass and apply myself."

"Yes. That's exactly what I think."

And if that's all it takes to change his mind and get him back on the right track to studying and not failing, then I just earned my tuition in ten minutes. *If only it were that easy.*

"Then let's make a deal."

"What kind of deal?" My tone is skeptical at best.

"I'll study . . . but only if I've got you sitting across from me to stare at."

My brain goes blank for a second, and then the thoughts come fast and furiously. First, a flash of victory. *Graduation, here I come. My tuition is* paid. And withstand the distraction of Ryker to get my own studying done? Finally, that dumb feeling of guilt creeps in and I shove it away. *This is for his benefit. I'm not doing anything wrong.*

I might have expected the guilt, but I didn't expect his condition. I need to say something. I can't agree right away because he'll know something is off. Past history would have me turning him down cold.

"We can't study together every day. Seriously. That's . . . not going to happen."

"Why not?"

I'm still struggling for a legitimate reason, and I blurt out the first one I can think of. "Because I like to take my contacts out, put my glasses on, put my hair in a bun, wear my pajamas, and ditch my bra."

Of course, as soon as I say the word *bra*, Ryker's gaze drops to my boobs.

"Feel free to ditch the bra anytime. It's not going to bother me at all. Actually, I'll be perfectly honest—I've got zero motivation to study on my own, but a braless Justine sounds like amazing motivation."

Covering my chest with both arms in an attempt to escape the intensity of his gaze, I force myself back to the subject at hand. Is he playing me? Or is he serious?

I'm still not ready to give in and make this seem too easy. Strategy. This is all about negotiation. "Look, we can only study together a couple times a week. I study every day, and I can't have you up in my business all the time. I don't want *anyone* up in my business all the time. I don't actually like people enough for that much human interaction."

His response is so quick, it's like he was anticipating me shutting him down. "Three days during the week and one day on the weekend. A couple extra days before the Professional Responsibility midterm, and then we go hard for all of our finals."

When he says *go hard*, my mind immediately dives into the gutter. *Bad, Justine.* I force the illicit thoughts away and focus firmly on the subject at hand—*studying*.

"You know you need to ace that Professional Responsibility midterm, right? Because otherwise Babcock is going to screw you over. You need irrefutable proof that you crushed that test so if she does screw you over, you can appeal the grade. You pissed her off, and she's not going to forget."

He nods. "I know. That's why I'm thinking we have to focus harder on that one."

When did this become a *we* thing? But then again . . . Professional Responsibility is my least favorite class of the semester, so it's not like I'm going to be all that motivated to study for it on my own either. Maybe this will actually be beneficial for me too.

"So, do we have a deal?" Ryker holds out his hand to shake, but I hold mine up instead. "You also have to study for the class we don't have together. What was it?"

"Election Law. Easy shit. My dad wants me to go into politics, so it's actually not that bad. I'm taking it pass-fail."

"You better not fail it, because that would be moronic."

"I can't fail Election Law. That's practically impossible."

"Fine." I reach out and slide my small hand into his much bigger one, and he grips it firmly. I'm so focused on the feel of his hand wrapped around mine that I almost forget to add, "We have a deal."

His smirk tilts up the corners of his mouth, and I snatch my hand back. *Okay, no touching. That needs to be a rule.*

I hope to hell I know what I'm doing. Because another kiss like the one in the library can't happen again. I'm getting paid to help him study, not to date him. I need to draw the line and keep it there.

He picks up a highlighter, and my eyes are riveted on the muscles of his forearm and his watch. *Why is that sexy?*

Shit. I'm so screwed.

Desperate for a distraction, I reach for the bag between us.

"What'd you get?"

Chapter 17

Justine

Before I can call Merica and spill about the Ryker study date, her name pops up on the screen of my cell. Part of me expects a barrage of questions more intense than those the professors throw at us with the Socratic method, but apparently she can't actually read my mind because all I get is a yawn.

"I slept through my night class, and now I've gotta ask Kristy Horner for notes."

The name Kristy Horner brings an automatic groan to my lips. She's the most vocal of my classmates about the fact that she slept with Ryker, and apparently had several repeat appearances. *Don't care*, I snap at myself. I just wish it was the truth. I'm still deciding how to respond when Merica continues.

"Maybe I'll use this opportunity to strike up a casual conversation about Ryker's dick and finally get my answers."

"Ugh. Please don't. That's just . . . really?"

"What? You keep telling me you're not going to take

one for the team and find out, so what choice am I left with?"

"To live on blissfully without the knowledge, continue to be happy with your boyfriend?" *And let me stop thinking about the size of Ryker's penis when I'm only supposed to be thinking about his grades*, I add silently to myself.

I open my mouth to tell Merica everything, but she launches into another tirade about the horribleness that is Kristy Horner. I stop at a train crossing, half listening, and my gaze lands on the white bakery bag on the seat beside me that holds half a blueberry muffin.

Because Ryker wanted to buy me something to make it a date . . . even though he has no idea that the only reason I was there is because I signed a contract with his dad.

Another shard of guilt lances through me. *Nope. Not thinking about it.*

After the way our study date—no, study session—started, I expected the rest of the night to be filled with me trying to ignore more innuendo and smug smirks with very little actual studying getting done. That wasn't the case, and it totally threw me.

I don't like it when people surprise me. I put Ryker into a little slot marked *overprivileged douche bag*, and if he doesn't fit there, then I'm not sure where to put him. This deal I made with his dad depended on him staying in that slot.

Instead of focusing only on my work, I spent way too much time noticing how delicious the five o'clock shadow shading his jaw looks, and how he pushes up his baseball cap and messes up his blondish-brown hair before readjusting it while he's reading. Then there's the way he taps his highlighter twice on a page when he's committing a concept to memory.

All things I shouldn't be noticing. But the one big thing I already knew stands out above them all—he's too hot for his own good. More than one girl walked by our table multiple times, eyes on him as she did.

It would have annoyed me, but Ryker didn't even notice. He's completely oblivious to the stares he gets from the women—and men—in a room.

"Jus? Are you even listening to me?" Merica's voice comes through my phone louder.

"What? Oh, sorry. Mind wandering. I'm stuck at a train crossing."

"Damn trains. So, you're cool with Saturday night?"

Crap, I really did miss part of the conversation, and she's going to give me hell if I ask what she said. My listening skills outside of class fall somewhere between decent and marginal on a good day, and with thoughts of Ryker in my head . . . well, let's just say I'm working with a handicap.

Get out of my head, Grant.

"Sure, sounds great," I reply, deciding to just roll with it. Merica isn't into much that I dislike. It's not like we're going to end up at one of those learn-to-paint-like-an-amateur-Monet classes that seem to be all the rage right now.

Merica squeals on the other end of the phone line. I have no other description for the sound she's making. "Yes! I'm so freaking excited. Talk tomorrow?"

Her palpable excitement gushes through my phone, and for a moment I wonder what the heck I just agreed to. *I guess I'll find out this weekend.*

"Of course."

"'Night, hottie."

"'Night, Mer."

When we hang up, it hits me that I never got a chance to tell her about what happened with Ryker.

Nothing happened. Just studying. Stop obsessing over it.

Right, like that's possible.

Chapter 18

Ryker

I pull into the underground parking garage of my condo building and climb out of my Camaro. I don't make it five steps toward the elevator before another car door slams shut and a voice calls out to me.

"Hey, man, you coming for poker night tomorrow?"

Turning to face Ian Everett, I pause. "Hey, I wondered what the hell happened to you. Haven't seen your car around for a few days."

Ian's blond mop is messy and looks like he just spent the last few hours with several women. As he comes closer, I decide I'm probably right. The lipstick smear on his chin tells me plenty.

"I've been crashing with this chick from Supply Chain Management. We had a group project and she . . . well, you know how that shit goes."

He's right, I do know how that shit goes, but it's been a while since I gave up the comfort of my own bed for an entire night. And I never bring them here. It might sound cliché, but my condo is my sanctuary. I don't even really like people knowing where I live. Especially not since Veronica Muzio decided to camp out on my doorstep for three days when I stopped answering her calls. Building security was at a loss, and explaining to her that she needed to move the fuck on wasn't fun. I don't need that shit happening again.

Tapping a finger on my chin, I tell Ian, "I think you missed a spot, unless that red is really your color."

He laughs and shrugs before swiping the side of his hand across his jaw to remove the makeup smear.

We head for the elevator together, shooting the shit. Ian's in his last year of his MBA, being groomed to move into the junior executive program of his father's company after he graduates. We've known each other since our undergrad days when he tried out a pre-law class and decided it wasn't for him. I didn't get it back then, but now, I wish I'd made the choice to go to business school instead of law school.

But then you wouldn't have met Justine.

It's like Ian's a mind reader. "So, what's up with you? New chick on your dick?"

"Not exactly."

The elevator lets out on our floor.

"That doesn't sound promising."

I shrug, not wanting to admit that I'm still trying to gain any ground with Justine after two years of blow-offs.

"Yeah, well. I'm working on it."

Ian's eyebrows hit his shaggy mess of bangs. "Working for a woman? Damn, Ry. You losing your touch? What happened to all that easy ass you've always gotten?"

"You know what they say about too much of a good thing, right? Well . . . maybe I'm trying something different."

My friend crosses his arms over his chest and eyes me. "Different like fucking dudes? I'm equal opportunity when it comes to other people, but I'm not gonna try that shit myself."

The suggestion is so ridiculous that my gut-level laugh echoes through the hall. When I've finally caught my breath, I shake my head at Ian. "Not a chance. I'm trying the slow-and-steady method for this one."

My words seem to truly confuse him because Ian's face twists up with confusion. "Slow and steady? That's a thing? What happened to *hit 'em and quit 'em*?"

"Hasn't worked with this chick, and I don't expect it to work with her anytime soon."

Ian pushes off from the wall and gestures to my door. "You're gonna tell me this shit over a beer, because I've never heard a fairy tale like Ryker Grant striking out with a woman."

Six beers between us later, Ian is laughing his ass off over how many times I've been shot down by Justine.

"You're telling me that you've been asking this chick out for two fucking years and you've only kissed her *twice*? Seriously? How did I not know this?"

"Because I didn't think it was worth sharing." I lift the bottle to my lips and wish it was something a hell of a lot stronger.

"She got a gold-plated pussy or what? Jesus, man. That's desperate shit."

Lowering the bottle a little harder than necessary, it cracks when it hits the table. Turns out I don't like to listen to Ian talk about Justine's pussy. Not a surprise.

"Laugh it up. Someday some chick is going to knock you on your ass, and you're not going to know what the fuck happened."

"Yeah, but you don't even know if it's worth it, man. I mean, she's gotta be hot, but isn't this just the challenge? What if you get her and it's not worth it?"

There's no way that's going to be the case, but I don't tell him that.

"I guess I'm going to find out after I finally get her, won't I?"

Chapter 19

Justine

When I slide into my seat for Advocacy on Tuesday morning, Kristy Horner turns around in her chair and pins me with an accusing glare. "Whatever you think you're doing, it's not going to work."

I pull my laptop out of my backpack and fire it up. If I wait for Kristy to spout her snarky comments first, the slow machine won't be ready to take notes until five minutes after the lecture starts. I wait until I have my casebook out before I finally reply.

"What are you talking about?"

"Ryker. I heard you two were together last night at Unwired."

You'd think we're in high school with how fast word travels these days. And since when does Kristy Horner have friends who study at Unwired? Her posse is solidly Starbucks half-caf, venti whatever-whatever.

I hate that I feel like I have to justify myself to her at all, but this nonsense needs to be nipped in the bud right now.

"We were studying. End of story. No big deal."

Kristy isn't a dumb girl, so there's no blonde stereotype here. She wouldn't have made it this far if she was. Her gaze is shrewd when she studies me like I'm a science experiment.

"You don't like him. Everyone knows that. So why, after two years, would you all of a sudden start studying together?"

"Maybe you should ask Ryker."

"Do you really think I couldn't get him back anytime I wanted?" Her tone carries the flavor of a threat.

"Maybe for a night. Seems like that's all he ever wanted you for anyway."

Her eyes narrow and her mouth pinches into a flat line when I shoot the words back at her. *Direct hit.*

I flip open my casebook to the spot I have marked with a Post-it, and I'm saved from continuing the conversation when Professor Alexander begins his PowerPoint presentation at the lectern.

Kristy turns around, but she's not going to let this go. It might just be a feeling, but it's a strong one.

It doesn't help things at all that Ryker is waiting for me after class and Kristy is ten feet away when he asks, "Are we studying tonight or tomorrow?"

Kristy's blond hair performs this shampoo-commercial-worthy swing when she pivots around at the sound of Ryker's voice.

His blue eyes are on me, not missing the constant darting away of mine, and he follows my gaze and looks back with confusion. "What's wrong?"

Not wanting to have this conversation where she can hear us, I do something that later registers as idiotic—I grab Ryker's hand and drag him away. Kristy isn't the only person watching us now.

The first door I come to is the Law Review office. It's open, but the back interior office door is closed. That means the editor-in-chief is probably in there, but with the noise-cancelling headphones she takes everywhere, she won't hear us.

Ryker laughs as I shut the door behind us. "What the hell, Justine?"

"One of Kristy Horner's friends saw us together last night."

"And that means you need to drag me off to a deserted room to whisper about it? I'm not protesting, don't get me wrong, but you better be careful or people are going to start to think you actually like me." His lips curl up in a smirk and he takes two steps toward me, crowding me into the corner.

My breathing hitches as he comes closer, but I force myself to focus on what I was going to say, not how amazing he smells.

"Someone saw us last night."

He presses a hand against the wall above my shoulder, and only a few inches remain between us.

"So what? Are you ashamed to be seen with me or something?"

"No." I shake my head. "It's not that. Didn't you and Kristy . . . I mean . . . don't you have a thing?"

"A thing?"

"You know . . . casual hookup? Do you really want to piss her off so you can't go back there? You realize she hates me, right?"

Ryker drops his hand from the wall, steps back, and crosses his arms over his chest. All humor fades from his expression, and his eyes are hard on mine when he finally replies.

"You're telling me you don't want her to know we study together so I can preserve some easy fuck? Really? Wow, Justine, good looking out for me, but I can take care of my own shit. Thanks for the concern, but it's not necessary." He drops his gaze to the floor before looking back up at me. "How the hell can you be this blind? Why would I be worried about Kristy when I'm trying so fucking hard to get you?"

This time it's me who stiffens. "We're studying. That's it."

He uncrosses his arms and leans in again before skimming a thumb along my cheekbone. My skin lights up at his touch. "If you think that's all this is, you're oblivious."

I need to put space between us. Not let him kiss me again. But the memory of both times his lips have been on mine are burned into my brain, and my body won't move.

Instead, I repeat the only words I can seem to conjure. "We're just studying."

Ryker drops his hand as his jaw turns to granite. His tone is just as hard. "Tonight. Same place. Same time. I'll see you there."

I shake my head. "I have to work until eight."

"Tomorrow." His blue eyes blaze. "You're not getting out of this. We have a deal."

"I'm not trying to get out of anything." My words come out flustered. "I just . . . have to work. I can do seven tomorrow."

"Good. I'll be there."

"To study," I remind him.

He steps back, his smirk firmly back in place, and I

think he's going to touch my face again but he looks down at his watch.

Something that feels a lot like disappointment twists through me. *Really, Justine? Calm down.*

"Whatever you have to tell yourself, Justine."

Chapter 20

Justine

I think it's encoded in my DNA to be early everywhere. Maybe it's the years of racking up tardy slips when my mom was in charge of getting me to school. The only days I made it on time were the ones I stayed with Gramps. Just one more in a long list of reasons that living with him was a hundred times better than living with my parents.

I'm at the same booth at Unwired we used before, and once I have my laptop set up and my books out, a big form casts a shadow over me. Looking up, I expect to see Ryker with his ready smile and bright blue eyes, but instead I see a vaguely familiar face that I can't place immediately.

"Hi?" It comes out as a question because he's looking down at me with an expectant expression.

"I wondered if I'd ever run into you again."

Okay, so I've met this guy before, but I have no idea who he is.

"Umm . . ."

His smile falters. "I'm just going to blame it on a few too many vanilla vodka and root beers that night if you don't remember me."

The comment jogs my memory. The bartender. From the night we celebrated at Ziggy's after finishing up finals. The one who wouldn't let me pay for my drink.

Details come rushing back, including the memory of me finally saying yes to Ryker, our kiss, my orgasm, and him standing me up the next day.

"Sorry. I guess my memory isn't quite as good as yours. How are you?" I don't know what else to say to this guy. He was nice and flirty. I can't remember if he told me his name or not. My mind is still drawing a blank there.

"No problem. I'm just really good with faces. It's a bartender thing."

"I bet."

"You study here a lot? I've just discovered this place, and I don't know how I missed it for the last couple years."

His backpack slung casually over one shoulder tells me he's a student too. "Are you in grad school?"

He shrugs. "Third year of med school. Can't wait to be done."

"Oh, wow. That's gotta be tough."

With a look at my casebook, he comes to the right conclusion about me. "Law school?"

"Yeah. Third year too, and I can't wait to be done either."

"I haven't seen you around campus, but I guess that makes sense since we're on opposite sides."

"True. I don't venture far from the law school."

"And you don't venture out to Ziggy's very often either."

I gesture to the pile of books and cluster of highlighters on the table before replying. "I'm more of a studier than a drinker."

"I can respect that." He nods to the seat across from me and shifts the backpack on his shoulder. "You mind if I join you? I've got some studying to knock out too."

A deeper voice interrupts before he can slide into the booth. "I mind, Caruthers."

My head jerks up to see Ryker standing just beyond the bartender. He turns, and I remember that they seemed to know each other that night at Ziggy's.

Ryker steps between Caruthers and me and leans down to brush a kiss across my cheek. "Sorry, babe. I got stuck at a train crossing. Didn't mean to be late."

Chapter 21

Ryker

Whatever Justine and I have going, I'm not letting some slick bartender get in my way. The kiss is instinctive and when I pull back, her eyes are wide and soft. I like that look on her.

I don't spare another glance at Caruthers as I slide in the booth across from Justine and pull out my laptop. He's already forgotten.

"Well, uh, maybe I'll see you around. Feel free to stop by Ziggy's anytime, and I'll make you a drink on the house." His words are clearly directed at Justine.

The guy has balls the size of boulders if he's got no problem hitting on her right in front of me, especially after I just laid my claim in a very obvious way. But I'm not going to waste any more time on him. More than anything, I'm curious to see how she's going to reply. It's a test of sorts, given by the universe—one that I'm content to sit back and observe.

"Thanks. I appreciate the offer, but like I said, I don't spend a lot of time at bars."

"Then maybe I'll see you around here again. Have a good one." Caruthers hefts his backpack higher and gives me a challenging nod that I return out of habit.

I watch Justine as he leaves. Her eyes don't follow him, which means that even if he wanted to be competition, he isn't. No, her eyes are on me.

"What was that?"

"What was what?" I reply, even though I know exactly what she's talking about.

"You kissed me. Like some territorial marking. In public." Her words are coming in spurts.

"Yeah."

"Why?"

Dropping my highlighter between the pages of my casebook, I cross my arms and meet her confused gaze. "Because I wanted to."

She pushes a thick wave of dark hair over her shoulder, her eyes never leaving mine. "That's not a reason."

"It's all the reason I need."

"But—"

I cut her off before she can protest. "You could've said yes to getting a drink with him, but you didn't. You know why that is?"

"I don't know . . . that's not my scene."

Uncrossing my arms, I lean forward, my elbows on either side of my casebook. "That might be true, but you said no because we've got something happening between us, and you're going to ride it out just like I am."

She picks up a highlighter, gripping it tightly in her fist. "We're just studying. That's all."

"We both know that's bullshit." I pull my laptop out and slide it onto the table between us. "But feel free to keep lying to yourself, and I'll keep kissing you anytime I want. Deal? Now, what do you want to start with?"

Justine releases a sound that's close to a growl and buries her hands in her hair. Instead of tearing it out in frustration, she twists it up into a messy bun and shoves a pen in to hold it.

It takes a spot on the list of the top ten sexiest things I've ever seen a woman do.

She scrubs both hands over her face, and I can't help but like the way I unsettle her. That's exactly what I want.

I wait while she stares at the pile of casebooks next to her. "Professional Responsibility. It's my least favorite, so I want to get it out of the way first."

"Sounds good."

We both flip open our casebooks and work through the reading, talking about the cases and typing out notes for class. Every time she readjusts her hair or bites her lip, I'm reminded how badly I want to get my mouth on her again. Everywhere. But at the same time, I'm strangely turned on by how hard she focuses. This is study date number two, and I understand how Justine has kept her grades so high. She's a machine, and totally relentless in her analysis and memorization.

I was right before—her brain is just as sexy as the way she fills out the V-neck she's wearing. I want to see her in a dress, or even a skirt like she wore that night at the bar. I want a chance to explore her body and her brain.

My mind is wandering when I'm supposed to be finishing up reading this case, but I'm out of time. Justine looks up and cracks her neck before she starts rattling off the points she thinks Babcock will cover in class.

My fingers pound the keys on my laptop as I try to get

down all the details, but Justine's stomach growls louder than my typing.

"Did you have dinner already? I'm frigging starving."

She shakes her head, and her tone is wry when she says, "But I've got a mac-and-cheese bowl waiting for me at home."

I don't think before I reply. "That's not real food. You need protein. Vegetables. You know? Let's finish up Trusts and Estates and go grab something."

Justine slaps her casebook closed. "I beg to differ that it's not real food, because mac-and-cheese bowls have been a major part of my diet for the last six years. Cheap, quick, and easy. What's not to like?"

"Babe, there's nothing cheap, quick, or easy about you. If you were . . . well, we both know the last two years would've gone differently."

Her eyes go wide at my words, which are nothing but the truth. When she says nothing in reply, I realize I've knocked her off-balance, which works for me just fine.

Changing the subject, I ask, "How about Chinese? Panda House isn't far."

Her eyes light up when I mention the student favorite of all the Chinese restaurants in town, but I wonder if she'll actually accept.

"Panda House?" Excitement tinges her tone. "I guess that would be okay. But work first, and then food."

The buzz of victory rises through me. *And that's how it's done.*

I keep my face expressionless as I nod and we both crack open our Trust and Estates books. We continue to study in companionable silence, but inside I'm fucking thrilled.

I'm finally taking Justine on a real date, whether she realizes it or not.

Chapter 22

Justine

I'm starving, and Panda House Chinese is my weakness. It's not fair that Ryker played that card, especially after the territorial kiss to ward off the bartender Caruthers. But I'd probably go to dinner with the devil himself at Panda House if he caught me at a moment when my stomach is growling.

Now, with plates heaping with the deliciousness that Panda has to offer sitting in front of us, we're eating in non-awkward silence. It's not until I'm halfway through my food and slowing down when I take a look around us.

The stares. They're coming from tables in every direction. And several of them I recognize.

Ryker lowers his chopsticks and follows my gaze. When he looks at me, it's with an unreadable expression. "Finished?" He says nothing about the fact that we're apparently the main source of entertainment in the restaurant tonight.

Am I done being stared at like an attraction at the zoo? "Sure am. You?"

"I'm just getting started here." That expression of his?

It stays unreadable, but his words tell me that he sees the stares too—and if I'm not mistaken, he likes them.

I decide to throw it out there in the open. "Do you like this? Being the center of attention?"

"When I've got the most beautiful woman in this room across from me? What's not to like?"

I should scoff at the line. It's not light years away from the ones he has been using on me since first year, but for some reason, it feels different. More intimate. It doesn't put my back up the way it did before.

"I'm sure you say that to all the girls," I joke.

"No. I don't."

A thrill zips through me at his response, but I have no idea how to reply to that, so I dig my fork into my fried rice deliciousness and keep eating.

The server comes by as I'm stuffing my face in lieu of conversation. When he sets the bill folio down, Ryker lowers his chopsticks and grabs it before I can even do a mental count of how much money I have in my wallet.

He pulls out a credit card and slips it in without even looking at the bill, then hands it back to the server, who hasn't had a chance to walk away yet.

"I'll be right back with this," the kid says before hurrying off.

I fish my wallet from my purse and pull out one of the two tens inside and slide it across the table.

"Here you go. I can throw in more for the tip."

Ryker does exactly what I expect and pushes it back toward me. "I got it."

"I'm not letting you buy me dinner."

"Because it'll make this too much of a date?" He tilts his head, and his expression dares me to tell the truth.

"Yes," I admit. And I can't cross that line.

Ryker leans back against the booth and crosses his arms. "I think you're the most intelligent woman I've ever had dinner with, so that means you should be able to figure out when you're on a date."

"This isn't a date," I protest. "This is two study buddies grabbing a meal because we were both starving. At least, it was until you decided to do that." I nod toward the spot where the bill had been laid.

"Justine, I hate to break it to you, but we're on a date."

"No, we're not."

The situation is turning ridiculous, but it's obviously not an argument I'm going to win. That doesn't mean I have to let it happen again. Note to self: be quicker on the draw when it comes to bills.

Wait, wouldn't it be easier not to go to dinner with him? Why didn't my brain go there first?

Guilt washes through me because Justice Grant isn't paying me to spend time with his son outside of the studying context. But Ryker won't stay in the neat little box where I'm trying to keep him. The kisses, dinner . . . he's blurring the lines. This is about focusing on the goal, not letting myself get distracted.

I steal another glance at Ryker from under my lashes. *No matter how sexy and tempting the distraction is.*

Chapter 23

Ryker

Justine tries her car three times in the parking lot before I get out of my Camaro and walk around to the driver's side window and knock on the glass. She opens the door and looks up at me with frustration lining her features. I don't like that look on her.

"It won't start."

"Let me try it."

Justine slides out of the driver's seat, and I take her place. A few turns of the key tells me a jump probably isn't going to solve the problem, but it's worth a try.

Five minutes later, after Justine tries to start it a few times hooked up to the Camaro, I'm unfortunately proven right.

"I'll give you a ride home and you can call a garage in the morning about having it picked up."

Her expression falls. From the looks of the car and everything else I've gathered about her, I know this probably isn't an expense she has figured into her plans. It's clear her budget is tight, judging by the Lipton tea she brings to study and her diet of mac-and-cheese bowls.

When she drops her head against the steering wheel, she confirms my thoughts.

"I didn't exactly figure a tow truck and a repair job in my budget." She lifts a hand and slaps the dash. "Why? Why couldn't you just hold out a few more months? Six on the outside? Don't you have any sense of loyalty?"

The desperation in her voice as she talks to her uncooperative car cuts into me, but I keep my mouth shut. Right now, I don't think there's anything I could say that's going to change the situation.

"Grab your stuff. I'll give you a ride, and you can think about what you want to do in the morning."

"Things don't always look better in the morning, you know."

Justine's dark eyes are shiny, but I'd bet my Camaro she'd never let those tears fall in front of me. *Good. I don't want to see them.* Something tells me that they'd gut me more than the last girl who tried tears with me when I told her we weren't actually dating. Ironic that now I've got a girl telling me the same thing I've told others.

"I know, but at least it'll be light out, and you might think of some more options. You strike me as a pretty resourceful girl."

She forces a smile to her face, but it's pained. Turning, she grabs her backpack off the passenger seat and shoves a few more things in it.

"Then I guess I'm taking you up on your ride because right now, I really don't feel like schlepping my stuff to the bus stop."

"I've got you covered, Justine. It's gonna be okay." I say the words, but I wish I could make them true. I don't like seeing her struggle.

We climb in, and I back out of the parking lot. "Am I taking you to the same place you lived last year?"

From the passenger seat, she shakes her head, her arms wrapped around the backpack on her lap.

"No, I had to find a cheaper place. I'm over in the Gilroy Student Housing Complex."

Yanking my eyes from the road, I look at her. "I thought that place was being torn down this year."

When Justine shrugs and her grip tightens on her backpack, I chastise myself. *Pride, Ry. Tread carefully*.

"Nope. They decided to hold off until next fiscal year because the demo costs were higher than planned. They've got one of the buildings rented out. It was dirt cheap, so I was pretty lucky to get in."

Lucky isn't exactly a word I would use to describe the complex I'm remembering. *Shit hole* is a better description.

Ten minutes later when I pull into the parking lot in front of the building, I confirm my opinion. This place is a dump. The yellow, orange, and blue panels that make up the corners of the buildings are faded almost beyond recognition and are falling off in chunks. Basically, picture the crappiest '60s no-tell motel you've ever seen and downgrade it another step. I remember coming to a party here when I was a senior in high school and being shocked at the shitty conditions. That was over six years ago, and things have only slid further downhill since.

"I'm down at the other end. Last one on the first floor."

I guide the Camaro in the direction Justine indicates and pull into a parking spot marked by faded yellow lines and a crumbling curb.

"Shit!"

My gaze jerks to Justine, but she's already out of the car and dashing toward the building before I realize what the problem is. The door looks like someone kicked it in.

I yank open the door of the Camaro and charge after her. The girl's an idiot to go running into a break-in scene. Wrapping a hand around her wrist, I pull her back.

"What the hell are you doing? Someone could still be inside."

She struggles against me, then twists out of my grip with what must be some kind of evasive move like they teach in self-defense classes.

"And if they're still inside, they haven't gotten away with stealing my stuff!"

Her struggles intensify, so I wrap her in a backward bear hug, locking both arms around her waist before I pick her up off the ground. "Not fucking happening," I growl into her ear. No way in hell am I letting her take a chance of getting hurt because of her adrenaline-fueled reaction. "Get back in the car and call Campus Safety. I'll go in."

She continues to fight me for another minute, and I almost expect elbows to start flying, but she finally stills.

"Okay. Fine. I'll call." She speaks through gritted teeth.

I lower her to her feet facing the Camaro. "Go."

She turns to glare at me but follows my orders. Once she's safely inside the car, I use an elbow to push open the door and flip on the front light switch with a sleeve-covered fist.

Much like I expected, the apartment's best days were several decades ago. On the other hand, it's clean and neat. It doesn't take long to deduce what was stolen, but I continue my walk through the place just in case there's something else that's obvious or the person is still hiding inside.

The apartment is silent, and other than a rumpled shirt and a pair of shorts on the bathroom floor, it doesn't seem that much is out of place. Rather than linger and wonder what else could possibly be missing, I head back outside, pulling the door shut behind me. With the door busted, there's no way in hell Justine is sleeping there tonight. The rest of the cars in the parking lot resemble the one we left in the parking lot at Panda House—older and edged with rust.

Justine is out of the Camaro with her arms crossed over her chest before I make it to her door. "What did you see? Are they gone? What does it look like inside? Is everything gone?" Her questions come fast, telling me the adrenaline is still rushing through her system.

"There's no one inside, but it looks like they stole your TV. Maybe some other stuff. You'll need to go through it when the cops get here. You called?"

She nods. "Yeah, but I don't know how much it'll help. This is the third break-in this week here, and it's all been petty theft. They didn't take my TV. I didn't have one." She rubs her hands up and down her arms as I take her in.

"Third break-in? Are you fucking serious?"

"Yeah, since school started. No leads."

I open my mouth to ask her why the hell she'd stay here, but I already know the answer. She's too broke to go anywhere else and too proud to ask for help.

She walks closer to the front door, which is splintered at the bottom where someone kicked it in with what looks like heavy boots and some serious anger problems. "Why? Why would someone do this? It's not like I have anything worth stealing," she murmurs as she covers her hand with her sleeve to push the door open.

I follow her inside and survey the interior closer this

time. Justine's gaze catalogs every single possession, and she's right—she doesn't have much to steal.

She checks the bedroom and bathroom, and shakes her head when she emerges. "I had my laptop with me, and I don't see anything else missing that I can tell." Her gaze travels around the room once more. "I would notice, right?"

She looks up at me, and the pinched and worried set of her face kills me. She shouldn't have to deal with this kind of shit.

"Have you stashed anything in here where only you could find it?"

She shakes her head. "No. Nothing. Who would do this?"

"Some asshole who gets off on destroying property. You're lucky they didn't trash the inside too. Maybe someone scared them off before they could."

A shaft of anger stabs through me when I think about someone breaking in while Justine was home. She's not staying here, but we also can't leave it unlocked. I wouldn't be surprised if this place was cleared out by morning by her neighbors.

"Maintenance is going to have to fix the door before you can leave tonight."

Justine turns to me, her arms wrapped around herself. The adrenaline is slipping away and fear is taking hold. "I have to call Merica. She'll let me stay on her couch."

"Wait until Campus Safety gets here. Let's take it one step at a time, okay?"

She drops her arms to her sides. "I don't need you to babysit me. I can handle this myself. I'm a big girl. I'll be fine."

"Let me help. You don't have to be such a badass all the

time."

That's when I see her shaking. *Fuck it.* I drop my hand, wrap both arms around her, and pull her into my chest. She shakes harder.

"It's okay. No one is going to hurt you. They're going to have to come through me first."

Justine relaxes, but only for a moment, because blue and red lights cut through the dark of the night. She tenses and pulls away, and I'm almost certain she's blinking back tears.

The two green-and-white cruisers park to the left of my Camaro, and two officers climb out of the cars. The one who appears to be in charge looks from me to Justine, who is back to standing with her arms wrapped protectively around her middle.

"Miss, are you the one who called in a break-in?"

Justine nods and talks to the cops for several moments before leading them inside. I stay out front, waiting by the Camaro, deciding how I'm going to broach the subject of her coming to stay at my condo. She's going to say no every which way I can come up with.

That's when my second idea takes root, and this one just might have a shot.

A few minutes later, the uniformed Campus Safety officer leads the way out of the apartment, and I walk over to where he's talking with Justine.

"We'll get someone down here from maintenance within the hour to board up the door and then get it replaced tomorrow. The door, handle, and lock are all toast."

"Thank you. I appreciate that." Justine's voice isn't as strong, and my instincts say it's time to get her the hell out of here.

"Do you have somewhere else you can stay tonight?" the officer asks.

Before she can reply, I interrupt. "She's got a place, sir. We've got it taken care of."

The officer finally looks at me again and nods. "Good, because staying here isn't a good option. This place is becoming the easy target for thieves, and you're lucky nothing was taken, Miss Porter."

Justine chokes out a laugh that sounds harsh in the quiet night. "Yeah, I'm getting that."

"Let me make the call to maintenance so we don't have to stand around here all night." The cop walks toward the cruiser and pulls out a phone, and I step closer to Justine.

"Anything you need to get from inside? Because we're getting out of here as soon as the maintenance guys show up."

She shoves both hands into her hair before turning away and pacing. "I need to call Merica. I think she might be in her night class still. And I have no car. *Shit.*"

"You're not staying with Merica; you're coming with me. You don't need a car."

She spins around, and I'm glad to see the normal fiery Justine coming back. "And where do you think you're taking me? Your place?"

I know she's gearing up to shoot me down, so I drop plan B on her.

"No. We're going to my parents' house."

Chapter 24

Justine

The gate slides open and Ryker guides his Camaro up the long, winding driveway. I didn't even know that there were houses in this town that had gates. It seems even stranger to be driving with Ryker's hand resting on my leg. The touch started out as comforting because I couldn't stop my leg from shaking when I got in the car, but then he never moved it and I didn't protest.

The break-in rocked me, and I can't help but feel like my one safe place has been violated. When the anger began wearing off, all I could picture was what would have happened if someone had broken in while I was home. The shaking hasn't stopped since.

I don't often seek comfort from others, but I'm glad I wasn't alone tonight. It doesn't matter how strong I tell myself I am; I'm also self-aware enough to know that I have a breaking point. Tonight might have cracked it.

Still, I'm surprised Ryker didn't insist on taking me to his condo. Probably because he knows I would have insisted on calling Merica.

BAD JUDGMENT

When he said he was bringing me here, I couldn't find the words to say no. Justice Grant is one of the kindest people I've ever met, and if I'm being honest, I've always wondered what it would have been like to have a man like him as a father. I've never met Mrs. Grant, so I have no idea what to expect from the woman I've seen in the family pictures Justice Grant keeps in his chambers. The perfect family, that's what those pictures could have been captioned.

The only family pictures I have are snapshots of me and Gramps together. My parents never bothered.

The house comes into view, and it's just as perfect as those pictures. White and huge, with a red front door.

We park in front of one of the four garage stalls, and Ryker climbs out of the car. I'm not sure I'm ready for this. When I don't get out right away, he comes around and opens my door.

"Let me get your bag for you."

A thought strikes me. "Do your parents know we're coming? Did you call them?" I flip through the last hour in my head, and he had the opportunity when I was inside with Campus Safety, checking once more to see if anything had been stolen, but I don't remember him saying anything.

"My mom won't be home, and my dad won't care. He likes you."

Warmth creeps into my chest at the approval in those words, and I climb out of the car to follow him to a side door. A little of my anxiety drains away at not having to meet his mother tonight. She looks so flawless in the pictures, and I've often wondered if there's any way she could be as kind as Justice Grant.

Inside the garage, there are three shiny black cars and one under a cover. A hint of red peeks out from under the gray nylon. Ryker doesn't slow, just heads for the door and twists the knob.

"Dad, you around?" His deep voice echoes through the house, bouncing off dark, shining wood floors and stark white walls. The ceilings are at least ten feet tall—maybe taller. I hear movement ahead, and Ryker walks toward it and turns the corner.

"What brings you out here tonight?" Justice Grant's voice is comforting and familiar after the crap night I've had.

I peek around the corner as well, and his brow furrows with confusion when he sees me. His gaze darts between me and Ryker.

"And Justine. This is quite the surprise."

"Justine's place got broken into and she couldn't stay there. Luckily, I was giving her a ride home from dinner and came up with the great idea that she stay here tonight. I'll crash in my old room. She can take the guest room." Ryker's arm comes around my shoulders, and he pulls me closer to his side.

More confusion and questions enter Justice Grant's eyes, but I'm not at liberty to answer most of them in front of his son. The fact unleashes a wave of guilt inside me. *What must he think of me?* I need a chance to talk to him alone.

"That's awful, Justine. I'm so sorry to hear that. Where are you living? Did you call the police? Have they found who did it?" Justice Grant fires off questions, and Ryker takes the liberty of answering for me.

"She's in Gilroy, and apparently the university has let it get run-down to the point where break-ins are common. Campus Safety barely blinked about it. It was bullshit."

"I thought Gilroy was being torn down?"

"Next year." I explain the same thing I did to Ryker, and by the end of it, Justice Grant looks about like he did when he was told someone disagreed with his judicial opinion.

"That's ridiculous, especially if Campus Safety isn't patrolling it appropriately. I'll have to discuss it with the university's board of trustees."

Well, shit. What if they decide the place isn't fit to be lived in and kick us all out? I don't have somewhere else to go right now that I can afford without a roommate, and I really don't want to have to find another one.

I guess if I had to, there's always Merica's couch to crash on. *Why didn't I call her before I let Ryker talk me into coming here?* The only excuse I can come up with is my brain is completely fried from the double stroke of bad luck hitting home tonight. Besides, it wasn't like Ryker was asking me if I wanted to come here; he just told me I was. *Why did I let him do that?*

Moment of weakness, I assure myself. That's all it was.

"Let's get you settled upstairs. My wife would love to meet you, but she's out of town on an extended project. She's much better at this hospitality stuff than I am, but we keep the room ready regardless. The housekeeper was here yesterday, so it should be dusted and aired out."

I smile, trying not to convey just how out of place I feel right now as he continues.

"And you've eaten already, so we don't need to worry about that, unless you'd like some dessert. Or would you like a drink? A glass of wine? Something stronger? It sounds like you've had a rough night."

It's strange to see Justice Grant in domestic mode, but he's just as thoughtful as he's always been. I'm not sure what to say in response, and I look to Ryker to gauge his expression.

He's already looking down at me. "Want a drink? Might help you get to sleep. I know we need to be up early for class."

"Uh, sure."

"Preference?" Justice Grant asks.

I don't think now is the time to ask for vanilla vodka and root beer, but that's all I really drink. I'm not sophisticated. I don't know anything about wine, so I take the easy route. "I'll just have whatever you're having. I'm not picky."

"Then cognac it is. You'll enjoy it. This one is Ryker's favorite."

I nod, even though I don't have a clue what cognac is, but I want to sleep without having nightmares about someone breaking into my house while I'm inside it. I can just imagine the icy, gut-wrenching fear would have been ten times stronger than the anger and helplessness I felt when I saw the door was kicked in. If Ryker hadn't pushed me to study tonight at Unwired, I would have been studying at home. Inwardly, I shudder at the thought of what could have happened.

"I'm going to get Justine settled upstairs, and we'll be back down," Ryker tells his father.

"I'll pour some cognac in the library and have it waiting."

I follow Ryker as he leads me up a wide staircase in the front entryway of the house and then down a hallway to the right. The walls are all stark white, but not plain, because there's molding about three feet up from the floor and what looks like picture-frame-shaped molding below it. We stop at the end of the hall where there's a door to the right and a door ahead of us. Ryker twists the handle on the door on the right and steps inside.

It's a beautiful room in shades of silvery gray and pale purple. A large four-poster canopy bed dominates the space with gauzy silver fabric hanging from it. The matching dark wood dresser sits on the far wall, and a pale purple chair and footstool sit between the dresser and the bed. The silvery curtains are open, but I can see nothing beyond the darkness of the night.

"This is the guest room. Sorry about the purple-and-gray explosion."

"It's beautiful." And it is. Actually, it's the most beautiful bedroom I've ever been in.

Ryker sets my backpack on the bed and nods to the door a few feet from the bed. "You've got a bathroom through there that connects with my room. My room is next door, the one at the end of the hall." He steps toward me and lifts a hand to my face before brushing a stray lock of hair away from my eyes. "If you want to just crash instead of having a drink with my dad, that's cool. No pressure."

What I want is for him to kiss me again.

I freeze at the thought. I can't be thinking things like that. And not just because we're standing in his parents' house.

But Ryker doesn't kiss me. He stares into my eyes, trying to read my thoughts, and I'm glad he doesn't have that power. I saw the confused look on Justice Grant's face when Ryker curled his arm around my shoulders. He has to be wondering what the hell is going on between his son and me.

I need to talk to him alone. I need to explain that it's nothing.

Because it is nothing. Right?

Maybe if I keep lying to myself, it'll come true. Fake it till you make it, right?

"I'm good with having a drink. Give me five minutes?"

Ryker's thumb smooths over my cheekbone before he drops his hand from my face. "Whatever you need."

He leaves the room, but not without a backward glance that sears me to the core.

I'm so screwed.

Ten minutes later we're heading downstairs and I'm following Ryker through the halls of the house. It looked big from the outside, but the inside seems even larger. We find Justice Grant in a room that nearly stops my heart. It's wall-to-wall, floor-to-ceiling books.

Library envy. It's a thing. And I have it. Acutely.

"Wow. This is amazing. Did you collect all of these books?" I can't hold back the question.

Justice Grant pauses after pouring brown liquor into an ornate glass to match the other two on the small side table. His eyes find mine and he smiles.

"I've been a collector of books for many years. Some are gifts from family and friends, some purchased, and some were left when we bought the house years ago. Now I'm running out of shelf space and having to thin down my collection in order to add the ones I want."

"It's a beautiful room." My eyes scan the shelves before landing on the cozy window seat I'd like to curl up in for hours to read.

Ryker steps forward and grabs two glasses off the table

and hands one to me. "Let's see how you like cognac."

I'm not offended that he assumes I've never had it, because it's the truth. I stare down at the contents of the glass and wonder how I'm supposed to go about drinking this stuff. Do I take it like a shot or sip? I watch both Ryker and his father, and they swirl the liquid before sipping. I mimic their motions, but almost slosh the liquor over the side.

I check both their faces to make sure they didn't catch my almost faux pas, but neither did.

Putting my lips to my glass of half-swirled cognac, I fear I'm going to hate it or want to spit it out and embarrass the hell out of myself. But surprisingly, it hits my tongue and tastes a little like candy in a glass. It goes down easy, and I don't have an urge to choke or spit. *Winning*.

As we sample our cognac in silence, I wait for someone to start a conversation. Justice Grant takes the lead.

"I spoke to your mother just before you got here, and she misses you very much."

"Thanks for the update," Ryker says, continuing to sip his drink.

I know Mrs. Grant is a big-time partner at a law firm in town called Grant Bentham Beckett. I'm going to go out on a limb and guess that she's one of the founding partners.

"She's a litigator, right?" I ask.

Justice Grant nods. "Yes, she handles very complex civil litigation, and her cases generally take years of work to settle or take to trial."

"Wow. That sounds . . . intense."

"Let's just say Mom wasn't around much while I was growing up."

"She was around as much as she could manage," Justice Grant adds. "Being a founding partner is no easy job, and we've always been very proud of her accomplishments."

Ryker releases a harsh laugh. "I guess that's one way to describe it."

It seems there's no love lost between mother and son . . . which seems strange, and none of my business. I try to change the subject.

"So, an entire family of lawyers. Are there more in the family tree, or is it just this branch?"

"My father and grandfather were also judges. My wife's grandfather was a lawyer as well."

"Wow. Family tradition then, it seems."

"What about your parents, Justine?" The question comes from Ryker, not from Justice Grant. He already knows some of the details, including how they destroyed my credit by using my social security number before I even turned eighteen.

Looking down at the remaining liquor in my glass, I swirl it before sipping. When I look up, Ryker is watching me and waiting for an answer.

"We're not close. I haven't seen either of them since I was fifteen and my grandfather was awarded custody."

"Wow. I'm sorry. I didn't know." Sympathy is obvious on Ryker's face, but I don't want his pity.

"It's no big deal. I just don't talk about them because there's nothing to say."

I brace myself for more questions I don't want to answer, but Ryker's phone goes off in his pocket. He pulls it out and glances at the display with a frown.

"I need to take this. I'll be back." He strides out of the room before he answers.

What the hell?

"Would you like some more cognac?" Justice Grant

asks as he reaches for the bottle.

"Please." I hold out my glass for him to pour me another measure.

"So, do you care to tell me what's going on with you and my son, because it appears there's more happening than just studying?"

His forthright question is one I've been expecting, but still have no answer for.

"Umm. I— You know—" I stammer out words while I scramble to think of some explanation that would make sense. Honestly, I don't know what's going on between us.

"Justine, it's not a problem. I didn't put any rules around our deal beyond those we discussed. If there's more happening, I'm not going to say I'm unhappy about it. Quite the opposite. You're a smart girl, and my son could do much worse." He looks down at his drink. "In fact, he has done much worse. So bringing a girl like you home, one who I know is hardworking and dedicated to making her mark on the world, is far from a problem."

"It's going better than I anticipated. He's smart, but you already knew that. I guess . . . I honestly didn't expect to like him, and it's kind of throwing me off. But there's no need to worry. We're not . . . together, like you're thinking. We're just friends. I have everything under control."

"I have all the confidence in the world in you."

Before I respond, Ryker returns to the room. "I hate to do this, but I have to go. A buddy of mine ran into some trouble and needs my help. I should be back in an hour."

"Who is it?" Justice Grant asks.

"Ian. I'll be quick."

"Anything I can do to help?"

"Can I borrow the truck?"

The truck he was supposed to use to help me move. And now he's borrowing it from his dad to help some friend late at night. Anger blooms inside me, rooted in bitterness and hurt. Why had he screwed me over when it came to something so important, especially after that night in the bar?

"Of course. Take the truck. Justine and I will have another drink, and then this old man is going to bed. I've got a big trial kicking off tomorrow morning, so I need to be ready."

"Thanks, Dad." Ryker looks at me. "Sorry about this. I'll be back as soon as I can. If I don't make it back before you go to bed, I'll see you in the morning."

I stare up at him, and all I can think about is that damn truck and how quick he is to go to someone else's rescue. "I think I'll have another drink."

Ryker's eyes lock with mine, and he knows exactly what I'm thinking about. I think I see a flash of guilt on his face before he turns and leaves the room without saying another word.

Justice Grant pours me another large glass of cognac, and I savor it as the liquor pools in my belly while he answers my questions about his books.

My head is fuzzy by the time I make my way back up to the silver-and-purple room, but there's one thing I've decided—there really is *nothing* happening between Ryker and me, and that's the way things are going to stay.

Just. Business.

Chapter 25

Justine

I wake up disoriented and confused. The mattress under me is like a cloud, and the blanket tucked up to my neck is soft and warm and smells like lavender and sunshine. That's when I know I'm drunk—probably from the last glass of cognac I brought up to my room—because sunshine doesn't have an actual smell.

Blinking, I take in the room around me and remember where I am. Ryker's parents' house. My bladder is protesting, so I slip out of bed into the bathroom and take care of business.

Did Ryker come back from his late-night rescue of a friend?

I don't know why I care because *we're just friends*, but that doesn't stop me from quietly pushing open the door that leads from the bathroom to his bedroom.

A king-sized bed takes up a portion of the large room, and even in the darkness I can make out a shape in it. Question answered. Ryker came back.

I tell myself I don't care either way and tug the handle

to pull the door closed, but the hinge squeaks in protest and the shape moves.

Oh crap.

A deep voice, husky with sleep, comes out of the darkness as he sits up. "You need something?"

Caught.

"Sorry, got turned around. Wrong door."

My lie sounds believable, even to me, and I hope he buys it. I move to pull the door the rest of the way closed, but Ryker's voice stops me.

"Come here."

Into his room? In the middle of the night?

Bad. Plan. Don't do it, Justine.

But my bare feet are already following his command, stepping from the bathroom tile onto the wood floor.

"What?"

"Come here," he repeats.

Now that I'm inside the room and my eyes are adjusting to the light, I can see him more clearly. The sheet and blanket pool around his waist, leaving his upper body bare. There's just enough moonlight coming through the window at this angle to make out the defined muscles of his pecs and deep ridges of his abs.

God bless men who work out.

What? No. Bad, Justine.

Ryker motions for me to keep coming closer and pats the side of his bed. My stupid body responds to his wordless commands, and I pause beside the bed.

"I'm sorry," he says.

"Sorry for what?"

Our voices are hushed, as if we're both afraid of waking his father.

"For not being there for you when I said I would be. I'm not that guy."

They're the words I've needed to hear for months, and they're finally hanging in the air between us.

"Then why did you? You never even said." The question has been driving me crazy since the morning I sat on my stoop, disappointment, hurt, and humiliation sloshing in my belly along with the remains of too much liquor.

"I can't tell you why, but you have to know that it wasn't something I could avoid or have planned for. I've owed you an apology for so long, and without an explanation, I know it's a shitty one."

He can't tell me why. Something about the bullshit excuse takes the strength from my knees, and I sit on the edge of the bed. My T-shirt rides up, and I become acutely aware that I'm wearing nothing but that and my panties.

And I'm sitting on Ryker's bed.

In his parents' house.

If that's not a string of bad decisions sewn together with even worse judgment, I'm not sure what it is.

I press both hands to the bed in a move to stand up, but Ryker's palm slides over the top of one, pinning it in place.

"Don't go. I know you're pissed, and you still have every right to be, but don't walk away from me again."

"You can't tell me why, but you expect me to just forgive you? I sat out in front of my apartment for over an hour waiting for you! Do you know how much that sucks? Do you know how much I regretted what we'd done the night before? It was concrete proof that me turning you down over and over was the right choice."

Ryker releases a whoosh of breath. "I know. You're right. I played into everything you think I am, but dammit, Justine, that's not fucking fair. Things aren't black and white. Shit happened that I couldn't control."

"Shit happens," I repeat slowly. "Great excuse. I'll remember that one for next time."

I push off the bed again, but Ryker grabs my arm and tugs me down. I lose my balance and fall against him. He wastes no time taking advantage of the opportunity, and flips over to pin me to the bed.

"You're not walking away from this."

My T-shirt rides up further, and the hot press of his skin against mine clears my brain of any protests I'd been about to make.

"Are you naked?" I ask, my voice unsteady from the booze. The heat of his body is soaking into me, and I'm pretty sure the head of his penis just brushed against my belly. Naked. Skin on skin.

"Yes."

Oh my God.

I freeze, unsure what to do. Ryker Grant, who I've decided I have *absolutely nothing* going on with, is lying on top of me naked. With a hard-on. And it's touching me.

And instead of struggling to free myself, my body wants to wrap around him for more contact. Heat builds between my legs, and my panties are damp. In minutes they're going to be soaked, and he'll be able to feel it.

"Your heart is pounding, Justine."

"You're lying on top of me naked, *Ryker*."

"You like it."

I go quiet. What am I supposed to say? *No, I hate it. Get your sexy-as-hell body off me because I need to go back to my room and get myself off before I'll be able to get any sleep?* Yeah. No. Not happening.

"You should probably get off me now." My voice drops into a whisper.

"I don't want to move."

His face lowers closer to mine, and I can feel his breath on my skin. He doesn't ask for permission. Doesn't offer to move. Instead, his lips slide along my jaw, leaving tendrils of sensation in their wake.

My panties? Let's not talk about the state of them.

When his lips hit the shell of my ear and his teeth graze the lobe, I can't stop my body's response. My hips buck upward, seeking the delicious friction I need.

And I get that friction by rubbing my clit against the hard length of Ryker's cock.

I should be embarrassed. Should be horrified. But I've stopped thinking, and I'm operating on pure instinct backed by booze-fueled courage. I haven't had another orgasm as good as the one I stole in the back hallway of the bar—and the good Lord knows I've tried. All summer. It's like I've got all this pent-up need burning inside me, waiting for him to unleash it.

"Fuck, Justine. That feels so goddamn good. I can feel those sweet little pussy lips against my cock."

I've never been a girl for dirty talk, or so I thought, but when Ryker voices those rumbling words in the darkness of this room, my nipples harden and I buck harder against him.

I can't stop myself. I want it, and he's going to let me take it.

"You like that, baby? Rubbing against my cock. You gonna come for me? Let me hear that sweet sound?"

"Yes." I moan, and he takes my lips as I work my hips against him.

"Come for me, and then I'm gonna eat that pussy and finally get a taste of what I've been dying for all these years."

It doesn't take much to send myself over the edge. The orgasm slams into me and radiates outward through my body. I keep up the pressure, the friction, grabbing every little bit of pleasure that I can until it finally fades away.

Only then do I realize that my hands are locked around Ryker's bare shoulders, my nails digging into the skin of his back.

I release my grip immediately and mumble, "I'm so sorry," as embarrassment fills me.

What the hell did I just do? I used Ryker as my own personal sex toy and got off dry-humping him like a teenager. Mortification burns my cheeks, and I know if it were light in this room, my face would be red.

"Nothing to be sorry for, baby. And we're not done."

He presses his cock against my pussy, setting off aftershocks of pleasure, and a moan escapes my lips.

"I love hearing you come for me. I can't get enough of that sound."

He moves down the bed and kneels above me. My eyes zero in on his cock. It's thick and long and rises up to almost touch his belly button. The dick print didn't do it justice, because apparently he's a shower and a grower.

My mouth, which has never watered at the sight of a penis before, floods with moisture, and all I can think is how badly I want my lips wrapped around the crown. I know from the touch of it against my belly, the skin is smooth and hot.

Since when have I ever been desperate to put a dick in my mouth? Since never. It must be the haze of orgasm messing with my head.

But I can't get rid of the thought. I've got two choices—get the hell out of here, or stay.

Chapter 26

Ryker

Now that I've heard Justine come, a question is battering around in my brain—did she come that night I pinned her up against the wall in the back hallway of the bar? I have to know, but I'm fumbling with how to ask the question because her eyes are locked on my dick and she's practically licking her lips.

Fuck, my dick would look amazing between those lips.

I yank my thoughts back to the question at hand. "That night at the bar? In the hallway when I kissed you? Did you come? I didn't think anyone could come that easy."

I wish I could see her face, because I would bet anything that her cheeks are bright red.

She mumbles something I can't make out.

"What was that?"

"This is so humiliating," she whispers. "I just dry-humped you. Like we're fifteen or something."

I smile at her words. I sure haven't gone this slow with any woman since I hit sophomore year of high school, so she's not far off in that assessment.

"I want to make you come again."

Deciding the best way to stem her embarrassment is to do exactly that, I press a quick kiss to her lips before sliding down her body until only the soaked panties she's wearing separate my mouth from my goal.

"I want to taste you. Touch you. Make you come harder than you've ever come before. I want this wet pussy in my mouth. On my tongue. I want you to come on my face this time."

Justine's eyes widen but there's no protest from her lips, and even a slight nod.

She wants it too. I know she does. Because I'm right there with her.

I keep my eyes on hers as I hook a finger in the material of her panties at each hip and draw them down. Sweet fucking heaven—that's what I reveal. A tiny dark strip of hair and bare pussy lips are before me.

"You're so fucking pretty." I glance up to meet her eyes. "Right down to your tight little pussy."

She likes the dirty talk. I could tell when she was rubbing against me and my words sent her over the edge. Well, she'll get plenty of it from me because it turns me on just as much.

I lower my mouth and waste no time getting that first taste by sweeping my tongue between her lips.

Sweet. Fucking. Heaven. She's tart and tangy and everything I wanted her to be and more. I know I should start slow and take my time, but the taste of her goes straight to my head. I *devour*.

Justine's quiet moans and cries are the only incentive I need to keep going. I'm going to make this so good for her that she'll never be able to think about her pussy without remembering how good it felt with my mouth on her.

I'm going to ruin her for other men. No one will ever make her come as hard as I will.

I move my hand to slide a finger inside her and the muscles clamp down on me. A second finger has her writhing against my mouth, and I wrap my lips around her clit and suck. Her moans quiet, and I look up to see Justine holding a pillow over her mouth to silence the sound.

I keep going, sucking, licking, tonguing, and fingering her until her legs tense and a muted cry reaches my ears. Her inner muscles convulse around my fingers, and I don't stop until her fingers curl into my hair and lift my head.

Justine's wide eyes are hazy with pleasure, and I love knowing I did that. I want to be the only man who can do that for her.

When did I decide I was keeping her?

Shit, does the answer to that question really matter? Because Justine's not the kind of woman you can decide to keep if she doesn't want to be kept. My future—well-planned out not so very long ago—is now as hazy as her eyes. I don't know what the fuck I want to do with my life, but I know Justine has specific plans for hers.

I push up from between her legs, keeping my eyes on hers as I lean forward and kiss her. Against her lips I ask, "Do you like how you taste, baby? Because I think you taste amazing."

She doesn't reply, only jams her fingers into my hair again and yanks me closer, taking the lead. The kiss lasts for long minutes until she pulls back. My cock is throbbing, and there's nothing I want to do more than bury it inside her right now.

But Justine jerks away and slides out from under me. "I

have to go. I can't do this. We have to stop."

I grab her hand as she stumbles to her feet, stalling her hasty exit. "Can't do what? We just did."

Justine shakes her head. "We have to stop. This can't happen. I can't afford for this to happen."

I have no idea what she's talking about, but she's full of shit. "This is happening, whether you can afford for it to happen or not. You can't imagine how bad I want to make you come again. There's nothing wrong with what we're doing."

She squeezes her eyes shut as she turns away, tugging at the hold I have on her hand.

"Let me go."

"No."

She turns back, face blank. "You don't have a choice."

There's something in her eyes I can't read, and as much as I want to drag her back into my bed and keep her there all night, I don't want to do it fighting her every step of the way. I've been chasing her for over two years, and she's pushed me away at every opportunity. I thought things would change. I thought we'd found level ground, but she's still pushing me away.

Frustration mounts and I drop her hand. "You need to realize you can only push someone away so many times before they stop coming back."

"I never asked you to keep coming back." Justine's words are quietly final as she slips out of my room through the bathroom, shutting the door behind her with a creak of the hinges.

Maybe she didn't ask me to, but that has never stopped me. Am I really going to let her push me away and not chase her this time?

And what did she mean, she can't afford for this to happen? What does she have to lose?

My mind works overtime as I lie in bed, alone. She lost her scholarship. I'm almost positive she didn't take a job at the strip club. She must have gotten student loans . . . but if she didn't, then how the hell is she paying for school? Her job at the business school library can't possibly cover the tuition costs, and based on her reaction about her car and what she said about getting lucky to find a cheap place to live, I know she's not rolling in cash.

So, what the hell is left?

Chapter 27

Justine

I'm up early. The house is quiet, but I make my way downstairs anyway. I need to talk to Justice Grant again. I can't wait to get this out in the open, and yet I've never dreaded having a conversation more. What is he going to say? Is he going to be furious?

As I make my way to the kitchen, the rich scent of coffee hits my nose. Someone's up, and I'm guessing it's not Ryker.

I follow the smell and find Justice Grant sitting on a bar stool at the kitchen island, sipping his coffee with a newspaper in front of him. He looks up when he hears my footsteps.

"Good morning, Justine. Did you sleep well?"

The honest answer to that question is yes and no. Yes, I slept well because I had an orgasm to end all orgasms, but no, because my sleep was plagued with vivid dreams about someone breaking into my house and what would have happened if I hadn't left Ryker's room last night.

"Just fine." It's the only answer I can give him.

"Good, I'm glad. Join me for a cup of coffee? I imagine Ryker will be up fairly soon. He doesn't sleep late. Never has."

And there goes the mental excuse I've always attributed to why he stood me up that morning after the bar. I assumed he was too drunk and hung over and just slept too long, but given the cryptic answers about not being able to tell me why he couldn't be there . . . I know it has to be something else.

"Thank you. I'd love some coffee."

Justice Grant moves from his stool and strides to the cupboard. Once he has the mug, I hold out a hand. "I can do that, sir. There's no need to wait on me."

"You're a guest in my home."

Once I have the mug before me, with milk and a dash of sugar, I take the seat beside Justice Grant, guilt pooling in my belly about what happened last night, making the coffee unappealing.

I need to tell him something. I can't believe I let last night happen.

Wrapping my hand around my mug, I squeeze before looking over at him. My stomach drops to my feet but I open my mouth and push the words out anyway. "I think we might need to talk about Ryker."

Justice Grant's eyebrows furrow together and I pause, gathering my words to explain . . . somehow. I open my mouth to continue when Ryker walks into the room.

My heart lurches into my throat. *Shit*.

"Morning, Dad. Justine. Can you be ready to leave in a half hour?"

Memories of last night batter me, and I can't look him in the eye. What we did. What he said. *His father is next to me*. I try to push the images away, but only partially succeed.

"Good morning. You want coffee?" Justice Grant replies.

"Yeah, I'll grab it." Ryker looks to me, and I know he's waiting for an answer to the question he asked.

"Yeah, sure. I can be ready in ten, actually." I have an extra pair of jeans and T-shirt shoved in my backpack, and there isn't much else I need to do other than throw my hair into a messy bun and put on some eyeliner and mascara.

"Sounds good. I need to grab a few things and we can get moving."

He nods at me, and I squeeze my mug tighter and stand. "I'll be back in a few then."

I know rushing off isn't exactly the boldest move, especially leaving Justice Grant wondering what the hell I was going to say, but I have no idea what else to do. I need to pull myself together and figure out exactly how I'm going to face Ryker, and what I'm going to say to his dad.

Chapter 28

Ryker

Awkward silence fills the car as we wait for a train to pass by, and I turn to Justine.

"Are you ever going to look me in the eye again? Or explain why the hell you can't afford for something to happen between us?"

Her backpack lays on the floor at her feet, and her hands fidget in her lap. Her gaze darts toward me when I speak, but doesn't stay.

"Do we really need to have this conversation now?"

No woman has ever frustrated me this much. "You can't bolt from the car like I'm sure you will as soon as I park, so yeah. Now's a great time."

Justine's cell phone buzzes in the pocket of her backpack, and her hands go for it immediately.

"Hello?"

The man on the other end is a loud talker, so it's not hard to hear him. "This is Officer Crawford from Campus Safety. We have a suspect in custody for the break-in last night."

"For real? Who? Why? Did you find out why?"

"The suspect hasn't admitted to anything yet, so I can't confirm, but we wanted to let you know as a courtesy. Maintenance will be installing a new door and dead bolt today, so you shouldn't have any more problems."

"Thank you. I appreciate the call. That's great."

"We'll let you know if we get more information out of the suspect. Have a good day, Ms. Porter."

She hangs up and stuffs her phone back in the pocket of her backpack. "At least I know I can go home today. That's good news."

I look at her with disbelief. "Are you shitting me? You're going back to that rattrap of an apartment? The university shouldn't even be able to rent those out. They should be condemned."

Justine crosses her arms over her body, a mulish look casting over her features. "It's where I live. It might not be up to your standards, but not everyone can be as picky. You heard him, he said they had a suspect in custody, so it's not like I'm going to have any more problems."

I shove a hand through my hair and stare at her. "A *suspect*, Justine. You're in frigging law school. You know damn well the person they picked up might not be the one who did it. And there have been multiple break-ins. It might not have been the same person for each of them. The fact that they've got someone in custody doesn't make that place any safer than it was last night when your door was kicked in."

The gates lift from the train track, and I shift the car back into drive.

"I'm going home."

"It's not safe. Do you own a gun? Because you're going to need one living there."

Her gaze jerks to me. Finally. "You can't have a gun on campus."

"Then what are you going to do the next time someone kicks your door in and you happen to be inside? Campus Safety isn't going to get there quickly enough to do a damn thing if some guy wants to rape and murder you."

She sucks in a harsh breath. "Thanks a lot for putting that out in the universe, like an asshole. Besides, *nothing is going to happen*."

"Three break-ins since the semester started is just ridiculous. You can't stay there."

Crossing her arms over her chest, she stares me down. "Not your business."

I pull up to another red light and turn and meet her glare. "I fucking care about you, so I'm making it my business. You think my dad can't get that place shut down and force the issue?"

Her dark eyes blaze hot. "You think I can afford to live somewhere else by myself? I live on a budget. Now, I have no scholarship. I only have what I've worked my ass off to save and a tiny inheritance. My choices are severely limited."

"Then why didn't you get a damn roommate?"

"Because my last roommate screwed me over by bailing halfway through the semester and not paying her bills! Everyone I trust already has a place to live and a roommate! I'm not going to spend my last year of law school couch surfing when I could have my own place. It may not be glamorous, but at least it's quiet and it's mine."

"Then how the hell can you even afford to still be in school?"

Justine's eyes go wide and her mouth shuts so abruptly,

her teeth click together.

"You didn't go to another strip club after the Vu. Did you?"

She looks away, suddenly fascinated by what's going on outside her window, shutting me out.

The light changes, and I take the roundabout and dodge traffic before pulling into the parking garage next to the law school. Justine still hasn't replied when I find a spot on the top level.

"You're not going to tell me anything, are you?"

Her gaze drops to the backpack she's clutching in her lap, her shoulders hunched.

"Will you even look at me?"

She fumbles for the door handle and yanks it open. I follow suit, not about to let her walk away from this.

She's already near the trunk when I step in her path. "Justine, stop. Just fucking talk to me. I want to help. Let me fucking help."

It's like she's completely shut down. She won't look at me, and it's driving me nuts. Every time she blew me off before, she did it with a direct stare, and I could always read her eyes. Now, I've got nothing.

I lift my hand and cup her chin before she can sidestep me. Her dark gaze is confused and shaken. "Let me help," I repeat. "You don't have to be so damn strong all the time."

She closes her eyes for a moment before reopening them and focusing on me. "I can't do this with you. Not here. Not now. I need to get to class."

Dropping my hand, I shake my head. "Because that's all that matters to you, isn't it? Your grades and your degree. Do you care about anything else? Anyone else?"

Those dark eyes flash with what looks like a sheen of

tears, but she doesn't let them fall. Justine hefts her backpack again and strides away toward the stairs.

What a fucking mess of a morning.

Chapter 29

Justine

Class starts in seven minutes, and I'm in the bathroom like I'm some schoolgirl instead of months away from graduating with a law degree. I splash my face with cold water to snap me out of it. Thank God for waterproof eyeliner and mascara.

The door creaks open, and just like freaking high school, the one girl I don't want to see walks in. *Kristy Horner.*

"Wow. You've looked better."

"Thanks a lot." I grab a handful of the paper towel and dab my face dry.

"He's not worth crying over. Trust me, I know."

I shoot her a *what the hell are you talking about* look. "I'm not crying over anyone."

She leans against the wall and studies me. "Right. And three people haven't told me they saw you arguing in the parking garage with Ryker this morning. If you want to keep your private life private, I suggest you don't have a throwdown in public."

"Thanks for the advice." I toss the paper towels in the trash and grab my backpack off the counter.

"I'm just telling you this to save you some heartache down the line. Ryker's mother is old money, and she's not going to want her son with . . . someone like you. And while Ryker might seem like such a rebellious badass, he's still living on the gravy train, and he's not going to risk it by taking you home to Mommy and Daddy."

I don't know what possessed me to speak, but the words are out before I can call them back. "He took me home last night for drinks with his dad, so I guess that proves your theory wrong."

Kristy jerks back like I slapped her. "He took you *home*. To his parents' house?"

"Justice Grant's cognac is pretty dang good. He didn't even mind that I didn't have a clue how to drink it properly."

Kristy's eyes narrow to slits. "He's a liar and a user. He'll throw you away long before we ever make it to graduation. I'd bet my GPA on it."

What a bitch. I straighten my shoulders and stare her down. "Like he threw you away? Bitter much? I wouldn't go betting your GPA on something you clearly don't understand."

"Get ready to do a lot more crying in the bathroom then. You're not nearly as special as you think you are."

I force a smug smile to my lips. "Maybe not, but apparently Ryker thinks I am."

Her lips flatten into a hard line. "I guess we'll see, won't we?"

I leave the bathroom wondering what the hell got into me. Why did I rile up Kristy? She's just going to spread rumors about everything I just said far and wide across campus.

When I slip into Advocacy, the one class I don't have with Ryker, students are flipping casebooks open and taking notes on the first PowerPoint slide, even though the lecture hasn't started. Kristy lowers herself into the seat ahead of me, not bothering to look at me this time. Well, that's a positive change.

When Professor Alexander takes the lectern and begins the lecture, my fingers don't move as fast over the keyboard, because I'm stuck on how I'm supposed to respond to Ryker's question this morning about how I'm paying for law school.

He's not going to let it go.

And I can't tell him.

I still have absolutely no idea what to do when class is dismissed and my sketchy notes stare back at me from the screen. The last thing I need to do is start getting distracted. *Keep your eye on the prize, Justine.*

Maybe I just need more caffeine. I've got a half hour between classes, so I head down to the café to get a shot of espresso. Everyone else seems convinced that coffee can solve the world's problems, so I'm willing to give it a try.

"Hey, hottie! We need to talk." Merica is coming toward the café, book in hand and a determined look in her eyes.

Oh crap. "Hey, sorry, I just got out of Advocacy. Today was mind-numbingly boring."

"Try taking Federal Income Tax. Boring doesn't even begin to cover it. All I know is the IRS is the devil and that whole tax code needs to go in the shredder. Let's just have one rule instead of a fucking zillion that I have to memorize for the final. Why did I think this was a good idea?"

I could remind Merica that her stepfather insisted she take the class, but it's not exactly a reminder she's going to appreciate.

We get into line behind ten other students, and Merica pins me with a direct stare. "So, what's this I hear about you and Ryker arguing in the parking garage? And you getting a ride with him? Have you seen the package? Can you confirm the rumors?"

I would have thought it was impossible to laugh, but leave it to Merica to have giggles breaking free from my throat. It's good to know that some things don't change, including the fact that my best friend is amazing.

"Don't even start that rumor," I reply, unwilling to confirm or deny, even though I have the inside information she's after. Now is not the time or the place. Besides, I'm not thinking about Ryker Grant's penis ever again. Never. Ever.

Nothing like setting yourself up for failure, I chide myself, knowing that I'm spouting nothing but nonverbal lies.

"Then tell me the truth so I won't have to use my overly vivid imagination."

Only six students ahead of us now, and I'm praying the barista picks up his pace, because at least two of them are not even pretending to ignore us. The girl in front of Merica just straight-up turned around.

Merica glares at her. "Do you mind? We're having a conversation."

The girl glares back and shoves her earbuds in her ears, and my best friend's attention is immediately back on me, one eyebrow raised.

"I stayed at his parents' house last night. It's a really long story."

Merica's eyes bulge wide. "You did what?"

I fill her in on the break-in, but not the dirty details of last night. That's not something I want to get into in the middle of the student café.

By the time I'm finished, Merica's mouth is hanging open. "You're coming over tonight to tell me the rest and we're drinking box wine."

"You have no idea how badly I need that. I get off work at seven."

"I'll be ready and waiting. Tonight I'm trying that bread maker my mom gave me for my birthday in an attempt to turn me into a domestic goddess. This situation calls for carbs too. You should probably wear yoga pants."

"I love you, Mer."

"Love you more, Jus."

I'm outside the law school and heading for the bus stop to get to work when Ryker's Camaro slows at the curb.

"Get in."

My hackles are up as soon as the words are out. "Don't talk to me like that."

"You don't have a car. Your shift starts at the library in twenty minutes, and you're going to be late if you take the bus."

I stop in midstride. "How do you know that?"

"I called the library and flirted with the girl to give me your schedule."

"Are you serious?"

"Dead serious. Now, get in the car so I can take you to work."

I make a noise low in my throat that sounds a little too close to a growl. "You're impossible." But still, I stalk toward the car and yank open the door I jumped out of so quickly this morning.

"Determined."

"Maybe you should apply that trait to school."

"I already am, thanks to you."

He pulls away from the curb but instead of heading toward the business school, he takes the second exit out of the traffic circle.

"Where the hell are you going? I need to get to work."

"And I know you've got twenty minutes, so I'm going to make use of them." He turns and flashes me a grin.

This. This right here is why I've avoided Ryker for two years. Because when his attention is focused on you, it makes you want to soak it all up. The more time I spend with him, the more I realize that not only am I not immune to it, I'm more susceptible than ever. That's dangerous.

Ryker turns into the lot outside the performing arts center, shifts the car into neutral, and pulls the emergency brake before turning to face me.

"I miss the taste of your pussy already."

Oh my God! Did he really say that?

"You can't say things like that to me." My words come out higher pitched than I expect.

"Then how are you going to know how fucking bad I want you? I can't stop thinking about it. I want more."

And I can't have more.

"We can't do this."

His grin fades. "Fuck if we can't. We *are* doing this."

I have to use the only kind of honesty he's going to understand and pray that he respects it. "No, because if you're thinking about my pussy and how much you want my lips wrapped around your cock or burying yourself inside me, you're not thinking about school. And guess what? I'm not too proud to admit that I can't concentrate if I'm thinking about it either. This is exactly why I've been shutting you down. This year is too important to screw up because you want to scratch an itch."

"This isn't an itch, Justine. I've been there, done that. This is something completely fucking different."

Dammit, I want to believe him when he tells me how different this is—and that terrifies me.

"You need to focus on school. I need to focus on school. We're not doing this."

"What are you scared of? Tell me the truth. Not some bullshit answer." His blue eyes drill into mine, demanding an honest response. So I give him one.

"I'm afraid that you're the ultimate distraction, and I won't be able to help myself. I'll just get sucked in deeper and deeper until I forget why I need to keep my priorities straight."

His stare intensifies, and I wish I could read his mind. It's like he's working out a complex analysis in his head.

"Then let's make a deal."

"What kind of deal?" Suspicion coats my every word.

"The kind that incentivizes us both."

I glance at the clock in the dash. "You've got five minutes, and I need to get to work."

"This will only take two, because you're going to say yes."

"Cocky bastard," I murmur under my breath.

He pays no mind to my comment. "If we both get As on the Professional Responsibility midterm, we both a get a reward."

"What kind of reward?"

"I get your lips wrapped around my cock, and you get all the orgasms you can handle—any way you want them."

I fight to keep my blush from creeping up my neck. "And how is that going to help?"

"Because we'll both study our asses off—me, because I want you, and you, because you would anyway . . . and you want my cock, even if you won't come out and admit it. We'll keep studying like we have been, and after the midterm, we both reap the rewards."

"Just study?"

He meets my skeptical stare head-on. "I can't promise I won't kiss you again. You can't expect me to agree not to touch you at all. But we will study. Both of us. You think I'm going to fuck up my grades if you're the prize? No way in hell."

"And your other classes?"

"I'll fucking rock those too. We both will. I'm going to prove that not only are we hot as fuck in the bedroom, we're going to kick ass in class."

How can I say no to that? Honestly, he's almost making this too easy. He gets the best grades of his life and makes his father happy, and I get everything I'm willing to admit that I want and everything I'm not. For the first time in my life, I can have my cake and eat it too. What other answer can I possibly give than yes?

I wait only a few moments before I tell him what he wants to hear. "Okay. You've got a deal."

I hold out my hand and he wraps his fingers around

it, but rather than shaking it, he pulls me halfway over the center console before burying his other hand in my hair and lowering his lips to mine.

His tongue steals inside as he takes control. I'm lost in the kiss, forgetting everything, including the time, when he finally pulls back.

"We're going to make a hell of a team, Justine. Now let's get you to work."

Chapter 30

Justine

I make it to work five minutes early, and my first order of business is to figure out what I'm going to do with my car. It's still sitting in the Unwired parking lot, and a quick call there and a chat with a manager tells me they'll give me another few hours before they have it towed to a lot and send me the bill. Just the thought of how expensive it will probably be to fix has me considering all my options.

Regardless of what's wrong with it, even the cheapest repair job is going to max out my budget and cost more than the car is worth. The next call I make hurts, but my choices are limited. It looks like I'll be using some of the four hundred dollars from the junkyard to buy myself a bike.

It also means that I'll be hopping the bus to Merica's house and arriving a little later than planned. No worries, though. It won't be the first time I've bussed it, and I'm certainly not the only student on this campus to be sans car. The hipsters think it's super cool to ride vintage Schwinns and shun anything with four wheels and an engine.

I'm nearing the end of my shift when a guy comes up to the counter and stands in front of me, waiting a solid thirty seconds before he clears his throat as I'm highlighting the facts of a case.

I drop the highlighter and jerk my attention to his face. *Have I seen him here before*? Messy blond hair, green eyes, a smirk that rivals Ryker's—*stop right there.*

"Can I help you?"

"You're a law student?"

I glance down at the two other casebooks stacked beside the open one. "Your observational skills are impressive."

His eyes narrow as he studies me. "You got a name?"

Mine narrow right back at him. "Does it matter?"

"I just want to know if you're who I think you are."

Well, that's creepy. "Can I help you with something? Library related? You know, because that's my job, not answering your questions and confirming suspicions."

He pulls out a phone and before I realize what he's doing, I hear the click of the camera app and a small flash bursts from the front.

Yes, very creepy. My hand goes to the staff phone on the desk next to my books. Two calls to campus police in one week is more than I need to deal with.

"What the hell are you doing?" And where the hell does this guy get the audacity to take a picture of me?

"I told you, I want to know if you are who I think you are."

"I'm calling campus police. You need to leave. Now. And delete the picture."

He's tapping out something on the screen and within moments, a self-satisfied grin stretches his face. "Figured I was right." He looks up at me. "Great to meet you, Justine. Now I see the appeal."

Excuse me? It's official. He's really fucking creepy.

"How do you—" I start, and he turns his phone around so I can see the screen.

The top of the chat window says "R-Fucking-G" and I have only one guess as to who that could be. Glancing down at the messages, I see a new chat bubble pop up just below the picture and the one that says—*yeah, that's her.*

The new chat bubble reads: *Don't forget, she's mine. Hands off.*

Yes, I know exactly who that is. I lower the phone into the cradle.

"Okay, it would've been way less sketchy if you had just told me you're a friend of Ryker's."

"Nah, this was more fun."

This guy is a nut. "Is there something you needed?"

"I heard you on the phone earlier. You're really having a junkyard come pick up your car? That blows, girly."

"One, don't call me girly. And two, thank you for the concern, but it isn't anything I need anyone worrying about. Three, if you tell Ryker—" I lean forward on my elbows and lower my voice. While he's waiting for me to continue, he ducks his head closer. "I'll check out a hundred books in this library in your name and make them all two years overdue, and you won't be able to graduate until you pay the fines."

He jerks back and straightens. "Whoa. Calm down. I'm not trying to cause any trouble. I just want to know if there's anything we can do to help."

We undoubtedly means him and Ryker, and I don't need Ryker to know anything about this.

"Thanks, but no thanks. If you'd just keep this to yourself, I'd appreciate it. I don't need my business spread all over town. First off, it's nobody's problem but my own, and second, it's not that big of a deal. It's not like I wasn't going to junk it eventually. My timeline just sped up a little."

Why am I telling him this? Stop sharing unnecessary information, Justine.

"You need a ride home from work?" He looks down at a big and undoubtedly expensive watch on his wrist. "Ryker told me you might, and I figure I can waste another hour before the walls start closing in on me."

I glance at my phone for the time out of instinct, even though I have no intention of accepting a ride from some random guy I don't know—regardless of whether he's Ryker's friend.

While I'm debating, his thumbs are flying and he's tapping out something on his phone. Moments later, my cell vibrates on the counter with a text.

RYKER: Take the ride from Ian. He's a good guy and he knows I'll rip his balls off if he tries anything with you.

The blond, who I now assume is Ian, waits for me to look up from my phone with a smirk. "Just take the ride, Justine."

These guys are freaking impossible. But I do need to get to Merica's because I'm in desperate need of wine, carbs, and my best friend's advice. I wonder for a moment if Ryker told him where I live.

"I'm headed to a friend's house. She lives about ten minutes east of campus."

He shrugs. "No big deal. It's just completely out of my

way."

"Then I'll take the bus, no big deal."

Ian eyes me with a raised blond brow. "I'm giving you a ride. Be ready at seven and we're out of here."

Exactly fifty-five minutes later, I punch my timecard in the office and head for the side door. I've decided I'm not accepting a ride from Ryker's friend, especially not after the four text messages I didn't respond to. The ones that said:

RYKER: Take the ride.
RYKER: Don't be stubborn.
RYKER: Ian says you're junking your car.
RYKER: Don't do anything until I talk to you.

Ian is a little tattletale. I asked him not to mention it, and he blabbed to his buddy anyway.

When I hit the parking lot and head for the bus stop, I see a bright red sports car parked at the curb where the bus should be in ten minutes.

I take a seat on the bench inside the clear plastic shelter, and the passenger window on the car rolls down.

I knew it would be him.

"Get in the car."

Ian's blond hair is mussed like he's been shoving his hands through it while he waited.

"I appreciate the offer, but it's totally out of your way, and I don't take rides from people I just met. I'm good with the bus."

"No, you're not."

"Yes—"

Ian cuts me off. "Look, you're not my girlfriend, so this arguing shit is really obnoxious when I'm not getting any pussy. Just get in the car so you can get where you need to go without having to sit on the bus for an hour. I'll have you there in ten minutes."

This guy is impossible, but it doesn't make accepting his offer any less rational. I mentally toss my hands in the air and give in.

As soon as we're off campus, he flies along the back-country roads. With his car's sleek lines and arrest-me red paint color, I doubt that Ian is really interested in the posted speed limit. Staring out my window, I wonder if we're truly going to make this entire ride in silence. Small talk isn't my greatest skill, and I have no idea what to say to him, but within moments I'm wishing I'd come up with something.

"So, are you fucking him for the money or are you fucking him for the position his dad has?" Ian's question is without preamble, and surprisingly, I don't detect a hint of malice. His tone is solidly matter-of-fact.

I yank my gaze off the fields to land on him as he expertly shifts the car and slows for a stoplight. "Um . . . neither, because I'm not fucking him at all."

Ian's head swings toward me, surprise—no doubt at my honesty—arching his eyebrow. "No shit? Damn, he's losing his touch."

"We're studying. We're . . . friends. That's it." If I don't sound one hundred percent confident, it's because I don't know what we are any more. And the deal Ryker and I made this afternoon . . . how does that change things?

I catch Ian's eye roll at my answer before he shifts into gear and attempts to break land-speed records for zero to sixty miles per hour. Or maybe that's the way Ian drives. I'm beginning to suspect it's the latter.

"What's your hang-up? You're sexy as shit. He's been obviously sniffing around for way too fucking long for you not to realize how bad he wants in your pants."

"Aren't you blowing the bro code here? Spilling his secrets?"

"Nah, it's no secret. You're not an idiot, which you'd have to be if you hadn't figured that out already. But since you're in denial, there's nothing I can do to really help his cause. So, moving on . . . You have any hot friends who like to bang on the first date?"

Confirmed, this guy is a nut. "Umm. I don't know?"

"Are you asking me or telling me?"

"I don't think I want to tell you." The turnoff to Merica's apartment is coming up, so I point. "Right at the light and then the first right after that. I'm going to Knob Hill."

"And who are you going to see in Knob Hill?"

"Not really your business."

We pull into the parking lot and I direct him to Merica's building, where, predictably, she's standing on her balcony, wrapping hot pink Christmas lights around a palm tree. She's already done the pink flamingos.

She pauses to take in the sexy car, and when I open the door, her eyes widen. "Hot ride!"

Ian is glancing up at her. "What's her name?"

"She has a boyfriend. Thanks for the ride." I shut the door and head for the stairs.

He rolls down the window. "Tell her I'm taking her out on Friday night. I'll be here to pick her up at eight."

"She has a boyfriend! Thanks for the ride!" I repeat, this time with more force.

He smirks at me as he backs out and roasts the tires before taking off.

Merica's watching, a bemused expression on her face. "It's definitely time for wine, and you to tell me what the hell is going on."

Chapter 31

Justine

The scent of fresh-baked bread hits me when I walk through Merica's unlocked door. *Carbs.* Thank God. I need them.

Merica comes in from the balcony and slides the door shut behind her. She cocks a hip and puts a hand on it.

"You've got a lot of explaining to do."

"Did you already pour the wine?"

"Of course."

An hour later, I finish my third glass of wine and Merica stares at me slack-jawed. A half-eaten loaf of amazingly delicious bread and the remains of a demolished stick of butter sit between us.

"Ho. Ly. Shit. How did you keep this to yourself? Seriously. Why didn't you tell me?"

"I told you, Justice Grant told me I couldn't. But I decided I had to invoke the unwritten, unspoken *best friend* exception, even if I'm technically violating the contract."

"Screw the contract. This is way too important to worry about that."

"But what the hell am I going to do? I feel like I'm crossing a line here."

"Ryker's the one that threw down the deal, though, right? He's the one pushing you to study with him. So what if he's motivated by pussy and blow jobs now? He's a guy—they're always motivated by pussy and blow jobs. Now you know he's going to get the grades and you get your tuition paid. You're not doing anything wrong, Jus."

Which is exactly what I've been attempting to get myself to believe. *I'm not doing anything wrong. Right?*

"You really don't think I'm crossing into the gray area here?"

Merica reaches for the box of wine and slides it over the edge of the table before holding her glass underneath the spout and pressing the button. When it's filled an inch from the brim, she releases the button and raises it to her lips.

"You wouldn't be wrestling with this so much if you didn't think you were. But I think you need to cut yourself a break. You've busted your ass for every single thing you've ever gotten. You got dealt a shitty hand in so many ways, and to lose a full ride at the beginning of third year? That's just another epically shitty blow. Life is just a series of decisions. What other acceptable choice did you have? None. I know it, and you know it. So make your peace with the fact that you did what you had to do and move on."

I'm afraid to give voice to the last concern rolling around in my head. I refill my glass and take a long swallow before I find the courage to put it into words.

"But what if this actually becomes something . . . real?

Then what?"

Merica studies me, probably catching all my nervous tells. "Do you think it's going to?"

"I don't know. We're going in totally different directions. I want to work at Legal Aid and make a difference. I don't think he has a clue what he wants to do with his life. At this point, I just know that I don't hate spending time together. I actually . . . I kind of like him, even though I didn't want to."

Merica's shrewd gaze assesses me—hearing all the things I'm saying and all the things I'm not. "Do you think you could fall for him?"

It's a question I've been avoiding asking myself because I'm afraid to even consider the possibility. "I don't know. I just . . . I'm worried about what would happen if in some crazy parallel universe, I did."

"There's no point in borrowing trouble now. Just roll with it. Maybe you both kill the midterm, have your fling and the sex sucks, and you move on."

A smile tugs at my lips because I can't imagine the sex could possibly suck. But she's right—I'm always planning my life out seventeen steps ahead, and right now, I just need to focus on the next goal in front of me, not a bunch of stuff I can't control. Like she said, why borrow trouble?

Merica lifts her glass again and after she sips, she taps a nail on the side. "Now tell me, how big is that package he's packing? Is it everything Becca said it was and more?"

I choke on my wine mid-swallow at her question. After I finish coughing up a lung, I stare her down. "Did I not just tell you I might *like him, like him*?"

She nods.

"And you're still asking me this?"

"Of course. Friends don't let friends date guys with small penises. If it's avoidable, that is."

"Let's just say I have no complaints."

A grin stretches across her face. "I knew it! For all that you've avoided men, you wouldn't jump back into the game for a small cock." She holds her glass aloft. "But this does deserve a toast. To Justine, may you get everything you've ever wanted, including all the best orgasms."

I lift my wineglass and clink against hers. "Cheers."

"So tell me, who was that hottie in the car? Are you thinking of taking them both on? Are you up for the two-dicks-and-one-chick situation?"

The base of my wineglass smacks against the table as I sit it down. "Hell no. There will be only one dick approaching this chick."

Her laugh fills the room. "That's what I thought. Well, if Jimmy ever gets boring . . ."

I grab another chunk of bread and toss it at her head.

Chapter 32

Ryker

When I said I'd be able to concentrate and do nothing but study with Justine, I was way too fucking optimistic about my willpower.

It's been weeks. Weeks of staring at her across this table at Unwired, doing my reading for all my classes, taking notes, working on outlines, and studying for this Professional Responsibility midterm. I've got calluses on top of calluses from beating off every night. Fuck, I've never gotten this much action from my hand since I was thirteen and hadn't yet discovered the magic of pussy.

Justine, on the other hand, does a better job of looking unaffected, but I can see the frustration in her posture. I've choked back more sexual innuendo and compliments than I can count, and I think she actually misses it.

In these weeks of studying, things have changed. I don't just want her lips wrapped around my cock. I don't just want her legs wrapped around my waist as I sink deep inside her. Because if that's all I wanted, I could have gotten it.

Now I'm addicted to her. Every fucking thing about

her. Not just her eyes and hair and tits and ass—but her jokes, her quips, her observations. Just her.

Fucked. That's what I am. Totally and completely fucked. I'm hung up on a girl for more reasons than the physical, and I know that's where the trouble lies. I need her to feel the same way, and I have no fucking clue if she does.

We've become friends, but even now she keeps me at a distance. She rides her bike to Unwired, not letting me give her a lift, even when it's dark and it pisses me off that she's riding alone at night. She pretends not to notice that I wait for her to get a head start, and then I follow her home in my car because I hate that she's still living in that shithole Gilroy complex. But there's nothing I can do or say to change her mind. The girl has more pride than any man I've ever met.

And why the hell does that turn me on even more? Maybe because I've dated too many girls who were impressed with the money my family has and my parents' positions. With Justine, I know that none of that holds any appeal for her. She's not impressed by anything other than how much effort I'm willing to put into school.

Justine snaps her finger in front of my face. "Hey, are you paying attention? I've been talking for five minutes, and you're staring into space like you're out of it. What's your deal?"

"I was staring at your lips."

Her eyes widen, and for the first time since we struck our revised deal, I'm referring to the prize on the line.

Going all in, I add, "They're distracting as hell."

Justine's gaze drops to the table. "We're studying."

"The midterm is in three days, and we're both getting As."

"That doesn't mean we should stop studying now and take any chances."

I drag my focus back to the case in front of me. "Okay." I read the next three sentences before I speak again. "There's a costume party Saturday night. At Green's Square. You going?"

Justine looks up as she pops a Pez candy into her mouth from her Captain America dispenser. She crunches the candy before responding.

Yep, I'm fucked, because I even think that's sexy as hell.

"Merica wants to go. She's got a sexy Tinkerbell costume she made last weekend. She's been trying to talk me into going as Wonder Woman."

The thought of Justine in tights and a cape . . . I shift on the cushion of the booth as my cock sits up and takes notice. "I'm putting my full support and approval behind that idea."

She smirks. "Figures that you would."

"Babe, you're already Wonder Woman without the cape and tights. With them, you'll be a fucking wet dream come true."

Justine's cheeks flush before she drops her gaze back to her book.

Just wait until after the midterm . . .

Chapter 33

Justine

I didn't think it would be this hard. I truly didn't. But sitting across from Ryker four days a week and pretending I'm just studying has been hellish.

He's not just the pretty face I wanted him to be. He's smart. He's witty. He's . . . dangerous. And without the sexual innuendo I expected him to be constantly throwing into conversation, he's become even more intriguing. Not that I have a problem with innuendo. I don't. But when I was expecting it, and then instead I get studious-and-determined Ryker . . . it's like Justine's kryptonite has been located and identified.

Two weeks ago he stopped playing fair. He showed up in *glasses*. Dark rimmed, sexy as hell, and totally unexpected. If someone would have told me that Ryker could get any more attractive, I would have said they were on crack. But I was wrong. Completely and totally wrong.

I keep edging toward this sign in my head that reads Danger, Do Not Cross This Line.

I know I told Merica that I *liked him liked him*, but even

then I didn't truly understand the full magnitude of the situation. Now I'm facing actual feelings that aren't all tied up in the physical side of things. We're only days away from our midterm, and Babcock has already told us she'll have the grades back before Halloween.

Every time I think about the midterm, I think about the deal we struck. One that I made for more than just the reasons he did, but regardless—I'm anxious to cash in on both my prize and his.

There's nothing I've been able to do or say to change the facts. I want him.

I've been having sex dreams lately, for goodness' sake. *Sex dreams.* About Ryker. I've never been this strung out in my entire life. But now we've got emotions running together, and I'm afraid things are going to get really, truly complicated.

But as long as his grades and mine stay up . . . what harm is it?

Chapter 34

Justine

RYKER: *Are you ready for tonight? Because I know I am. This guy got his A. Now I get the girl.*

I stare down at my phone, and I know what he's talking about. My heart hammers and my stomach flip-flops.

Babcock was late posting the grades and I've been hitting refresh all day like a crazy person. Nothing. Nothing. Nothing.

I made myself back away from the computer and do my reading for another class.

As soon as I read Ryker's text, I run to my computer and pull up the grade portal. The browser seems to take forever to load.

Come on. Come on.

What if he got an A and I didn't?

I'm nervous every time I check my grades, but never more so than right now.

I screw up my login and password twice before I have to wipe my hands on my jeans and enter each letter slowly. The page loads and I click on Professional Responsibility.

Another agonizing ten seconds pass before my grade pops onto the screen.

I got an A.

A lump rises in my throat.

Holy. Shit. This is really happening. Tonight.

Why does it seem so much more intense right now because I know exactly what's coming? Anticipation turns into chill bumps covering my bare arms as I glance at the Wonder Woman costume hanging in my tiny closet. Merica has an ace hand at sewing, and she spent the entire last weekend making it.

How do I answer his text? What do I say?

We've built what has become one of the most important friendships I've ever had, and now we're going to complicate it to hell and back. I'm afraid to lose this—lose him—but I'm even more afraid not to take the next step.

Deep breath in. Deep breath out. I can do this. I can have it all.

At least, that's what I'm going to tell myself.

Crossing back to my phone, I formulate a reply.

JUSTINE: *What if I didn't get an A?*

Ryker's response is instant.

RYKER: *Stop bullshitting me because we know that's not possible.*

JUSTINE: *Well . . .*

I jump when my phone rings instead of vibrating with a text.

Ryker's voice comes through the phone. "Tell me right

now—are you having second thoughts?"

"I'm having all the thoughts. I don't know if they're first, second, third, or fourth."

Silence hangs on the phone for a moment. "We made a deal."

I squeeze my eyes shut. "I know."

"I'm holding you to it."

My eyes fly open at his adamant tone. "What if I changed my mind?"

"You didn't." There's no hesitation in his reply and his words are underlined by conviction. "You want this just as much as I do. You're just afraid to admit it."

That's where he's wrong. I'm not afraid to admit it anymore. I'm just afraid of the consequences. Either way, I'm holding up my end of the bargain.

"I'll see you at Green's?" I say, not giving him the answer he's looking for.

"Damn right, you will. You're going home with me."

"'Bye, Ryker."

The line goes dead without him responding.

Anxiety creeps up my spine. How is tonight going to go? Merica will be here any minute to pick me up on her way home from class so we can get ready at her place. Full-on hair and makeup—the works.

I lift the costume from the hanger carefully, knowing that Ryker will be slipping it off me tonight. A riot of emotions ricochet through me.

I can do this. I can have it all. That's my mantra.

Let's just hope it's the truth.

Chapter 35

Justine

"The car will be here in three minutes!" Merica calls as I stand in front of the mirror in her bathroom.

"I'll be out in a second," I yell through the door.

"You look hot, so don't change anything."

If I were the kind of girl to take mirror selfies and post them on some social-media platform, now would be the perfect time. Like Merica said, I make a pretty hot Wonder Woman, even from an objective standpoint.

I wonder what Ryker will think. Scratch that, I already know what he's going to think. My boobs look amazing, and the tights and bodysuit hug my every curve. I rarely feel overcome with confidence, but a combination of Merica's skills and the earlier call from Ryker have me walking out of the bathroom feeling like I can conquer the world.

Green's Square, the token Irish pub in our college town, is decked out for Halloween and packed with girls dressed in the sexy version of every traditional costume imaginable. Luckily, it seems that Merica and I are the only Tinkerbell and Wonder Woman duo, at least so far.

I spy Kristy Horner in the crowd, dressed as a slutty angel with the coolest wings I've ever seen, and she gives me a once-over before looking away.

Think whatever you want, Kristy. We look good.

My eyes scan the room for Ryker, but I don't see his tall frame. Merica drags me toward the bar, inserting herself between two guys who step aside as soon as they get a look at her as naughty Tinkerbell. I squeeze in next to her, ready to have a distraction in the form of a drink in my hand. Luckily, Merica's not afraid to flash a little cleavage to get a bartender's attention, and we're served in no time.

We scoop up our Halloween drink specials before scanning the surroundings to snag an empty table.

Where is Ryker? Shouldn't he be here by now?

I'm not sure what I'm more afraid of—that I'll lose my nerve, or that I'm going to drag him out of here as soon as he walks in.

Three glasses of Halloween concoction later and there's still no sign of him. Where the hell is Ryker? Did *he* change his mind?

Merica stands. "I'm going out for a smoke, but you're going to swear on your life that you won't tell Jimmy."

"Do you even have a smoke?" I ask.

"I'll bum one. There are plenty of people here." She slips out of the booth, leaving me with the glass in front of me and a growing sense of unease.

Did he change his mind?

No. That's ridiculous. He wouldn't.

A shadow falls over the table moments after Merica is out of sight, and I look up, expecting to see a familiar face. And I do, but it's not the familiar face I wanted to see. It's the med student I talked to at Unwired who bartends at Ziggy's.

"Hey, you. Good to see you tore yourself away from the books for a night." His entire face lights up with a smile, and he slides in across the booth from me.

"Indiana Jones?" I ask, taking in the hat, white linen shirt unbuttoned at the throat, brown pants, and bullwhip curled at his side.

"Dr. Jones to you."

His quick response steals a laugh from me.

"What's your real first name? I know your last name is Caruthers."

"Jonah." He reaches his hand across the table to shake mine. "It's nice to finally be officially introduced . . ."

"Justine Porter." I slip my hand into his and shake. I try to pull back, but he doesn't release his grip.

"I kept hoping I'd see you again at Ziggy's."

"Bars aren't really my thing."

"So you just come out for special occasions?"

"Pretty much."

"I've got to say you make a pretty fabulous Wonder Woman. Makes me wish I'd dressed up as a superhero so we could fight evil together."

"Sorry, man. I've already got that covered." Ryker sits down in the booth beside me and throws his arm around my shoulders.

My gaze jerks to him, and sure enough, he's got on a

pair of jeans and a Captain America T-shirt that stretches impressively over his chest. It might not be a full-blown costume like my Wonder Woman get-up, but damn . . . he gives Chris Evans a run for his money.

"Figured as much, but you can't blame me for trying," Jonah says, pushing up from the bench seat.

"I was running late. Sorry, babe." Ryker presses a kiss to my temple. He looks at the man exiting the booth. "Thanks for stopping to say hey, Caruthers."

"Yeah. Anytime. Have a good night."

Jonah melts into the crowd and Ryker turns to face me, brilliant smile in place. "I really can't blame the guy for trying every time he sees you. You look fucking incredible tonight. And all mine."

His words and the fire burning in his eyes send bolts of heat through me, settling between my legs.

I want him.

Pulling myself together, I form a response. "Thank you. You look pretty damn good yourself. Captain America? How'd you pick that one?"

"It's one of your favorite Pez dispensers. I figured if you were going the Wonder Woman route, I had to pull out the superhero card."

The fact that he noticed something like that surprises me, but should it? Very few details seem to get by him. Ryker isn't the guy I initially thought he was. He's so much more.

He pulls his phone out of his pocket and slides it in front of me. I look down at the screen, and blink. He's logged into the student portal where our grades were posted.

Professional Responsibility – Midterm – A – 4.0

I look up to meet the intense blue gaze. "I believed you when you texted me. I didn't need proof."

"I wanted you to see it anyway. Because you know what? I'm fucking proud. We're a kick-ass team, Justine, and I'm not just saying that because I've never wanted anyone the way I want you."

The heat he unleashed grows exponentially. *I'm in deep trouble.*

"We do make a pretty good team." I attempt to keep my words nonchalant, and marginally succeed.

"I thought you said you were having second thoughts?" He scans every inch of my face, and I know this answer matters to him.

"I said I've been having a lot of thoughts. This is new for me, okay? When we made this deal, it was far off in the future. Something to worry about later. Now it's later, and I can't stop wondering—can we really balance it all? Studying and school and . . . whatever this is?"

Ryker's expression sobers. "This isn't a conversation I want to have in the middle of a bar."

He's right, but the unsettled feeling inside me won't subside until we have this conversation.

Ryker stands. "Let's get out of here."

"You just got here." I blink up at him, surprised that he already wants to leave.

He laces his fingers with mine and pulls me out of the booth and up against him.

"And I got what I came for—you."

His single-minded focus on me turns the heat to liquid fire. When was the last time anyone ever made me feel this way? Never.

"Okay."

I let him lead me out of the bar and we pass Merica, who now has Jimmy in tow, as we reach the front door.

"Hey, hottie." She studies us both, her gaze locking on our clasped hands before jumping to my face. "You heading out?"

"Yeah."

"Have fun and don't do anything I wouldn't do." Merica leans in and squeezes me in a hug before whispering in my ear. "You deserve this. No regrets."

I hug her back and she curls into Jimmy's side. "We'll have to do a double date another time."

The men nod at each other, and Ryker and I head outside.

Clouds of smoke from the laughing students gathered outside billow on the night air as we take the sidewalk around the bar. I spy his Camaro parked behind the bar in a handicapped spot.

"Feeling brave tonight?" I ask, looking from him to the car.

"I wasn't about to waste any more time looking for a place to park."

"What held you up?"

"Just some family stuff." He walks me around to the passenger side and opens the door.

I pause before lowering myself inside. "Everything okay?"

Ryker's nod is short. "Nothing to worry about." He closes the door as soon as I'm settled and rounds the hood before hopping in. But he doesn't start the car like I expect him to.

Instead, he turns to me. "Tell me right now if you're changing your mind. I have to know."

I shake my head. "I'm not changing my mind. We made a deal."

His expression sobers. "And we both know this isn't about making a deal anymore. This is me wanting you. All of you. Wanting to know how you feel under me. Wanting to know how hard you're going to come when I'm buried inside you. I want it all, Justine. Including the chance to show you how fucking amazing life can be when you let a few distractions in."

He's absolutely right. This has become so much more than just a deal. He's talking about a future. A future that's becoming a seductive temptation for me.

You can have it all.

But can I?

Justice Grant paid the first two months of my tuition, and the third payment is due next week. What would he say if he knew that I was planning on sleeping with his son and continuing to take the money?

What does that make me?

"What do you say? Can you take a chance on me? On us?"

Ryker's questions are sincere, and there's only one answer I can give, even with the feelings of guilt snowballing in my brain.

"Yes. I say yes."

Triumph brands his features. "Good. I'm taking you home."

With every mile that passes as we drive toward his place, my mind races to find a solution to my growing moral dilemma. I can't accept the tuition money and have Ryker too—at least, not without paying it back.

I didn't want to have debt when I got out of school, but if that had been my only option, and I'd been able to get a loan without crippling interest rates, I would have taken it.

All I have to do is make a new deal with Justice Grant—everything has to be a loan. He's getting what he wants—Ryker's grades are staying up—so how could he say no to the proposition? I don't think he'll hold this against me. He's not that kind of guy, and he all but told me that he had no problem with the idea of Ryker and me being more than study buddies. At that time, though, I didn't expect for this to happen.

So can I really have it all?

Yes, I decide. *I can.*

It just has to be a loan. That's something I can live with.

While Ryker guides the car downtown, I pull out my phone and my fingers fly, composing an e-mail to Justice Grant.

I keep it short and vague.

Justice Grant,

I've reconsidered our agreement and I'd like to discuss changing the terms. I think you'll find them acceptable all the same.

Sincerely,
Justine Porter

I send the e-mail and shove my phone back in my purse, relieved when the niggling feelings of guilt evaporate. Everything is going to be okay.

Ryker waves a keycard at the gate that blocks the entrance to the parking garage of a fancy condo complex, and it opens. Pulling inside, he slides into a spot and shifts the Camaro into park.

Turning to me, his blue gaze pins me to my seat. "No regrets. That's the one promise I want from you. No regrets, no matter what happens."

Can I make that promise?

I nod my head, the single motion spurring the words. "No regrets. I promise."

Chapter 36

Ryker

I've waited years for this. Justine Porter, standing in my living room, one hand on the shoulder of her Wonder Woman top, her lower lip caught between her teeth.

I'm going to have her every way I've ever imagined. She's mine now, whether she realizes it or not.

"Strip. Slowly."

Her eyes go wide at my command before sharpening on me. She releases her lip and cocks a hip.

"How long have you been saving that up?"

"Way too long. But since I saw you at the Vu, it's been at the top of my list."

She walks toward me, pressing a fingertip against my chest. "You wanted to see me on that stage? Working a pole?" Her tone is seductive, and my already stiff cock goes rock hard.

I shake my head in response. "I would've dragged you off the stage before I'd let any other guy see you strip."

Her dark eyes glimmer with heat. "But you wanted a private show?"

"Abso-fucking-lutely."

Justine steps back, and I don't know if she'll let her inner temptress out to play, but I watch in approval as she reaches for the shoulder of her top again and shimmies one and then the other down her arms. She leans forward, exposing that spectacular cleavage and those luscious tits, but I want more because that's the kind of greedy bastard I am.

"More. I want to see it all."

I wait for her to balk, but she doesn't. Justine pulls the spandex further down her arms, and her tits are spilling out of the low-cut black bra. The straps dangle by her elbows as she reaches up to cup her tits.

"Fuck me." She would have made a mint as a stripper, but I definitely would have killed someone.

"I thought that's what we were here for."

"Take off the bra." I need to get my mouth on her nipples. I've jacked off so many times wondering what color they are.

She reaches behind her back to unclasp the bra, but holds it against herself for a beat before letting it fall.

"Sweet fucking Christ," I breathe. High and firm, topped with pale pink nipples. Even better than I imagined.

Knowing I won't be able to hold out long enough to give her what she deserves if this striptease continues, I stride forward and snatch the bra from her grip. My hands wrapped around her upper arms, I back her up against the floor-to-ceiling window.

Justine's palms press against my chest, gripping my shirt. "I thought you liked the tease."

"I fucking love it. Too much."

I take her lips, covering her mouth with mine and pressing my lower body against her. I want her to feel what she does to me. Justine is no passive participant in the kiss—she steals the role as aggressor, pulling away to bite my lower lip before sucking my tongue back into her mouth. Her hands find their way around the back of my neck, and take control once more. It's a constant battle for supremacy, and I've never been so ready after one kiss.

Only Justine.

That shouldn't surprise me in the least.

I knew she was different. Whether consciously or on a gut level, I wouldn't have spent two years in pursuit if she hadn't been fucking amazing. And now she's mine.

I may not have had her yet, but I don't care. I know what's coming is going to be the best night of my life, and I'm going to do every damn thing in my power to make sure it's unforgettable for her.

I want her addicted to me.

It's only fair, because I'll never get enough of her.

Chapter 37

Justine

Ryker's hands roam my body, lighting up my skin. I'm buzzing with the headiness of everything—his kiss and his touch. I've never had this kind of reaction before, and even though I don't have tons of notches on my bedpost, I know this is totally different.

I want my clothes off. I want him inside me. I want it now.

Foreplay later. What does that make it? After-play? Round two? Whatever.

He rolls my nipple between two fingers and I squeeze my thighs together, failing to quell the ache.

Dropping one hand from the back of his neck where I've been holding on for dear life, I slide it between our bodies and palm his cock.

The best way to get what I want without having to beg for it? Make it what he wants.

"Fuck, baby." His breath catches as he drops his forehead against mine. "You want that?"

I can't lie. "Yes. Hurry."

Ryker drops his gaze to mine, but before I can read his expression, he steps back and twines his fingers through my hand that was just wrapped around his erection. "I changed my mind. I want you in my bed. Under me. I want to hear my name echoing down the hall as you scream when I make you come."

My inner muscles clench, and in that moment, I'd let him take me anywhere as long as he follows through on his promises.

As I trail him down the dark hallway, his grip on my hand silences any lingering hesitation. I'm not second-guessing anything now. Instead, I'm taking everything I can get.

When we reach the doorway, Ryker stops, turns, and wraps both hands around my waist before picking me up and carrying me toward the giant bed. Once we're close, he twists around and drops onto it, falling backward with me on top of him.

I waste no time as my hands go for the hem of his shirt and tug it up. He raises his arms and within seconds his chest is bare, and I'm taking advantage. This time it's my hands covering every inch of his skin, learning him, tasting him. It lasts only a minute or so before he grips me again by the hips and rolls us over.

The rest of my costume, and my panties, are gone in moments. All I'm wearing is confidence and a smile.

Ryker pushes off me to stand, fingers working the button and zipper of his jeans. He shoves them down and his cock springs free. *Commando.* Why is that so damn hot?

Just like it did the night in his bed at his parents' house, my mouth waters at the sight of his perfect erection. I want it between my lips. I want him so on edge that he can't control himself when he finally slides inside me.

His blue eyes burn with heat, and I wonder if he's picturing the same thing. I sit up as he steps forward, reaching for him, but Ryker's hand grips my wrist before I can make contact.

"No. I'm gonna come in that tight little pussy first, and if I let you get your hands on my cock, I'm a goner." He steps toward the nightstand and digs in the drawer. He tears open a foil packet, rolling a condom down his length before returning to spread my knees and step between them.

Instead of thrusting inside me, he pauses. "Speak now or forever hold your peace, Justine. We can't go back after this, so you better make damn sure it's what you want."

I'm past the point of no return, and I'm done questioning my choice. Good, bad, or indifferent, I'm doing this.

"Don't make me beg."

A darkly satisfied smile tugs at his lips. "Oh, you're going to beg."

Before I can say another word, he presses the head to my entrance and buries himself inside me.

Holy. Hell.

Full. So full.

Everything after that initial sensation is washed in a blur of impending orgasm and need. Stroke after stroke, he powers into me. Hands under my ass, he lifts me up, changing the angle and ratcheting up the pleasure. I'm screaming his name as I come the first time, and begging incoherently until he ruthlessly pushes me over the edge into a second shattering climax. Ryker's roar as he comes is imprinted in my brain.

He's right. I'm never going to forget this.

Chapter 38

Ryker

I wake up with nothing but cool sheets and an empty pillow beside me, and my first thought is that Justine left. She ran. She's gone.

I roll out of bed and stride into the kitchen, pissed that she would bail after last night. Pissed that she'd walk without even telling me to go fuck myself first. She's a woman and therefore mercurial in mood. But she's also Justine, so she's beyond unpredictable.

Anger is rushing through my veins and I'm headed for the counter to grab my keys, intent on tracking her down because I'm spoiling for a fight. You don't have a night like we did last night and then just disappear without a word.

Is this how all those girls felt when I bailed before morning? Is this poetic justice at work?

But all my introspection evaporates when I see Justine reaching up into the cabinet beside the stove, wearing nothing but my Captain America T-shirt from last night. It rides up, exposing the curve of her ass as she reaches to the top shelf to grab something.

I'm dumbstruck. Silently, I drink in the vision of her in my kitchen.

She hums to herself as she pulls down the nonstick spray and uses it on the frying pan. I still can't find any words as she sets the pan on the burner, tests the heat, and spoons in white batter in three spots.

Pancakes?

Justine Porter is in my kitchen, naked except for my shirt, making pancakes.

I must have done something very, very right in another life to be rewarded this way.

She turns and reaches for a drawer, I'm assuming to look for a spatula, but sees me and screeches.

"Jesus Christ, you scared the shit out of me!" She slaps her hand over her heaving chest in the vicinity of her heart. But let's be honest—all I see is braless tits bouncing in my shirt.

Striding toward her, I back Justine into the corner of my kitchen, trapping her in the circle of my arms, my hands pressing against the countertop on either side of her hips.

"I thought you left." The words come out harsher than I intended from the residual anger. I hadn't planned to say them at all. Hadn't planned for her to know I was freaking the fuck out, but they came out anyway. "I thought I was going to have to drive over to campus and bang down your door to find out why you bailed on me."

Both of her dark eyebrows arch up. "Really? I have a feeling that would be a case of the pot calling the kettle black, if you know what I mean."

"I wanted you in my bed when I woke up."

"And I wanted pancakes." She twists to look at the stove and the batter in the frying pan. "Which need to be flipped."

I don't give a shit about the fucking pancakes. Not when I've got her in my arms, all sleep-tousled hair, no makeup, and looking sexy as hell. But Justine is intent and more awake than I am. She ducks out from under my arm and yanks open a drawer to remove the spatula.

"They can burn for all I—"

Justine turns, and with lightning-fast reflexes, smacks me on the ass with it.

"What the—" I start, rubbing the stinging spot on my ass.

"They are not going to burn. I may not be good at much in the kitchen, but I make kick-ass pancakes."

She turns her back on me to flip them, but not after shooting me a smirk as I rub my ass again.

A couple of minutes later, Justine slides three perfect silver-dollar pancakes onto a plate and sets it on the bar. "You can have the first round. They're a little bit darker than I was going for on the one side, but that's your fault."

I might be a guy, but I'm not completely stupid. There's a sexy-as-hell woman in my kitchen, mostly naked, and she's feeding me. I'm going to eat the fucking pancakes.

"They look better than anything I can make."

"Then eat." Her smile is bright and cheery and proud.

I head for the cupboard to find the syrup as Justine pulls the butter out of the fridge. As I sit down and doctor up the pancakes, she starts another batch. I'm more interested in watching her than I am in eating, but I'm not about to let them get cold and have her hard work go to waste.

But that doesn't mean my brain is running down this road of how fucking good it feels to have her here.

One night. We had one night together, and all of a sudden I'm putting her in my kitchen every morning in my head.

What is it about this woman that gets me so tangled up? She's different. She's a challenge. I should be content now that I've gotten her in my bed, but I'm not. I take in every detail about her, but I still want to know more.

She flips another batch and joins me a few minutes later at the bar. We eat in companionable silence until she freezes with her fork in midair, pancakes headed toward her mouth.

"What's wrong?" I follow her gaze to the bowl of crap on my counter. It's supposed to be a fruit bowl, according to my mother, but I've only ever tossed mail, keys, change, and other random shit in it.

Justine's gaze is locked on the Pez dispenser I bought the night before I was supposed to be at her apartment to help her move. I was headed home from the bar and had to stop to get gas. When I went inside the gas station to get a soda and some chips, I spied a Pez display and couldn't resist. It was my attempt at being charming, and we all know how that worked out.

"What's that?" Justine asks, lowering her fork to her plate, uneaten pancakes still speared on the tines.

"Exactly what it looks like."

She pulls the cardboard and plastic package from beneath a pile of mail and stares.

Yoda.

Because who the hell doesn't like Yoda?

"You bought me Pez?" Her eyes find mine, and disbelief colors her tone.

"Yeah, I saw it and thought of you, so I bought it."

She's holding the package like it contains solid gold and not plastic in the shape of one of the most recognizable Star

Wars characters ever.

"When?" The question is quiet, and as soon as it falls between us, I don't want to answer.

But I'm not going to lie.

"The night before I was supposed to be at your house to help you move. I didn't blow you off, Justine. Something came up and there was nothing I could do. I didn't have your number, so I couldn't call or text. I still feel like shit over it, and I'm sorry."

My apology is the sincerest I've ever delivered, and yet I still can't tell her the truth.

She drops her eyes from mine to Yoda and back to me again. "You didn't intend to blow me off."

It doesn't come out as a question, but I know it is.

"No. Never."

"So, what the hell happened?" Her expression pleads for an explanation, but I can't give her one.

"I can't tell you. Just know . . . if there was anything I could've done to change that morning, I would have."

Chapter 39

Justine

I want to shake a real explanation out of him, but I can't. The proof that Ryker didn't intend to stand me up is in my hands.

What would Yoda do? I stare at the Pez dispenser and already know it's going to be my favorite addition to my collection. Ever. Because it's proof that I mattered to him even before I should have. Maybe that shouldn't carry so much weight with me, but it does.

Heavy silence blankets the room, and Ryker is waiting for a response. I don't really know what to say, but I have to let it go. Move on. I can't keep holding on to those feelings because I've got so many better—and scarier—ones floating inside me when it comes to him.

"Thank you." A smile sneaks onto my face. "I love it."

His expression relaxes and he leans toward me. "I'm glad." His lips brush across my cheek, and my body heats.

I turn to meet Ryker's seeking mouth, not caring that my lips are sticky with syrup. He devours me as though he can't get enough of my taste.

I want him. Pulling away, I drop my attention to the bulge in the shorts he's wearing. Last night we both got carried away, and I didn't fulfill my end of the bargain. My lips on his cock.

That's going to change right now.

I reach over to cup the thick length, and he flexes into my hand.

"Fuck, baby. I want that mouth."

My smile is as wicked as his voice is deep. "Then you should probably go sit on the couch and lose the shorts so you can have it."

The pancakes are forgotten as we both stand. Ryker grips my hand and pulls me with him toward the couch.

I'm not waiting. I'm taking. This is my turn, and I'm going to give him something he'll never forget. Tucking my thumbs into his waistband, I shove the shorts to the floor and give him a push.

"Sit."

Ryker follows my directions and drops onto the couch, his eyes never leaving mine.

If that's how he wants to play this, I can do it. Slowly, I sink to my knees with my hands on his thighs. I waste no time, gripping his shaft and lowering my mouth to the head, my tongue darting out to circle it. And still, my eyes never leave his.

Ryker's gaze heats with intensity and both hands move—one to bury in my hair and the other to cup my cheek.

"You're going to wreck me. You've barely started, but I know you're going to wreck me."

His words spur me on, as if challenging me to make them a reality. I close my mouth over the head, sucking and laving before going deeper and taking more. I slip one hand beneath to cup his balls as I work my mouth over his cock, sucking, licking, and reveling in the swell of power that fills me as pleasure steals over his features.

I made him look like that. Me.

And I want to see what he's going to look like when I wreck him. Breaking the stare, I throw myself into the blow job, spurred by his words and groans.

"So fucking perfect. You're gonna swallow me whole and take everything I give you."

I squeeze my thighs together to stem the ache growing there. I've never been more turned on by giving head.

His fingers grip my hair tighter, and I work him over faster and faster until he groans. "Fuck, I'm gonna come."

The words unleash a wave of satisfaction in me. Hell yes, he's going to come, and he's never going to forget this moment. I keep going, taking him deeper, letting his cock bump the back of my throat. He stills my movements, holding my head in place as he fucks into my mouth with short strokes.

Ryker's yell fills the room as his orgasm slides down my throat.

He drops forward, his head bowed over me. I slip my lips from his shaft as he presses a kiss to the top of my head.

When I rise from my knees, he pulls me down onto the couch beside him.

"Five minutes, and then it's your turn."

And he's a man of his word. Pancakes and orgasms for breakfast? Don't mind if I do.

Chapter 40

Justine

I never expected to be one of those girls. The ones who can juggle school and work and a relationship. But somehow, here I am.

I stare up at the supreme court building and then glance down at my watch. The bus dropped me off five minutes ago, but I've been using the time to gather my nerves.

I have to tell Justice Grant that I'm going to pay him back. He responded to my e-mail with this time to meet and discuss, so now I have to explain to him why I can't keep letting him pay my tuition without making it a loan. I didn't walk into this situation looking for a handout, but his offer was too good to turn down.

That was before everything changed. I can have everything I want, the guy and my degree, but I'm going to have to work for them both.

Good thing I'm no stranger to hard work.

Squaring my shoulders, I give myself one final pep talk before I head inside with my newly drafted contract in my bag.

He will understand, and he'll respect me for being so honest and forthright.

I need Justice Grant's respect. It's hard to explain, but it's the truth. He's the most upstanding man I've ever met, always leading by example.

I stride toward security and make my way through the hallways and up the stairs to his chambers. The door is open, so I enter without knocking.

"Justice Grant?"

The interior door opens, and he steps out. "Justine. Thank you for being so prompt. I have to say I'm confused by the message. Care to explain what's going on?"

Sucking in a deep breath and releasing it slowly, I spill everything, starting with the most important fact.

"I think I'm falling in love with your son."

Justice Grant's eyes go wide. "Is that so?"

I nod. "More than likely. I've . . . I've never felt like this before, and I know it's crazy and complicated and I have no idea what else to call it. So yes, sir, I think that's what's happening."

I'll never win an award for the most elegant declaration, but it's sincere.

"I see."

"So that changes things, as I'm sure you understand. I can't take the money for tuition unless it's a loan. What you've already paid and whatever you pay from here on out." I freeze, not having considered another possible option. "That is, if you keep paying. I guess this could change everything."

He smiles at me, his expression as kind as always. "Ryker got an A on his Professional Responsibility midterm when I know damn well Babcock wanted to knock him down a peg after that stunt he pulled the first week of class. If you think I don't know how he found the motivation to study hard enough to earn that grade, you must not think I'm very smart." He nods to the two chairs in a conversational arrangement in his chambers. "Let's sit down."

I settle into a chair and Justice Grant takes the one angled toward it.

"I think I understand where you're coming from, but I'm here to tell you that I consider whatever is happening between you and my son to be completely separate from our arrangement."

I exhale, glad he's not whipping out a scarlet letter to pin to my shirt. "I'm glad you feel that way, but I think you understand why I feel differently."

He leans forward, his elbows on his knees, and for the hundredth time I wish that I'd had a father like him growing up. How different would my life have been? But then again, I wouldn't be me. I don't know if I would appreciate everything I've achieved and feel as proud as I do.

Especially right now, as I pull a new contract from my bag and lay it on the Battle of Iwo Jima book on the small table between the chairs.

"What's this?" Grant sits up and picks up the contract.

One thing they don't teach you in law school is how to do actual legal work, like draft contracts. So I taught myself using the contract he'd drafted . . . and Google.

Grant's gaze moves across the words, and I'm holding my breath, hoping I didn't screw this up.

He flips over to the second page and then the third. I included all the boilerplate contract stuff he did, including the confidentiality clause I already technically violated by telling Merica. *Does that mean I'm going to be a terrible lawyer?*

His blue eyes, a few shades darker than his son's, rise to meet mine. "You put some serious thought into this, didn't you?"

"Yes, sir. But, I'll be perfectly honest, I have no idea how to draft a loan agreement. I just gave it my best shot. If there are things that need to be fixed, I'm happy to make the changes if you just tell me what to write."

He's digesting my explanation, but a small smile pulls at his lips. "You're going to be one hell of a lawyer, but the first thing you have to learn is never tell the opposing party you don't know what you're doing. Act like you've done this a hundred times. Confidence will take you further than any other skill you learn in law school."

I nod, soaking up his wisdom just like I did when I clerked in these chambers during my externship. "Duly noted. If you have any suggested revisions, I'm willing to take them into consideration."

His smile widens. "Better."

Justice Grant stands and walks to his desk, retrieving a gold pen. He crosses something out, and it takes all the willpower I have not to get up and stare over his shoulder to see what he's changing. A few moments later, he comes back and hands it to me.

I read his familiar handwriting, interpreting the semi-illegible scrawl that I've missed seeing.

He crossed out the interest rate and payment terms and replaced them with something *much* more favorable to me.

I glance up. "Are you sure? This isn't a very good investment for you, sir."

"Can you live with the terms?"

When I nod, he hands me the pen. "Then your signature is all that's missing."

I flip to the signature page, and sure enough, his is already there.

I lift my gaze to his once more, the gold pen weighing heavily in my hand. "Are you sure?"

"The best investment I can make is in the minds of the next generation. You're a smart girl, Justine, and more than that, you're genuine, honest, and kind. You could've just taken the tuition and not paid it back, and I wouldn't have been disappointed. But this shows me even more about your character, and I hope my son is smart enough to keep you happy and never let you go."

His words of approval warm me from the inside out. I scrawl my signature on the line.

He settles himself back in the chair and says, "Now, let's talk about getting you a job that will pay you enough so you can meet your obligations. Where are you working now?"

"The business school library."

"How would you feel about taking a clerk position at a firm? You'd be doing research, reading cases, and writing memos, similar to what you did here, but they'll pay you at least double what you're getting paid by the university. The work will be interesting."

"Which firm?"

"Grant Bentham Beckett."

Where Ryker's mom works.

"Oh, wow. I never considered that as an option. Is your wife back home from working on her project?" I can't imagine a more awkward way to meet Ryker's mom than in her place of work with no warning.

"No, she won't be back for a couple more weeks. You'd be working for a small group of appellate litigation attorneys who desperately need the help right now. I had actually planned to ask you if you were interested in the job after your externship, but I knew you were going to Legal Aid for the summer. Is that still your plan after graduation?"

"Yes, if I can find an opening somewhere."

"Then working at the firm for the rest of the year will help you pay off a good bit of this loan before graduation. I'm sure I don't have to tell you that you're not going to make much at Legal Aid."

"I know, but it's not about the money for me." And it wasn't. It never has been.

Justice Grant's smile is sincere, but I can tell he thinks I'm partially an idiot for not looking for a higher-paying job.

"It's admirable, for sure. They need good lawyers just like everyone else. So, how do you feel about handing in your notice to the library and starting at the firm next Monday?"

Today's Monday, so that's only a week's notice. I feel bad about it, but the offer he's made me is not only interesting, but will help me pay off a chunk of the loan before I graduate.

"How much will they pay?" I ask, needing to hear an actual number before I accept.

When he gives it to me, I school my expression not to show my shock. It's not just twice what I make at the library—it's over three times as much. I quickly calculate in my head, realizing I'll be able to get a good head start on knocking out this debt before I even graduate. And if Justice Grant says the work would be interesting, I believe him.

"Okay, I'm interested."

"Great. I'll make a call and have HR and the chair of the practice group e-mail you the details."

"I don't need to interview?" I'm shocked that it could possibly be this easy.

Grant shakes his head. "They'll accept my recommendation in place of an interview."

It always comes down to who you know . . . But in this instance, I'm not complaining.

"Thank you, sir. I'll watch for the e-mail."

We both stand and I shoulder my bag. He's walking me to the door in the outer chambers when he adds, "I'd like to keep this new arrangement between us still, but if you want to tell Ryker about the job, feel free."

I keep my voice calm and steady, but inside I'm cringing. *Should I argue that we need to tell him everything?* I glance up at Justice Grant, and I can't find the words to question him.

"Okay . . . if you think that's best."

"I do. For now, anyway. Especially given the confidentiality clause you kept in your agreement."

As soon as I'm out of the office, I'm kicking myself. *Why did I include the confidentiality clause?* Did some part of me want to put off telling Ryker? Clearly, his dad doesn't want him to know yet.

The guilt I'd just hoped to banish creeps back in.

It's not forever, Justine. He just said—for now. Everything's going to be fine.

I keep telling myself that for the next half hour as the bus takes me home.

Chapter 41

Ryker

I haven't had a girlfriend in years. I've had hookups and casual sex, but not girlfriends. So how the hell do I break it to Justine that that's exactly what she is? She's mine, I'm hers, and neither of us is touching anyone else.

Not that I'm worried about her touching someone else, but I feel the need to make it extremely clear when I walk out of the parking garage and see her standing next to a pickup as some guy lifts her bike out of the bed.

"Thanks! I appreciate the ride."

Justine, being the stubborn woman she is, still won't let me give her rides to and from school. So why the hell is she taking rides from strangers?

The guy leans down and gives her a quick hug and a kiss on the cheek before watching her ass as she pushes her bike toward the law school. Finally, he catches sight of me and looks away before jogging around the truck and climbing back inside.

I wait next to the bike rack, but Justine doesn't notice me as she settles her bike in and locks it up.

"Hey," I say to get her attention.

She jerks her head up and smiles when she sees me. "Hey. I didn't see you there."

"I noticed. Who was the guy?"

Confusion mutes her smile. "What guy?"

"The one in the truck you just got out of. If you needed a ride to class, I would've grabbed you."

She looks toward the road but the guy is already gone. I'm not sure how she missed the rumble of his exhaust as he revved the engine and pulled away.

"Elliot is a guy who lived in my dorm in undergrad. He saw me about a mile away and stopped to offer me a ride."

"A guy who lived in your dorm in undergrad." My tone takes on a dangerous quality. "Do you even know him? Trust him?"

Her brow furrows. "It was a mile. He offered a ride, I was cold, and I took it. Not a big deal, Ryker."

She's oblivious to the fact that if she'd offered to skip class and go home with the guy, there's no doubt he would have taken her up on it.

"Call me next time. It'll be snowing before you know it, so you're going to have to stop riding sooner rather than later. Might as well get into a new routine. And for the record," I lean in and brush my lips across her earlobe, "my lips are the only ones I want to see on you."

Justine jerks back. "Are you *jealous*?" The disbelief in her voice surprises me more than her words.

"Are you *surprised*?"

She blinks. "Yeah, I guess I am. And you know what? I don't know how I feel about that."

I glance at my watch. We only have fifteen minutes before class starts, which isn't long enough to make my point the way I need to. But I will. After class.

Chapter 42

Justine

Ryker's reaction to Elliot giving me a ride is still swirling through my mind as he wraps my hand around a large cup of tea from the café and pulls me into the elevator. I see the looks we're getting. His actions are making it abundantly clear that we're . . . *what are we exactly?*

The crowded elevator is taking us to the third floor, and Turner's class is not the place to pose that question.

Do I need an answer? Do I want an answer?

What if we're just friends with benefits? Am I okay with that?

The doors open on the second floor and, *of course*, Kristy Horner is standing there.

"Room for one more?"

No one in the elevator can miss the way she devours Ryker with her gaze.

Being that Kristy's blond, built, and hot, it doesn't surprise me when two of the guys step backward and make room. I squish toward the back corner, attempting not to whack the tiny girl behind me with my backpack.

Ryker takes a step back too, but Kristy presses her chest up against his anyway.

"Sorry, guys. Didn't mean to make it a crush."

Liar.

I can see her profile over Ryker's shoulder, but she's not paying any attention to me. The standard awkward elevator silence fills the car as it goes up one more floor before jerking to a halt.

Kristy takes this opportunity to fall forward against Ryker, both hands pressing against his pecs. The guy to her left reaches out to steady her, but she moves closer to Ryker instead.

I can't make out her whispered words, but it sounds like, *You always did know how to keep me steady.*

The doors slide open, and Kristy waits an extra beat before lifting her hands off Ryker's chest. She gives him a wink before strutting out, confident that every eye is on her.

I really hate that girl.

A niggle of . . . *something* sneaks into me along with the echo of Ryker's words—*"My lips are the only ones I want to see on you."*

Apparently, my hands are the only ones I want to see on him. But I say nothing and follow the crowd toward the classroom. Ryker reaches back and grabs my fingers, lacing his through mine.

He releases me when I stop by a single empty seat, and I drop my backpack on the counter without bothering to cushion the *thunk*. His eyebrows knit together, but all he says is, "I'll see you after class," before moving down the row to the next empty chair.

The lecture drones on, but I force myself to pay attention and take verbatim notes like I normally would. It's a good way to block out the stupid rush of jealousy I feel every time Kristy blatantly stares at Ryker. Is she feeling desperate now that he has clearly turned his attention elsewhere?

I shove the thoughts down. I need to concentrate. No distractions. That was the deal. But I didn't take into account my own feelings when I made that decree.

Yeah, he and I need to have a little chat after class. Maybe I'll feel better if I know where we stand.

Ryker is by my side as I finish packing up my laptop and shoving my casebook in my backpack. "Library?"

"Sure."

I lead the way out of the room and across to the third-floor entrance where the private study rooms are. Ryker looks in the windows until he finds one that's unoccupied, and flips the sign before letting me in.

"We need to talk." The words come out in a serious tone from Ryker's lips. But what surprises me most is that he beat me to it.

"I think you're right." I take a seat on one side of the table, in view of the window, and he takes a seat on the other side.

I open my mouth to say something, but Ryker jumps in first. "This thing between us? It's exclusive. No one puts his hands or mouth on you but me. Got it?"

Crossing my arms over my chest, I lean back in my seat. "Then same goes. Because you didn't exactly push Kristy Horner off you in the elevator."

"That's not the same—"

"Bull. Shit." I emphasize both syllables.

"She fell into me."

"On purpose."

"And?"

"And I didn't like it."

Ryker leans forward, propping both elbows on the table. "And I didn't like watching some guy you barely know put his lips on you. I've never been the possessive type before, but when it comes to you, I want to drag you away from any guy who tries to touch you. Fuck, Justine, there aren't two minutes that go by when I don't want to drag you away, period. Get you alone. Make sure that sweet little pussy is wet and ready for me."

My eyes widen at his words, and my body reacts predictably. How can it not when he's staring at me like that? And his possessiveness? Why does that make me even hotter? *I shouldn't like it. I shouldn't be this thrilled that he feels this way.* But I can't help it. I am. The flare of heat in his eyes says that he knows it too.

"You love it when I talk dirty to you, don't you, baby?"

His low, husky words jerk me out of my slide into lust. "We're in the library. We can't talk like this here."

Ryker glances to the little window in the private room and back to me. "No one can hear us, and what's more, no one will be able to see what I'm about to do."

Oh. Hell.

He stands and flips the lock on the inside of the door before grabbing my backpack and pulling out my laptop, opening it on the table in front of me. Next, he pulls out my casebook and sets it beside the keyboard.

"You're going to look like you're studying your little heart out if someone looks through that window. They're going to have no idea that I'm eating your pussy until you're ready to scream. But you're not going to scream—you're going to bite your lip and let that orgasm rip through you, and no one is going to be the wiser. After, you're going to go to class, your pussy ready for my cock, and then I'm going to take you home, make you sit across the table from me while we both do all of our reading. I'm going to feed you before I fuck you all night and you can scream as loud as you want."

I'm not sure he needs to say anything else, because I'm ready. I'll do whatever he wants as long as he gives me everything he says he will.

"Now, pick up your highlighter and start your reading. I've got work to do." And he ducks under the table and disappears from sight.

Today I opted for comfort over fashion, going with black leggings, black boots, and a tunic-length gray sweater. Simple, but it works.

Ryker doesn't waste any time tugging my leggings down and smoothing my sweater along my leg so there's no visible skin.

Is he really going to . . .

Cold air hits my bare skin as he tugs my panties aside.

"Fuck, you're already wet, baby. I've been dying to taste you since yesterday."

My grip on the highlighter tightens, and I stare blankly at the words on the page in my casebook, pretending to concentrate as the first swipe of his tongue laves me from bottom to top.

Oh God. I can't do this. I'm never going to be able to stay quiet.

I squirm in the seat as Ryker murmurs from beneath

the table. "You better make it look like you're studying, baby. You don't want anyone to know that I'm eating this pussy, do you? Hold still. You're not going to last long."

I open my mouth to protest that he can't possibly know that, but two fingers slide inside me, and I shut my mouth with a snap.

Oh. Shit. I'm going to come. In the library. I don't think I'll be able to do it silently.

His mouth latches around my clit, and when he sucks, I know I'm screwed.

"Oh shit. Oh shit," I murmur.

"Quiet, or I'm not going to let you have it. I'll stop right now."

I bite down on my lip and squeeze my eyes shut, hoping like hell no one looks in the window. The orgasm slams into me, and I drop the highlighter to grab the edge of the table.

"Good girl," Ryker says as he slides his fingers out of me, replaces my panties, and pulls my leggings back up my hips. I release my grip on the table to yank them up the rest of the way, my gaze darting to the window.

I'm not sure if I was expecting a crowd of gawking onlookers, but there's only one set of eyes. They're on Ryker as he comes out from under the table.

Fucking Kristy Horner.

I slam my casebook closed and she darts away, a look that could kill on her face.

"What? What's wrong?"

I don't even want to say it. It doesn't matter. She's not going to do anything. *Right?* Then again, he should know too.

"Kristy Horner was by the window. She saw me. Saw

you. Us. Whatever."

Ryker's satisfied smile falls away. "I'll take care of it."

"No." My voice strikes out like a lash.

"I'm sure as hell not going to let her tell anyone. This was my idea, and I'm not letting you get in trouble for it."

His concern for me quells some of the rising panic. "Do you really think she would?"

He shrugs. "I don't know. She's a piece of work, but she's not a bad person. I'll talk to her."

I narrow my eyes and pitch my voice as seriously as possible. "If she says she needs the same treatment to keep it quiet, I will shank her."

"Not happening, babe. Don't worry about a thing. I'll do damage control, and you get on with your day."

Chapter 43

Ryker

I track down Kristy Horner in the *International Law Journal* office. She's the editor-in-chief to my assistant EIC position. When I shut the door, she turns in her seat from the desk in the back.

"Wow, I guess you don't spend much time afterward with any girl. And here I was starting to think Porter was special." Kristy's tone is snide and triumphant.

"You're going to erase what you saw from your brain, and if you ever tell anyone, I will unleash hell on you."

Her face molds into its most comfortable expression—snotty princess. "There's nothing you can do to me if I decide to tell people. Gosh, what would Daddy think if you got kicked out of school because of that skank?"

My hands curl into tight fists. If she were a man, I'd drop her to her knees with one shot for talking about Justine like that. But I don't need to touch Kristy to take her down a peg.

"You're not going to tell anyone a fucking thing. You know why? Because all those slutty little porn shots you sent me might find themselves resurrected from the depths of my phone."

She sucks in a breath. "That's called revenge porn. There are cases."

"And these were unsolicited. Why should that be okay when men are humiliated for sending unsolicited dick pics? Actually, wouldn't that make a hell of an article for the student paper. I bet I could get the editor to write a piece on the double standard."

"Fuck you, Ryker."

"That ship has sailed. But if you say a single word about Justine, for any reason, I will fuck up your world."

Her glare could peel paint off a wall. "And what the hell makes her so goddamned special? You would never have threatened someone for me."

"She just is. And it's none of your fucking business anyway. Quit the bullshit games and leave her alone."

"Someday you're going to realize that you missed out on something awesome with us."

"That's a risk I'm willing to take."

I grab the door handle and yank it open. I've got better things to do than waste my time with her.

Chapter 44

Ryker

"Babe, you have to quit looking at me like that or I won't be able to concentrate."

Justine is sitting across from me at my kitchen table, and the look on her face says she's worried about studying.

I snap the cap on my highlighter and drop it on the table. "Seriously. Don't make me go study in another room."

"But I can't stop thinking about the library. Not the crappy part where Kristy Horner peeped through the window, but the part where you made me be quiet when I wanted to scream."

Yeah. There's no concentration happening here because now my dick is as hard as a rock. But I'm not going to let us be the distraction she's been worrying we would be from the beginning. I promised myself I wouldn't let this interfere with school, and I'm not going to.

Okay, so the library might've been a little interference, but . . .

"Let's make a deal. We both finish all our reading and I'll clear this table and fuck you across it. Then we'll eat."

Her eyes light up. "Will you cook something for me? Naked?"

A grin works its way across my face. Unexpected, and yet welcome.

"Maybe. But if the oven is involved, my dick is going in an oven mitt."

"Fair enough. You've got a deal." With a laugh, she grabs her highlighter and stares down at the page intently, glancing up at me from beneath her lashes as she bites her lip.

Fuck, but I like that look.

Chapter 45

Justine

"Oh. My. Fucking. God. Right there. Right there. Right there."

Ryker has me spread out over the kitchen table, my fingers wrapped around one edge as he powers into me thrust after thrust. Shoving his hand beneath my hips, he presses two fingers down on my clit.

"You gonna scream for me?"

The grip I'm keeping on my control snaps, and I give him what he wants. "Ryker!"

His roar follows mine and a few moments later, he slows. He leans forward, his hands covering mine, before he peels my fingers back, lacing them with his.

His hot breath hits my ear. "You're amazing."

The words I told his father are bubbling up inside me. *I think I'm falling in love with you.* But there's no way I can say them. Especially not now, when I'm in a near putty-like consistency and my brain is flooded with endorphins from the body-shaking climax.

Now is not the time. I need to think about this. Need

to figure out if I'm really falling down this rabbit hole, or if this is just me being an overemotional girl who is finally getting some off-the-charts fabulous sex.

Ryker has made no indication about how he feels. *But do his feelings or lack thereof change mine? I don't need him to feel the same way about me to validate how I feel about him.*

All these introspective thoughts are shoved to the back of my mind when he rises and pulls me up to standing with him.

"Pizza?"

And there it is. The confirmation I needed that he's a normal law school guy.

"Pizza sounds good."

I bend, intending to reach for my clothes that are scattered on the floor around the table, but Ryker tightens his grip on my fingers.

"You don't need those. Grab one of my T-shirts in my room. That way you can tease me with flashes of your ass when you get up and walk by, and I'll be so hard up I'll have to bend you over the nearest flat surface before we even get our first slice down."

I thought I was done. Floating in the bliss of my orgasm and replete. I was wrong.

My inner muscles clench, whether at his words or his touch, I don't know. But it's a fair guess that both are involved.

I head for his room to grab a T-shirt.

"Stay."

Has any word ever been quite so seductive?

I'm reaching for my leggings, buzzing on the aftermath of yet another Ryker-induced orgasm, when I look up to meet his blue gaze.

"Stay," he says again.

"Here? With you?" They're stupidly obvious questions that I shouldn't have to ask, but can't seem to stop them.

"Yeah. Here. With me. In my bed."

"We have class in the morning."

"So I'll take you home first to change, and then we'll go to class."

This new level of intimacy should scare the hell out of me. I should be backpedaling and coming up with all the excuses in the world why I can't stay here.

But would that just be me throwing up all the roadblocks I can think of because I know I'm falling too hard and too fast and it scares the hell out of me? Especially because I really want to stay?

"Come on, Jus. I want you with me. I'm not ready to let you go."

And that's the rub. I'm not ready to let him go either. Not even close.

I give him the only answer I can.

"Okay. I'll stay."

Ryker's arms wrapping around me and pulling me close against him so he can tuck my head under his chin is all I need to know I made the right choice.

Chapter 46

Justine

The e-mail comes in the middle of class Friday morning when I'm supposed to be taking the best notes of my life, but this is Advocacy class, so there's a lot of discussion that doesn't require note taking. And being that I'm the multi-tasker that I am, I'm checking my e-mail.

From: Vito Richards
To: Justine Porter
Re: Grant Bentham Beckett Employment Offer and New Hire Information

Dear Ms. Porter:
On the recommendation of Justice Grant and following review of your transcripts and résumé, we've determined that you would be a great fit for the position of Appellate Practice Group Research Assistant. We're looking forward to having you in the office on Monday at 2:00 p.m. to begin orientation and set up your work schedule.
You can park . . .

I skim over the rest of the details, but my mind is stuck on the big question. How did they get my transcripts and résumé? Justice Grant is the only logical source.

Monday at two p.m. They must have a copy of my class schedule or my old library work schedule too, or I just got lucky and they picked a time I can actually work.

My money is on them getting a copy of my class schedule. As a trustee, I can't imagine it would be difficult for Grant to get his hands on that either. I'm just surprised that he didn't ask me for it instead of procuring it himself.

Regardless, my palms sweat and my stomach flops in giant waves of nerves. *What am I doing? What am I going to tell Ryker?*

That's the question that's weighing down my conscience most heavily. How do I tell him I got a job working at his mom's firm without telling him it's to pay back his dad? *Just for now.*

I'm an idiot if I think I can keep it a secret for long. I have to tell him, and when I do, he's going to understand. *Right?* If the alternative is me dropping out of school, he would have to understand.

I decide I'm definitely going to tell him about the job. I can't keep that part to myself, nor am I willing to lie about it.

I turn the question over and over in my mind as discussion takes place around me. Any other class would tell you that the best solution is always honesty, but this is Advocacy. According to my professor, showing the facts and the arguments and law in the best light possible to prove your case and sway the opinion of the judge or jury—or whomever is sitting between you and the outcome you want—is the goal. That's what being a good lawyer is all about.

There's one concrete thing I've learned in law school—everything is a different shade of gray. There are a few bright-line rules, but everything else is a matter of interpretation. Even murder has its defenses. There are arguments on either side of every issue, and that's what lawyers get paid to do. Find the arguments. Make them persuasive. Do the best job you can to be an advocate for your client.

In this case, I'm probably taking the analogy a little too far because I'm being an advocate for myself. But doesn't everyone deserve an ally? Besides Merica, no one has been on my side since Gramps passed away.

As class wraps up, I decide that I can worry about how to tell Ryker about the new job later. I've got an entire weekend ahead of me to curl up inside, stay warm, study, read, and maybe . . . just maybe . . . spend another night with Ryker.

Yeah, I've got it bad.

Chapter 47

Ryker

I've never been to a farmers' market before. I didn't even know they were open after summer, but Justine was sipping a cup of coffee at the bar in my kitchen this morning wearing nothing but my T-shirt and when she said she wanted to go, there wasn't enough willpower in the world for me to say no. Add to that it was a little cold inside, making her nipples hard, and I might have been distracted about what I was saying yes to.

Either way, now we're here, and I'm carrying three bags of apples around the farmers' market because Justine is dying to make applesauce, apple pie, and apple crisp. Apparently it's a fall thing, and with everything going on this year, she hasn't had time to do it.

I'm sure as hell not going to complain if the woman wants to bake for me. Actually, I'd probably beg her to bake for me, which puts me in the realm of royally fucked. Things between us have already gone past any level that I expected, and my thoughts would probably freak her the fuck out. What would she say if she knew I was falling in love with her? Would she run the other way?

Justine is impossible to read, and I've worked my ass off not to scare her away. Right now, I feel like every day I get with her is a bonus, but the thought of losing her twists me up inside.

I'm trying not to think about it. Trying not to dwell on how much it would suck to lose her.

I'm not going to lose her.

"I think I've got enough," Justine says, looking from my full arms to the pile of apples displayed at one of the stalls.

"You sure?" I try not to laugh because she looks so damn cute when she's agonizing over this.

She nods emphatically. "Yes. I'm good. I've already spent twenty bucks on apples, and we still have to hit the grocery store to get everything else I need."

"If you're making me apple pie and all this other stuff, then I'm throwing in for the other supplies."

Justine narrows her eyes at me, and I can practically see the wheels in her brain spinning. "Okay, one more stall. And then we're leaving."

The young farm kid watching this entire exchange waits patiently while she picks out one last half bushel of apples. On the way out of the farmer's market, I stop and grab a gallon of apple cider, a dozen apple cider doughnuts, and a bag of caramel corn.

It's the best Saturday morning I've ever had, and it's all because of the woman sitting in the passenger seat.

I want to tell her, but I don't want to throw off the easiness of the day. I've got plenty of time . . . after all, I'm going to talk her into spending the entire weekend.

It's safe to say that my condo has never smelled this frigging good. It's also safe to say it's never looked this fucking amazing either. I can't take my eyes off Justine's curvy ass as she bends over to pull a pie out of the oven.

I know I'd get backhanded by the *Women's Law Journal* if I said that I loved seeing her barefoot in my kitchen. So sue me.

"Shit!"

She sets the pie plate on the top of the stove, and I'm by her side in three steps.

"Did you burn yourself? Are you okay?"

Justine's face isn't tinged with pain, but annoyance. "No, but the crust got too dark."

It looks perfectly golden brown to me, but I don't know shit about baking pies.

"It looks amazing."

She scowls. "It was almost perfect, but I left it in a minute or so too long."

I slide my hand around her hip and turn her to face me. "Baby, it's perfect. And if you wanted to make sure I'm hooked on not only your brain but your baking skills, mission accomplished."

The scowl fades away and a small smile takes its place. "You're hooked on my brain?"

I let a cocky grin take charge. "Obviously, it was your spectacular tits and perfect ass that got me first, but the first time you got called on in Torts and you went head-to-head with Professor Payne and answered every single question, I had to wait for my dick to go down before I could stand up."

"And you hit on me right after class."

My grin widens at the fact that she remembers. "Fuck yes, I did. Sexy and smart. You're the whole package. Why wouldn't I hit on you?"

She rolls her eyes. "You realize that if you'd dropped the cheesy lines and just told me this two years ago, I probably wouldn't have been able to hold out for so long."

My grin fades. "Bullshit. I don't think it would've mattered what I said; you would've shut me down every time. First year, I get. It sucks and it's hard. Second year, you were focused on even harder classes and Law Review."

Her gaze drops to the pie. "You're probably right. I wouldn't have said yes. There's no way I could balance it all. And right now, I'm terrified I won't be able to either." She looks up at me again. "I'm better at intense focus on one thing than I am at balance."

"It's going to be fine. I promise. School first, and we'll work everything else around it." I pull her in closer and drop a kiss on her forehead. "We got this."

She nods, but her hesitation lingers. Even so, I know pushing the subject isn't going to do me any favors. I'll get her there. Eventually.

"So, what am I going to have to do to get a slice of that pie?"

The smile that tugs at her lips is my reward. "I think we can make some kind of deal . . ."

Chapter 48

Justine

"Holy fuck. This is good." Ryker's eyes find mine across the table, fork hanging midair from his bite of apple pie.

A warm feeling of approval pools in my belly. "I'm glad you like it."

"Like it? I friggin' love it." He devours the remainder of his piece, and while he's scraping his plate clean, he says, "I bet you could've paid your tuition selling pie."

I don't know if it's an offhand comment or if he's fishing, but now that his plate is empty, his eyes are on me.

I force a chuckle. "Right. And making enough pie to sell for tuition would leave zero time for actually going to school."

"How are you paying your tuition?" His tone is curious, rather than accusing. "You've never told me."

A fist grips my stomach and twists. A fist of guilt, no doubt. I've been waiting for my opening because I know I need to tell him *something*. I *want* to tell him something. But how much can I really say? I start small, but I make sure every word I say is the truth. I will not lie to him.

"Your dad just helped me get a new job. At your mom's firm. I start Monday. My savings and working at the library weren't going to replace my scholarship, so I had to work out another solution." All true.

Ryker's expression shifts into something more rigid. "You're quitting the library to work at Grant Bentham Beckett?"

I nod. "The pay is better, and I need the money."

"You sure you've got it covered?" Even though he tries to keep his tone neutral, I can hear the skepticism breaking through.

I give him the most honest answer I can. "You don't need to worry about me. I'll be fine." Because I'm always fine. I always find a way to make things work.

But Ryker's not quite ready to let it go. "It just doesn't seem like you'd be able to work enough hours to come up with the money."

I smile. "I've got it handled. I promise."

And I do. Regardless of what happens with Ryker's grades, my loan is intact. As much as I want to spill every single detail so there are no more secrets between us, I have to trust Justice Grant. He said not yet, and I'm going to follow his lead. I've never had a father figure actually give me guidance, but I have to believe there's no one better than Justice Grant in that arena.

Ryker's expression is still unconvinced, so I move on to my next biggest concern. "What is working at a firm like? Have you worked at GBB? What do I need to know?"

He leans back in his chair, tension easing from his face. "Babe, you'll be fine. They'll love you. I worked there my first summer as a clerk. And while I decided it wasn't my thing, you'll probably be their newest rock star. Mostly you just have to figure out how to interpret minimal direction into real projects and hope like hell you did it right."

"What didn't you like about it?"

He looks away, his gaze lingering on the city beyond the window before coming back to me. "The politics, mostly. Maybe it would be different somewhere else, but with everyone knowing my mom, and her being a founding partner, and everyone being up in my family's business . . . it just wasn't for me."

"So you think it'll be different for me?" I ask, anxiety building about my upcoming initiation into law firm politics.

He reaches across the table and covers my hand with his. "You're going to be great, baby. Just pay attention, ask questions, and do good work. You won't have any problems. They'll love you."

His words dispel the bulk of my nerves, but not all of them. Everyone I work with is going to know Justice Grant got me the job. I push it away. There's no point in worrying about it right now.

"You want another piece of pie?" I ask Ryker, ready to move on from this subject, and yet hopeful that the next time it comes up, his dad will have given me the green light to tell him everything.

His smile is quick and genuine. "Hell yes."

As he digs into his second piece, telling me I'm a domestic goddess and I better watch out or he'll never let me leave, I know that I'm screwed.

I'm not falling anymore. It's a done deal.

Chapter 49

Justine

I thank the powers that be I had to scrounge together enough business attire last summer to work at Legal Aid, because without this black skirt suit and pressed white blouse, I'd be feeling majorly out of place as I walk through the doors of Grant Bentham Beckett and ask the receptionist behind the big granite desk where I can find Vito Richards.

As she puts in a call, I wait in the modern leather seating area and watch the stock quotes stream along the bottom of a flat-screen TV on the wall. The talking heads are muted but it wouldn't matter anyway, because Mr. Richards doesn't leave me waiting long.

"Ms. Porter," he says, hand outstretched. "It's great to meet you in person. Justice Grant has had so many great things to say about you."

I shake his offered hand. "Thank you. I'm really excited to be here."

And that's no lie. I truly am excited, despite the crushing nerves. This job is going to go a long way toward paying off my debt, and that's what matters right now.

He drops me off for orientation, and I spend hours filling out forms for HR and learning the computer system and programs. When I think my head's going to explode with all the information, Vito Richards opens the door to the orientation room and steps inside.

"Glad you're still here! I figured we would've scared you off with all the details."

I adopt a cheery smile, hoping like hell he can't tell how completely overwhelmed I am. "Of course not. I think I've got it all."

Richards nods. "Great. I'll walk you out and we can talk about your schedule."

I follow him out as he confirms what hours I can work and whether I want to try to work more hours than I did at the library. We pause at a cluster of chairs and a coffee table in the lobby, and I write down the hours he's hoping I can squeeze in. After a mental check of my schedule, I assure him it can work.

Altogether, I'll be putting in about fifteen hours per week, and maybe twenty if they decide to have me work some weekends. It's not many more hours than I'd work at the library, but I'm going to have to cut out of school as soon as class is over to hustle my butt downtown to get to work on time.

And without a car . . . that means I'm going to be at the mercy of the bus system unless I ask for a ride. Since asking for help has never been a strong quality of mine, it'll more than likely be the bus.

Not a big deal, I reassure myself. *I got this.*

Day two at Grant Bentham Beckett is my first actual work day. I had an eight o'clock class and made it here by eleven. Ryker wouldn't hear of me taking the bus, and dropped me off.

He pressed a kiss to my lips before I slid out of the car. "They're going to love you."

His words of confidence buoyed me through the doors and up the elevator to my new office.

Attorneys have the offices along the outside of the hallway with windows to the outside. Legal secretaries have cubicles running down the white interior hallway, and paralegals and research assistants have tiny interior offices with no windows, but at least we have doors. It comes through loud and clear as a design to reinforce the hierarchy around here. Ryker's mention of firm politics hovers at the forefront of my mind all day.

Vito's office is directly across the hall from my interior office, which is tucked behind the secretarial cubicle. I stash my bag in my office and retrieve a notepad and pen from my desk drawer before sticking my head in the doorway.

"Come on in, Justine. I was just talking to Ron about the projects we want to have you start on today," he says as I knock and peek my head inside the open door.

I enter the office, smiling at the man across the desk from Vito, and take a seat in the remaining vacant chair when Vito nods to it. He introduces me to Ron Lane, a fellow appellate partner I'll be supporting with research.

"We've got some exciting projects for you to work on, ones that we hope you'll find interesting and engaging."

He spends the next twenty minutes outlining the facts

of the major case he's working on, and I scribble furiously on my notepad to make sure I don't miss any details. I ask a few questions to ensure I understand the issues, but it's pretty straightforward. My electronic research skills are excellent, so I don't think I'll have any trouble tracking down cases for him.

When he flips the file closed, I'm poised to stand, but Vito isn't finished.

"I also have another case I'd like you to help with, even though the issues aren't typically something we handle."

Interest piqued, I flip to a new page on my notepad. "Whatever you need, sir. I'm happy to help."

"This one is a favor for a friend of a friend, and actually probably hits quite close to home for you."

I frown, wondering what kind of case he would have that would hit close to home for me.

"This isn't technically an appeal we're handling, but I said I'd look into any grounds for an appeal in a drunk-driving case that one of your fellow students got caught up in."

Chad. He has to be talking about Chad.

Vito's right, this one does hit close to home for me, even though Chad is gone and uncommunicative. Every text I've sent to check in on him has gone unanswered since the e-mail where he told me he was dropping out.

I know our friendship wasn't the strongest lately, but with our history, I expected a little more. But if there's a chance I can help him in any way, you better believe I'm going to do it, whether he wants my help or not.

"Whatever research you need, I'm your girl," I say, hoping it'll encourage him to move on more quickly to the details.

"As you probably know, Chad France was convicted of

a DUI this past summer based on an accident that took place right after finals."

There's no way I could ever forget. "I remember."

"He worked for a friend of mine who asked for a favor, but doesn't want to get involved due to conflict issues. I told him we'd review the case for potential grounds for appeal. It's a long shot, but it's worth another read. I'd like you to review the file and the court transcripts. Our best shot is finding a procedural error at this stage." He nods to a file box on the floor.

Oh, wow. No pressure there or anything, Justine. For Chad, I'll read everything three times just to make sure I don't miss anything.

"Do you have any ideas about what I should be looking for? I've taken Criminal Law and Criminal Procedure, but I'm no expert on procedural grounds for appeals in this situation."

"Just read through the files and see if anything stands out to you. The details are all there. I'll set up some time with one of the partners in the criminal law group, and he can give you a rundown on some of the most common errors and what you should be looking for."

That's exactly what I was hoping he'd say. Find me an expert I can ask a million questions. *I'll do my best, Chad. I promise.*

"Okay. That sounds good. Thank you."

"These are going to be great cases for you to cut your teeth on. Let me know if you have any questions as you dig in. Work on Chad's case whenever you get some downtime. It's not your first priority, but we'll do what we can."

"Understood. I'll get to them both; don't worry."

He smiles before I leave the office, lugging the heavy

box of files.

I waste no time once I'm back in my little white-and-beige cave. I'm sucked into my research and don't pull myself away until my stomach is grumbling and my watch says it's time to go home. But I can't leave without at least starting to look at Chad's case, so I flip the lid off the box. Dozens of file folders stand upright, and it's crazy to think that the fate of my childhood friend was decided among these pages.

The night at the bar comes back vividly in my memory. If Chad hadn't gotten hit and arrested, I wouldn't have needed help from Ryker. He wouldn't have kissed me. He wouldn't have stood me up. I wish I could erase it all for Chad's sake, but it's still crazy to think of how different things could have been. But then again, I have to believe that Ryker would have asked me out again. Would I have kept resisting?

Vito sticks his head into my office, interrupting my musings. "You should head home, Justine. You don't want to be the last one in the office on your first day. You'll be setting the standards pretty damn high."

"Sorry, I was just thinking about looking through Chad's case before I left. I would love to be able to find something helpful, and sooner rather than later."

"Save it for tomorrow. It's not going anywhere. What happened to him really was a crap deal. Only a fraction of a percentage over the legal limit, and he probably never would've been picked up had it not been for the driver who ran the light and hit him." Vito pauses. "I'm not saying he didn't commit the crime, but it's just hard to see a kid, who by all accounts was smart and a hard worker, go through something like this."

I nod, because I couldn't have said it better. I hated that this happened to him. "I'll dig through everything and see if anything stands out. When can I talk to someone in the criminal law group?"

"I'll set that up for later this week. Now, get out of here."

I'm heading down the stairs, my bag over my shoulder, when my phone vibrates in my hand.

Ryker: I'm outside. I'm taking you to dinner.

My mouth tugs wide with a smile as I tap out my reply.

Justine: I'm not going to argue with that.
Ryker: Then get your sweet ass down here.
Justine: On my way.

Everything else fades away as I head out of the building and see him waiting for me at the curb.

Chapter 50

Justine

Later that night, I'm in Ryker's bed, his hard body curled around me.

"I need to go home. I can't stay tonight again." There's nothing I want to do less than leave, but I know I need to keep some separation.

He curls a hand around my breast, and a zing of heat starts in my nipples and goes straight to my clit.

"You definitely need to stay because I'm not done with you yet. We've still got at least one more round before I'm letting you out of this bed."

I roll to face him. "Is that right?"

"Hell yes, that's right. You're not getting away from me yet."

"I can't just crash here every night." Getting this comfortable scares me when I'm clueless about what he's feeling.

"Is there some reason you have to really go home, or are you just freaking out about spending too much time here?"

Apparently Ryker can read me more easily than I

thought, or maybe I'm completely transparent.

"We're going to class together, you're taking me to work, we study together. You're going to get sick of me."

Ryker's blue gaze sears me. "You think after two years of trying to get you here, I'm going to let you leave my bed because you're worried about something that ridiculous? Not happening. I'll keep you here as long as I can. Hell, if I knew you wouldn't lose your shit, I'd just move you in."

"Uh, we're not— I mean. What?" My words come out a stammering mess.

"I hate that you live in crap student housing, Justine. I worry about you every night you spend there. Have the break-ins actually stopped, or has Campus Safety just stopped reporting them?"

As I gather the sheet to my chest, my teeth pinch down on my bottom lip at the concern etched on his features. I release it before replying. "They've stopped. I think. I mean, my place is fine."

I can't bring myself to admit that the nights I've spent in his bed have been the most restful sleep I've gotten since the night of the break-in, because at home, I spend too much time worrying away the hours I should be sleeping.

"You're staying tonight. I'm not asking. I'm telling you." His tone dares me to protest, and I know I should. I should tell him he can't order me to stay. But my protest would be halfhearted at best and completely bullshit at worst.

So instead, I cave. "Fine. I'll stay. Tonight. But tomorrow night I'm going home. I'm paying rent, so I need to sleep there."

"You can stop paying rent if you just—"

Oh no. That conversation isn't happening. I press a finger to his lips to stop him. *Because you're afraid you'll want to say yes?*

I shut down the inconvenient inner voice. I'm not considering it. This is too new, too untried. No matter how I feel, I'm not ready to jump off a cliff with no parachute or safety net. The last thing I want to do is move in, get comfortable, and then haul my stuff out again if something goes wrong. I've spent most of my life bouncing from place to place, never having a chance to put down roots. What if I put them down here and they get torn out?

"I'll stay tonight. Leave it at that, okay?"

Something about the tone of my voice keeps him from pushing. Instead, Ryker says nothing in response, probably because he's not going to make promises he won't keep, and I have a feeling this conversation isn't truly over. I know one foolproof way for him to leave the situation alone . . . I slide my hand between us and wrap it around his shaft.

Ryker groans as he hardens against my hand. "You don't play fair."

"Who says I'm playing at all? I take this very, very seriously."

Chapter 51

Ryker

I've avoided Kristy Horner and the *International Law Journal* office as much as possible this semester, but I can't any longer. Today is a full editorial board meeting to discuss our next issue going to print, and if I miss it, she'll have leverage to get me booted off the journal.

Before, the prospect didn't bother me, but now I've got something to prove. The only thing getting me through the meeting is knowing that I'm meeting Brandon at the bar for a beer later, and hopefully talking Justine into staying the night at my place. One day at a time.

When I walk into the office, I'm the last to arrive. Kristy is at the head of the table, with the rest of the editorial board filling up each side. I slide into the seat at the end.

"Thanks for joining us." Kristy's tone is snotty and annoyed, but I don't care.

I check my watch as the hands land on two o'clock. "Right on time."

She rolls her eyes, and no one in the room can miss the tension between us.

Kristy talks for forty minutes, giving a rundown on each of the pieces for submission, and debates the merits with herself without allowing anyone else to get a word in.

There's only one piece in the stack that I don't think should be included, and it's Kristy's. It's basically a regurgitation of the last note she published, with a slightly different spin so she can pad her résumé. I've got two choices—bring it up now, in front of the group, or take it up with her privately. As much as I want to call her out, I opt for the latter.

When the rest of the editorial staff leaves—after rubber-stamping everything Kristy chose for publication—I stay seated, leaning my elbows on the table.

"We need to talk."

Her blond eyebrow arches. "About what?"

"Your note. We're not publishing it."

"The hell we're not. I'm the editor-in-chief; I can do whatever I want."

"And ninety-five percent of it is a duplication of the shit you published last semester. Everyone in the room knew it, but no one has the balls to say anything."

Her laugh comes out as a huff. "You're going to challenge my work product? Really? After we published your half-assed piece last year?"

"I didn't make the call to publish mine, but you're making the call to publish yours. You're using the journal to pad your résumé, and I'm calling bullshit."

Her expression hardens. "My decision is final. Call it whatever you want."

"You need me to bring this up with Professor Tate? Because I will." Our faculty advisor is the only chance I have to knock Kristy down a peg. Last year, I would have kept out of it, but the way she's been taking swipes at Justine has pushed me past my limit.

Her mouth pinches into a scowl. "You wouldn't dare."

"Then I guess you don't know me as well as you thought."

She taps a fingernail on the table, as though considering what she's going to say next. "Maybe I don't, but you're still not going to do it. As a matter of fact, what you're going to do is leave this alone and get me a letter of recommendation from your dad for my clerkship application with the Sixth Circuit."

What the fuck? "Did you run out and find some crack before the meeting? There's no way in hell he's going to write you a letter of recommendation. I won't let him."

Her scowl twists into something nasty. "Yes, you are. And you know why? Because if you don't, I'm going to tell everyone all about how your dad is paying your new girlfriend's tuition, and that's why she finally spread her legs for you." She nods her head. "I guess it's lucky for you she lost that scholarship, or you would've never gotten a shot at her."

My expression stays neutral as her words tear through me, unleashing waves of rage. *What the fuck?*

Kristy's waiting for my reaction, but I refuse to give her the one she's expecting.

I stand, gripping the edge of the table so hard it creaks. "I don't know what the fuck you think you're talking about, but I don't want to hear Justine's name come out of your mouth ever again."

A harsh laugh tinged with something evil escapes. "You could've had me—someone your social equal—but no, you wanted that charity case. Apparently she's a hell of a lot smarter than you, because she found a way to get a free ride for fucking you. The student paper would *love* that story."

"Stop right the fuck now. You're full of shit." I want to reach across the table and shut her up myself, but I'll never put my hands on a woman like that.

"I bet you wish I was, but this isn't something I can make up. You know my mom works in the registrar's office, right? She's been drafted to help keep tabs on the payments coming in from the scholarship kids who lost their free rides. She told me that the last payment for Justine's tuition came from your dad—and it wasn't the first time. I thought that was pretty freaking interesting."

"And your mom is going to be out of a job tomorrow for sharing confidential information with you if you don't shut the fuck up."

My harsh tone isn't as effective as I expected, because Kristy laughs again and lowers herself back into her seat. "You're so blind, you don't even see it, do you?" She crosses her arms, rests them on the table, and leans toward me. "How many times did she shoot you down before she lost her scholarship? Don't you think it's odd that she didn't put up much of a fight after? Think about it, Ryker."

"Enough." The word comes out like a Doberman's bark.

Kristy shakes her head slowly. "She wouldn't give you the time of day for years, and then all of a sudden she's your new study *and* fuck buddy? You don't think those two things have anything in common? You're not usually this much of an idiot."

Anger vibrates through every cell of my body, and my fists clench against my sides. "You don't know what the fuck you're talking about, and if you say another word about this to me or anyone else, I will rain down hell on you and your mom."

Kristy's triumphant expression morphs into something ugly and cruel. *Why did I ever think she was attractive?*

"I guess we'll see what the dean has to say about it. Little Miss Perfect 4.0 might find herself out of school anyway. There's got to be some violation of the student code of conduct."

I meet her gaze with a glare. "You say anything to the dean, and I'll make sure my dad blackballs you from every job worth having after graduation."

Finally, a flash of uncertainty crosses her features. "He wouldn't dare."

"I swear to God, I won't stop until he does."

Kristy sputters, searching for something to say in response, but I'm not waiting around. I need some answers right the fuck now.

Chapter 52

Justine

I've spent two weeks working at the firm, with the majority of my time taken up by the first project Vito assigned me, which we finally wrapped up yesterday when he filed the brief.

The box containing all the information about Chad's DUI sits in the corner; knowing it remains almost untouched has been killing me. I need to know if there's any chance at an appeal. Yes, he was drinking and driving, but someone else caused the accident that led to his arrest. What's more, as far as I know, that accident is still considered an unsolved hit-and-run to this day.

I'm just about to dig into the court transcripts when Vito sticks his head into my office.

"There's a whole crew of us going out for drinks to celebrate an appeal we just won. You should join us, because filing that brief deserves to be celebrated as well. Drinks are on the firm."

I look around my little office at the stacks of files I've accumulated. "I appreciate the invite, but I'm sure the new girl should probably work instead of play."

Vito waves off my protest. "Not a chance. There's always tomorrow. You need a break, and you should see that firm life isn't all work. We have fun too. I don't want to give you the wrong impression."

I want to tell him that I honestly have no intention of ever working at a firm like this after graduation, so it doesn't matter what my impression is. When I open my mouth to decline, Ron peeks around the corner.

"You coming? We're just heading to AJ's across the street."

"She's coming."

Across the street, AJ's is filled with the happy-hour crowd, including one big table filled by people from the firm. It appears that this isn't really just a celebration for the appellate group, but a *drinks are on the firm, so come out and have one* situation. Merica told me what it was like as a summer associate—drinks every day after work, parties, ball games, concerts, you name it. Apparently the *work hard, play hard* mentality continues all year long.

Legal Aid was nothing like that. I mean, we had drinks together the Friday of my first week of work and the last Friday of the summer before I came back to school, but that's it—and we all paid for ourselves. There's not exactly an entertainment budget when you don't have money for coffee in the office.

I pick a seat next to Vito, as he's one of the only two people I've really worked with, but he doesn't stay long. He's up and talking to another partner, and a paralegal slides into the seat he vacated.

"Hi, I'm Janie. I meant to introduce myself the other day, but I've been slammed. I work for the appellate group too."

I shake her outstretched hand. "It's nice to meet you. I'm Justine."

"I heard! You're the one that Justice Grant sent us. That's so nice of him to always be helping out students. My daughter clerked for him when she was in law school. She graduated three years ago. Nice guy. It's just a shame about his wife."

"A shame?"

Janie looks like she's brimming with gossip as she looks around, making sure no one is going to overhear her. "She took a leave of absence. The firm never actually came out and said why, but we all know she's in rehab. They've kept it really quiet, and I'm sure the family has too. No one wants it to be public knowledge, especially with Justice Grant holding such an important position on the court. Some people just have a harder fight with their demons."

Rehab? "I had no idea."

Janie's eyes light with that special *oh, you didn't know* look. "Yes, it's really hard for them, I'm sure. She's been gone a few months. It all happened really quickly—one Friday she was in the office, and Monday the firm casually mentioned that she'd be out for an extended period of time due to a leave of absence. I have no idea what finally happened to push it over the edge, but something must have, you know?"

I'm absorbing the impact of what she said, and one thing stands out glaringly. "When did that happen?"

Janie tilts her head to the right as if searching her memory for the date. "I think it was the weekend of my youngest's college graduation. So the third weekend in May, maybe?"

The weekend Ryker was supposed to help me move. If they had to go check his mom into rehab, then that explains why he didn't show.

Janie's about to say more, but Vito comes back and she goes silent.

My mind turns this new information over and over while people drink and chatter around me.

I understand why he would have stayed quiet at first, but now? After everything?

Why didn't he just tell me?

Chapter 53

Ryker

Phone clenched in my hand, I hold it to my ear as frustration rides me. My father is still in court. My message is short and to the point.

"How long did you think you could keep the deal you made with Justine secret? Because if you were trying to keep it under wraps, you're doing a piss-poor job. We need to talk. I want answers."

I end the call, recognizing that it's a good thing he didn't answer. I don't trust myself to talk to him yet. Or Justine.

Fucking secrets. They always get out.

Kristy's threat to expose everything she told me plays on repeat in my brain as I turn my car in the direction of the bar where I'm supposed to meet Brandon. I need to figure out what the hell I'm going to do next, because I honestly have no fucking clue.

Chapter 54

Justine

I end up staying at AJ's longer than I expected, which means I miss the bus I intended to take. I'm stepping out of the bar when my phone vibrates in my hand, surprising me enough that I almost drop it on the sidewalk. I expect to see Ryker's name on the screen, but instead it's a number I don't recognize.

"Hello?"

"Justine, this is Jon Grant."

I recognize his voice immediately, even though Justice Grant has never called me before.

"Is something wrong? Is Ryker okay?"

Why is it when someone calls you unexpectedly, your first assumption is that something is terribly wrong? My pulse speeds up with every moment as I wonder what could have happened to Ryker. A million possibilities spin through my head, starting with some kind of horrific accident.

"He just left me a voice mail, and he knows."

My stomach drops to the cement beneath my feet.

"What?" The word comes out on a harsh breath. *He can't know.*

"Did you tell him?"

"No." Ice freezes where my spine is supposed to be. "I told him you got me a job at your wife's firm. I didn't tell him anything else." Guilt mixes with dread. *I should've told him.* "Which part of the deal does he know about? All of it?"

"He didn't say. I didn't want to call him back without talking to you first. This is going to be a delicate situation. How do you want to handle it?"

"I . . . I don't know."

"Do you want me to explain?"

I shake my head, but realize Justice Grant can't see it. "No. I . . . I'll figure it out. As long as you're okay with me explaining."

"You have my blessing to tell him everything. I'm concerned he's only got part of the story."

The icy fear grips more of my body with every word he speaks. "The worst part, right?"

"I don't know. I'm sorry, Justine. Let me know if there's anything I can do. I'm sure you can explain it to him and he'll understand." His tone is forced hope, and I think we both know it won't be as simple as that.

I want to ask Justice Grant more questions, but I know he doesn't have the answers.

I can only imagine how pissed Ryker is. I need to track him down. And . . . what? Tell him I had no other options? Use the awesomely cliché phrase *it's not what you think*?

"I'll let you know."

We hang up, and I stare down at my phone.

Why hasn't Ryker called *me* demanding an explanation?

I tap out a text.

JUSTINE: We need to talk. Please, just let me explain.

The little gray bubbles appear on the other side of the text screen for a moment and then disappear. *He read it.*

I wait for over a minute for the bubbles to reappear, but they don't.

Really? That's it? I'm not even worth a reply?

My phone shakes in my hand as I shove it in my bag. *Bus stop, here I come.*

Chapter 55

Ryker

Brandon is already at the bar with a beer when I walk in.
"Hey, man. What do you want? I'm buying."

"Shot of Johnny Walker."

Brandon's eyes widen. "Rough day?"

I drop onto the stool beside him and shove my hands through my hair. "Fucked-up day, that's for sure."

"What the hell happened?"

"I don't want to talk about it. I just need a fucking drink." And that's the truth. *What the hell am I going to do?*

He waves the bartender over and orders my shot—but makes it a double. "Best advice I have—get drunk enough not to have to think about it until tomorrow. I'll haul your ass home. My turn to be DD, right?" He pushes his bottle away.

The bartender pours the Johnny Walker, and I don't hesitate to knock it back.

Maybe Brandon's right. Getting drunk enough not to think about this until tomorrow sounds like a hell of a plan, even though I know it's not the smart choice.

I have to talk to Justine . . . but what the fuck am I going to say to her?

My phone vibrates with a text, and I pull it out of my pocket.

JUSTINE: We need to talk. Please, just let me explain.

So dear old Dad called her instead of me. I guess that's what accomplices do. I stare at my phone, but I have no idea what the fuck to say.

I toss it on the bar next to Brandon's instead.

"Glad to see you still have the same good taste as I do."

Our phones are identical, but his isn't staring back at him waiting for him to answer a text that changes everything.

"I need another shot."

He waves the bartender over, no questions asked, and starts talking about college football. I couldn't give a shit less about it right now, and my mind goes right back to the same place it has for months. Fuck, years. *Justine*.

Do I really need her to explain? She was desperate; I'll give her that. I saw that desperation with my own eyes when she walked into Déjà Vu looking for a job.

The shot glass is filled over and over, and I keep tipping them back. Brandon gives up on trying to talk to me and leaves his stool to talk to a redhead at the pool table.

Good. I'm not fit for company right now.

The front door *whooshes* open and a group of laughing people come in. *Students.* I recognize a couple of them. One in particular.

Fuck. Maybe she won't see me.

No such luck. Merica eyes me with curiosity as she

leaves her group behind and comes toward me. She nods to the empty shot glass on the bar.

"What the hell are you doing drinking alone?"

"Does it matter?"

I debate ordering another shot, but instead reach for a handful of popcorn in a basket Brandon left behind. I misjudge and it flips, popcorn spilling everywhere.

"You're shitfaced, aren't you?"

Before I can deny it, she has her phone out and her fingers move furiously over the screen.

It doesn't matter whether I'm shitfaced or not; I know exactly who she's texting. I snatch her phone out of her hands, hoping I'm quicker than her thumb on the Send button.

"Hey! What the hell!"

Merica reaches for the phone but I swivel around on the bar stool, keeping it out of her reach. The words are blurry on the screen, but I can read the message.

MERICA: *Ryker is drunk off his ass at Spartan's Brew House. You might want to get down here. I think something's REALLY wrong. Did you tell him?*

I'm staring at the last part of the message, letting the meaning sink in, when she yanks it out of my hands.

"What the fuck is your problem, dude?"

"How much did you know? How much did she tell you? About the deal she made with my dad?"

Merica's eyes widen but there's no confusion, only surprise.

She knew.

"She told you everything, didn't she?"

Merica scans the bar and looks back at me. "Look, you need to talk to her."

It's all the answer I need to confirm my suspicions.

How many times did Justine dodge my questions about how she was paying her tuition? How many times did she have the chance to tell me the truth? Too many.

"How did she tell you? Just casually mention she found a creative way to get her tuition paid after she lost her scholarship? I'm really fucking curious about how you tell someone that, because apparently she couldn't find the words to tell me."

"Who told you?" Merica asks, her eyes still wide.

"Doesn't fucking matter, because it wasn't Justine."

She lays a hand on top of the bar. "Your dad?"

"No." The word comes out harsh, because he should have told me. One of them *should've fucking told me.*

"Look, you need to talk to her. Or your dad. Because there's a lot more to the story than you realize. I mean, why do you think she took that job at the firm? She's paying your dad back. She's not taking shit for free."

Shock floods my system, and I try to fit this new information into what I already know. "What the hell are you talking about?"

She crosses her arms over her chest, shaking her head. "This is why you need to talk to them. Get your facts straight before you go off half-cocked. You don't think it would've been easier for her to just let him keep paying her tuition? She's going to take a job at Legal Aid where she makes next to nothing, and still she decided she couldn't be with you unless your dad agreed to make it a loan."

Her words sink in slowly. *A loan?*

"Are you sure?"

Merica arches an eyebrow. "Sure that you're being a jackass? Absolutely. Now, go fucking talk to her and try not to say something you're going to regret."

"I have to talk to her. Now."

Merica's right. This fucking changes everything, including any leverage Kristy has to threaten her.

"First smart thing you've said since I got here. Why don't you call a cab and go do that?" She pats me on the shoulder. "Next time, don't be a douche bag."

"Right."

She turns and heads back to her group. I grab my phone and look for Brandon by the pool table. He and the redhead are both gone.

That motherfucker.

It's not the first time he has bailed on me for pussy. Apparently some things never change. *Asshole.*

I return to the bar to pay both our tabs, and head out the back door.

I have to find Justine and talk to her in person. Now. I need to understand what the hell is really going on.

Chapter 56

Justine

I hear it before I see it. The horrible scraping of metal against metal as a car sheers along the guardrail on the opposite side of the road before coming to an abrupt stop.

A gray Camaro.

Oh my God.

Jumping to my feet from the bus station bench, I yank my bag over my shoulder and run toward the car. In my gut, I know it's Ryker.

The horn blares as I rip open the driver's side door. His face is pressed against the steering wheel, but thank God there's no blood.

"Ryker! Ryker! Are you okay?"

His head falls back against the seat and he blinks up at me. His face is red where it was pressed against the steering wheel, but there aren't any other visible injuries.

"Fuck. Shouldn't have driven."

"Are you okay? Are you hurt?" I scan him for any signs of blood or wounds, relieved to find there are none, but the smell of whiskey on his breath is strong. "What the hell did you do?"

"That was my question for you."

His words are slurred. *He's drunk.*

And if the cops come, he's *fucked*.

I don't know what possesses me, but I smack him across the chest with the back of my hand and then unbuckle his seat belt. "You're a fucking idiot. Now, get in the passenger seat. We have to get out of here."

He blinks at me but follows my instructions and climbs over the center console into the passenger seat.

I can't believe he did this. What the hell was he thinking?

I slide into the driver's seat and adjust it so I can reach the pedals. And then I get us the hell out of there.

We're closer to his condo than we are to campus, so I turn right at the next light, thanking everything that's holy that the car is still intact enough to drive and there are no cops on the road. The passenger side is going to be totally messed up, but he's got money to fix it. Money won't fix a DUI and a night in the drunk tank.

Mountains of guilt crush down on me as I drive.

This is my fault. He found out about the deal with his dad, got hammered, and climbed into the driver's seat wasted. But that doesn't mean I'm not pissed as all hell.

"You're an idiot, Ryker. What the hell were you thinking? Driving drunk? Do you not remember what happened to Chad? This could screw up your whole fucking future!"

"Didn't think I was that drunk." He groans, leaning his head against the window.

"You shouldn't have driven after drinking anything! You know better." I'm hurt, disappointed, and really freaking *pissed*. "And over this? Why didn't you just let me explain? Talk to me. Yell at me. Anything but this. I didn't think you were this guy. Was I wrong?"

Another groan.

I'm getting nothing in the way of satisfaction from him right now, so why even try?

I pull up to the gate of his condo parking garage. I have no idea how to get in, so I hit the call button and a voice answers. "How can I help you?"

"I have Ryker Grant here and he's forgotten his—"

"No worries, I'll let you in."

The gate rises in front of the car. Maybe they have a camera and recognize it? Either that or security's not so top-notch in this building. I couldn't care less at the moment.

Pulling into the spot where Ryker always parks, I turn off the car and get out to assess the damage. The whole passenger side of the car is scraped and paint is missing, but it's not as bad as I was expecting it would be. *He's stupid lucky.*

"Whoa, what the fuck happened?"

I whip around at the sound of the voice. Ryker doesn't need any witnesses, but I didn't have any other ideas about where to bring him. The voice materializes into the same blond guy who gave me a ride. *Ian.*

He jogs across the parking garage. His eyes widen at the sight of the car.

"Holy fuck! Where's Ry?" He jerks his gaze from the car to me. "What happened?"

I nod toward the passenger seat. "He's still inside. I don't know if I can get him out myself."

"Is he okay?" Ian jams both hands into his blond hair. "Shit, why didn't you take him to the ER?"

Crossing my arms over my chest, I stare this guy down. "He's wasted, not hurt, from what I can tell. And he's a dumbass because he *got hammered and drove*. Do you really think I should take him to the ER?"

"Shit." The curse comes out under Ian's breath. "What the fuck was he thinking? Let's get him out of here and upstairs."

He jerks his gaze between me and the car again before he reaches for the handle of the passenger door and yanks it open in a harsh creak of metal. Ryker tumbles out the side.

"Shit." Ian dives to grab his arms and drag him up. "Jesus, man. What a fucking shit show."

Ryker mumbles something that I can't make out, and Ian helps pull him to his feet. Should I stay? Leave?

Do I even want to stay? I'm pissed at him. How the hell could he do something so freaking stupid? Putting his entire future at risk like that?

I'm not worth it, a small voice says, and I know she's right. I'm not worth ruining his future over.

"Hey, can you hit the button for the elevator? We need to get him upstairs so I can call a med school friend. He might have a concussion." Ian has Ryker's arm wrapped around his shoulder and they're shuffling toward the elevator bay together.

I make my decision. I'll help get him up to his condo, and then I'm letting Ian take care of him. Realistically, I know Ryker's not going to want to see me. He couldn't even bother to answer my text and give me a chance to explain. Nope, according to Merica he went straight to the bar and got hammered.

When he's ready to hear my side of the story, he knows where to find me.

The three of us stumble our way to his apartment,

and I'm glad I remembered the keys. After I unlock it, Ian dumps Ryker on the couch. He groans and rolls over.

"He's going to have a hell of a hangover. Fucking idiot." Ian raises his gaze from his friend to me. "Are you sticking around? I'm calling my friend. He needs to get checked out, and I'm not taking him to the ER."

"I don't think he's going to want to see me when he wakes up." My chest squeezes tight with the words. It hurts more to say them out loud.

But what did I think was going to happen when he found out? I didn't expect him to put his entire future at risk. Guilt stabs into me.

Ian's eyebrows lift in interest. "So you do know what the hell happened."

"Not exactly."

I cross to the kitchen counter and dig a pad of Post-its out of the bowl of crap. *The one where he saved a Pez dispenser for me.* When I unearth a marker, I jot down a short, succinct note.

If you want to talk, you know where to find me.
P.S. You're a fucking idiot for getting behind the wheel.

I have to get out of this condo. I hate myself right now. Everything I did led us to this point. I'm not taking responsibility for Ryker's shit choice to get wasted and then climb in his car, but I'm also not without some culpability. Causation. We learned all about it in Torts. My actions were part of the chain of events here, and nothing I can do will change that fact.

I return to the couch and stick the note on the edge of the coffee table where Ryker can't miss it when he finally regains consciousness.

Ian glances over the words and looks up at me.

"I'm going to go out on a limb here and say he's going to be looking for you sooner rather than later."

"I guess we'll see."

And then I'm gone.

Chapter 57

Justine

You've got to be kidding me. This isn't happening again. It's not fair. All of these thoughts race through my head as I run through the parking lot, my feet aching from the hike from the bus stop because I forgot my flats.

The door to my apartment hangs open, and once again the door handle looks like it's been bludgeoned.

I creep closer to the open door. *What if they're still here?* Fumbling for my phone, I pull it out and pull up the number for Campus Safety. It rings twice before an operator picks up.

"Campus Safety, is this an emergency?"

"Yes. Someone broke into my apartment. I'm in the Gilroy Student Housing Complex. I think they might still be inside."

"Don't go into the apartment. Is there somewhere else you can go? A neighbor's?"

"No. I don't know any of the neighbors."

"Okay, that's fine. Just please get out of sight in case the intruders are still inside. We've had a lot of issues over there lately. You'd be safer if you left the premises."

I open my mouth to tell her once more that I have nowhere else to go and no way to get there, but a flash of movement distracts me.

"Ma'am?"

No way. It can't be.

"Ma'am?" the operator calls. "Are you okay? Campus Safety is on the way."

I hang up the phone and creep closer. The flash of long dark hair brings back memories of my childhood.

It can't be her.

I haven't seen my mom since the day the court awarded custody of me to Gramps. That was the last time she told me she wished I'd never been born.

The memory still cuts into me. *What kind of mother says that?*

She's thin almost to the point of being frail. A long-sleeved white T-shirt hangs off her shoulders, providing little protection from the chill of fall.

"Mom?" I try out the word that hasn't been on my lips in years.

Her head jerks around and her eyes find me in the darkness. I don't know what I expect to be the first words out of her mouth, but definitely not the ones she speaks.

"What'd you do with the money, Justine?"

"What money?"

We walk toward each other, and I'm numb. She looks exactly the same as she did when I was sixteen. *Shouldn't she look older?* More haggard?

But no, she still looks too beautiful for her age with long brown hair and dark eyes, and skin that's still dewy and tight. The same way she looked when she tried to force me to seduce some rich old guy so she could take pictures and blackmail him for touching a minor.

Cold. Calculating.

I still remember her words. *"It's time you start earning your keep if we're going to keep feeding you. Took you long enough to finally pass for eighteen."*

I told her to go to hell and ran to Gramps. That was the last straw for him.

She interrupts my trip down pothole-ridden memory lane. "Don't expect me to believe you don't have it. It took forever for the insurance company to finally pay out."

"What money?" Confusion and anger thread through my words in equal measure.

"The life insurance. They've been fighting it for over a year, and then they notified us the claim was approved. Except they didn't send us the check like they were supposed to. They said it went to you."

"Gramps had life insurance? And I was the beneficiary?" This is all news to me.

"Doesn't matter who the beneficiary is; that money is mine. He was my dad. I've been fighting for the payout. Submitting form after form until they finally gave in. Now, where's the fucking check?"

"Did you forge my name on those forms? My signature?" I don't know why I even bother to ask. Of course she did.

Another thought strikes me. "Did you break into my apartment before? Smash the door down? Terrify the crap out of me? All so you could look for some check I've never gotten?"

Her lip curls. "That was your dad. Now, quit lying to me. I want that damn check."

"Why would you break in? Why wouldn't you just ask me?"

Her brows pinch together in an angry slash. "Because I knew you'd lie to me just like you are right now."

Sirens wail in the distance. *Shit. Campus Safety.*

My mom's eyes dart toward the sound. "You called the cops? Why the hell would you do that?"

"Because that's what normal people do when they find someone breaking into their apartment!" My patience is gone. "You need to get out of here if you don't want to spend the night explaining to Campus Safety what the hell you were doing. And hope you didn't leave fingerprints, because I guarantee they're going to look harder than they did last time."

"I'm not going anywhere until I get that check. You can explain to them that you were wrong."

I cross my arms over my chest, pulling my metaphorical armor tight. "You broke into my apartment. I'm not telling them anything but the truth. There's no check."

"You always were an ungrateful brat. Haven't changed a bit. I should've aborted you."

The words hit me like a blow, stealing my breath.

With that parting shot, she spins around and jogs to the bushes on the far side of the parking lot before disappearing into the night.

I squeeze my eyes shut at the tears that spring to the corners. *Not here. Not now.* I suck in a shaky deep breath to calm myself. When I open my eyes, two Campus Safety units are turning into the parking lot. I scan the bushes and beyond as the officers park, but there's no sign of her.

What the hell am I going to tell them?

Chapter 58

Ryker

Fuck. My eyelids flick open but the light sends shafts of pain stabbing through my head. Jesus. Am I dead? Wouldn't that hurt less?

My face throbs like I caught a haymaker, my head feels like it might explode, my chest aches, and I basically feel like I ran into oncoming traffic. I roll over on my bed—

Wham.

Fuck. Me. My head threatens to split wide open when I slam into the floor face-first. Who is that sorry son of a bitch groaning like he's dying?

Oh yeah, that's me.

"You gonna live, asshole?"

The voice comes from behind me somewhere, and I recognize it as Ian's. I shift my eyes to the right, but even the movement of my eyeballs hurts.

Jesus, what the hell did I do?

A hand, which I assume belongs to my friend, shakes my shoulder.

"Dude, I gotta get to class and you need to get the fuck

off the floor and deal with your car. You don't have a concussion, but you've got a hell of a bruise on your forehead."

My car? A bruise?

My stomach sloshes as I roll to my side and look up at him. "Fuck, what the hell happened last night?" *And how much did I drink?*

"I don't know the details, man, but you fucked up. Bad. Whole right side of your car is trashed. You're lucky she found you and brought you home, otherwise you'd be in the drunk tank right now trying to explain to your dad why you just fucked your future."

I struggle to keep up with his words, and the disgust on his face takes me by surprise. "What did I do?" The question comes out quiet, and directed more at myself than Ian.

"You're going to have to piece that one together yourself, man. Upside, you didn't puke all over yourself, but you still reek like whiskey. It's coming from your pores now."

So that smell of sour booze is coming from me? "What the hell happened?"

"Told you—don't know. Might want to call your girl." His voice is further away this time, which explains why I hear the door slam.

Call your girl. Those words unleash a flood of shattered memories from last night.

I roll onto my back and see a sticky note hanging off the edge of the table. Snatching it, I read the words written in short strokes of black Sharpie.

If you want to talk, you know where to find me.
P.S. You're a fucking idiot for getting behind the wheel.

It's not signed, but it doesn't need to be. I'd recognize

Justine's handwriting anywhere.

Piecing together the memories in my head takes longer. *I really didn't think I drank that much.*

Someone else pounds on my door, and I haul myself up to stand. My head swims, and I think I might puke.

"Ryker, open this damn door right now." My dad's angry voice is unmistakable.

With shuffling steps, I make my way to the door, unlock it, and tug it open. His face can only be described as enraged.

"What the hell were you thinking?"

"Shouldn't you be at work?" I ask him.

"Shouldn't you be in jail?"

My dad's words catch me like a sucker punch to the gut, and dread creeps over me. "What the hell did I do?"

He shakes his head, and I can read disappointment and frustration on his face as well. "Do you even remember attempting to drive home from the bar last night? And smashing into a guardrail? Or how about the fact that Justine's quick thinking is the only reason you're not in jail? You leave me that message and don't even wait to hear the whole story."

That's when I remember everything . . . at least up until the bar.

"Did she call you?"

"No. I saw your friend Ian as I was coming up the elevator. He filled me in on the details."

"What happened?"

My father's scowl could peel paint from a wall. "You're going to have to ask Justine for that story, because she's the only one who was there. Whatever you did, you're going to make it right. She doesn't deserve your scorn for her choices. That girl changed everything once she fell for you."

My mind, already spinning, jerks to a halt. "Fell for me?"

My father shakes his head. "She's in love with you, and you're an idiot who doesn't realize what she gave up because of it."

My hands shake, and I'm not sure if it's an aftereffect of the booze or whether I'm losing my grip. Probably both.

"What did she give up?"

"I offered to pay her tuition if you kept your grades up. She called off the free ride in favor of making it a loan because she had to come clean with me and tell me she was in love with you."

She's in love with me?

"I have to fix this." I reach for my keys on the table and my father shakes his head.

"That car isn't going anywhere, and you need to clean up your mess. Call the body shop and have them send a wrecker. Take a frigging shower and attempt to look human again. You're smarter than this, Ryker. Act like it."

He's right. I need to clean up my mess like a man, and then I'm going to get the girl.

Chapter 59

Ryker

My trusty old Giant mountain bike carries me across town to campus. I dodge cars, pedestrians, other bikers, and nearly end up a hood ornament on a bus before I reach the Gilroy Housing Complex. As I approach Justine's unit, my gut twists and apprehension pumps through my veins. Her door is once again boarded up.

Her place got broken into again?

Anger, fear, and concern twine through my muscles, and I reach for my phone to call her, but it's not in my pocket.

Fuck. I pat down all of my pockets, but there's no point. It's gone. *How the fuck did I lose it?*

It's probably crushed in the road where I had to jump the curb to avoid the bus. I jam my hands into my hair, frustration pumping through my veins.

I stare at the door for another thirty seconds, but wasting time here isn't going to get me any answers. I check my watch. There's a chance she could still be at school, so I pedal my ass off in that direction next.

"You expect me to tell you a goddamn thing after last night?"

Merica rakes me over the coals with her words and the murderous expression in her eyes.

"She showed up at my house *in tears*. That girl hardly ever cries, and not only did you scare the ever-loving hell out of her last night by being a complete fucking *jackass* and doing something stupid, her mom broke into her apartment and then told her she should've aborted her!" Merica's tone is hushed so no one can overhear it, but it still comes off like a yell.

"Wait, what? Her *mom* broke into her apartment?" It sounds so wrong, I can hardly understand it.

"Yeah, apparently her dad did the honors last time."

"What the hell? Why?"

Merica shrugs. "Long story, but the gist of it is her parents are losers, and rolling from one con to the next is what they're best at."

Jesus. No wonder she never talks about them. "Where is she now?"

"Why should I tell you?" Merica eyes me before crossing her arms. "So you can let her down again? Because you don't realize that she hasn't leaned on anyone other than me since her grandpa died. She isn't the kind of girl who goes around expecting anyone's help. But there's something about the Grants that she must like because she let you and your dad in. She trusted you. Believed in you. And then you go and fuck it up without even giving her a chance to explain."

I jam my fingers through my hair. "What about her? If

she would've just told me, I—"

"You would've *what?* You took the news and had the worst possible reaction, and yet *she still saved your ass*. No one ever comes to her rescue. Not until your dad. And you're going to hold it against her that the one time in her entire freaking life that she really needed help, she finally bent enough to accept it?"

Dropping my hands to my sides, I meet Merica's angry stare and hope she can feel the intensity of the conviction running through me. "I'm going to make this right."

Merica must pick up on how fucking serious I am, because she finally relents. "Then you can find her at work. The job she took to pay back your dad rather than accept a handout."

I release a long breath. "Thank you."

"You better not fuck this up again. She deserves good things. Not this bullshit."

"I swear, I'm going to make this right."

I turn and head for the door. I've got a girl to track down and a big apology to make.

Chapter 60

Justine

My cell phone rings but I ignore it. I'm knee-deep in Chad's case, looking for anything that could potentially help him gain an appeal, and distracting myself from the epic shittiness of my life.

I'm doing a crap job at both.

Forcing myself to concentrate, I pick up the police report again.

A driver in a red sedan failed to stop at the signal . . .

My cell phone rings, breaking my concentration again. The screen shows an unknown number.

What? Did you really think Ryker would call? My note said to find me when he wanted to talk, but clearly he doesn't want anything to do with me. *What did I really expect?*

I grab the phone and answer it on the fourth ring as a way to shut down the pity party I'm about to throw.

"Hello?"

"Is this Justine Porter?"

"Yes, this is she."

"This is Officer Fitzwilliam from Campus Safety. We've got a development in your case, and we'd like you to come down to the station to talk about it."

I hold my breath, wondering if they've figured out it was my mother who broke in. I don't know what kind of misplaced loyalty kept me from turning her in, but when I opened my mouth to tell them, the words wouldn't come.

Gathering myself, I wrap an arm around my middle. "What kind of development?"

"I'd prefer to discuss it in person."

I glance at the clock at the bottom of my computer monitor, the possibilities racing through my mind. "I'm at work for another hour, but I can come after." I could use the time to compose myself for whatever they're going to say.

"Now would be better."

Dread sweeps through the room, leaving chill bumps on my skin. *That doesn't sound good at all.*

"Um . . . okay. Let me talk to my boss."

"Good. We'll see you soon, Ms. Porter."

Staring out the window of the bus as it carries me back toward campus, I flip through all the scenarios I might be walking into at the Campus Safety office.

What if they arrested her? What if they arrested my dad too? Why can't they both just stay out of my life? And how did I not know about this life insurance policy if I was the beneficiary? I guarantee I'll never see a penny of it, if it actually exists. My mom will make sure of that.

By the time I climb off the bus at the nearest stop, I've managed to gather myself and adopt a blank expression.

A student at the desk out front takes my name and tells me to have a seat. My butt hardly lands on the green vinyl seat before Officer Fitzwilliam rounds the corner.

"Come on back, Ms. Porter."

As I follow him down the fluorescent-lit hallway, my gaze jumps from his navy polyester uniform shirt to the black rubber soles of his shoes, to the industrial gray of the flooring tiles and back again. He gestures with a thick arm to a room on the right and I enter. For a moment, I hold my breath, wondering if I'm going to find my mother inside in handcuffs.

It's empty.

"Please have a seat. You want some water? Coffee?"

His demeanor is unreadable, and I decline his offers politely. "No, thank you. Can you tell me what's going on?"

Fitzwilliam's jaw moves with every chew of his gum, and he nods, lowering himself into the chair across the table from mine. He drops a file folder on the faux wood surface and crosses his arms. Anxiety creeps through me as I wait for whatever he's going to say.

I don't have to wait long.

"We believe we've identified the person who broke into your apartment."

I brace myself for whatever he's going to say next, but not well enough.

"We recovered several pieces of your mail from the scene of an accident this afternoon."

"My mail?"

"Yes, we assume they targeted you for identity theft. It's a common practice to steal the victim's mail for credit card applications and the like."

Everything clicks into place. He's got it all wrong. They

stole it hoping they'd find the check from the insurance company. *And they found it at the scene of an accident?*

"Excuse me, what kind of accident?" Did they get into a wreck?

"Around noon today there was a car-train collision on campus a quarter mile from Gilroy. The driver tried to beat the train and failed. Both the driver and passenger were taken to Red Cedar Medical Center. We were just notified that neither survived . . ."

His words fade as static fills my ears. I lift a hand to my mouth, covering my sharp breath.

Two fatalities. My mail.

I rock back and forth in my seat as cold slithers through my muscles and veins.

"Who were they?"

"We're working on figuring that out because they had no ID on them, only the mail. When they put your name in the system, it pinged my investigation."

Shooting out of my chair, I take two steps toward the door before my mouth catches up to speak. "I need to go to the medical center. Right now."

"Ms. Porter, there's no reason to—"

"I need to go there. Right. Now." I repeat. "Please. Can you take me? I don't have a car."

The desperation in my tone must be coming through loud and clear because Officer Fitzwilliam stands. And because he's a cop, he's also not stupid.

"Do you know who they are, Ms. Porter? It would certainly aid our investigation."

I'm beyond hiding anything from him. My words come out as a whisper. "My parents."

His expression tightens. "Come with me."

Chapter 61

Ryker

I've struck out over and over today. It shouldn't be that much a surprise given how many times I've struck out with Justine in general. That should be the one thing I can count on when it comes to her. She left work early, telling her boss it had something to do with the break-in at her apartment.

As much as I want to rush after her again, I head to the cell phone place, get a new phone, and wait for her to call me. And if she doesn't call, then I'm going to start over tomorrow morning and track her down in class, the one place I know she'll be.

My car is gone, and nothing in the empty parking space tells the tale of how close I came to fucking up everything last night. I was an idiot. Straight up, no excuses. Idiot.

If Justine hadn't been there, I would have headed down the same path as Chad—drunk tank, court, and the whole nine yards. But because the justice system doesn't work the same for everyone, instead of dropping out of school, I would have likely ended up with community service and a long letter in my file to the character and fitness committee of the State Bar Association about understanding that I made a huge mistake and that I had accepted my punishment and learned my lesson.

But instead, I got a second chance, and you better believe I'm not going to fuck it up.

Chapter 62

Justine

Nothing. I meant nothing to them. I've known it for years, but this just drives it home one final time.

Sobs rack my body, but it's not for the reason most daughters cry when they find out their parents are dead.

No. I'm crying for my lost childhood. All the good memories I never got to have. Every shit card that life dealt me.

Every day, I try to say positive. Try to focus on the good. Don't look back on the fact that I never got to be a kid. Not really.

You want dinner? Steal a box of cereal from the corner store.

You want a Christmas present? Better pick someone's pocket to pay for it.

You broke your wrist when your dad pushed you out of the way? Too bad. We're not taking you to the hospital because we don't need Child Protective Services in our business.

Who treats their child like that?

"I should've aborted you." The last words my mother

ever spoke to me.

If it weren't for my fucking mail, I wouldn't even know my parents are dead. They stole it to make sure whatever Gramps intended for me would go to them.

I am the product of neglect and selfishness. That's all I've ever known. How to take. How to watch out for myself. Is it any wonder that I don't know how to have a real, functional relationship with anyone?

And then my actions end up putting my boyfriend at risk of killing himself and destroying his future?

I shouldn't even be allowed to be around people. I'm toxic, just like my parents.

I hate them. Hate what they made me. Hate what I've let myself become.

The sobs subside to hiccups, and I'm thankful for the private room I'm in. No one in this hospital needs to see me break down. Then again, no one would care.

Pathetic. I've never been more pathetic in my life, and I hate the helplessness I feel.

At least I did one good thing today—every piece of my parents that can be used to save someone else will be donated. But even that act can't stem the tide of self-loathing within me.

Why can't I be numb? Why can't I be anything but what and who I am? I've got my knees drawn up in front of me, my arms wrapped around them as I attempt to shrink into myself and escape the pain and the bitter realities of my life.

Alone. That's what I am, and that's all I'm ever going to be.

I've been so focused on my goal—Gramps's goal—giving myself the future I thought I deserved.

But what do I really deserve? Everything I've done has

been aimed at achieving something wholly selfish—my degree, my success, my future. It's all been about me.

I've been so proud of my own accomplishments, but what are they worth if I have no one to celebrate them with?

My lungs feel as though they've been smashed in my chest, and the weight of everything I've done is crushing down on me. I need to escape before I suffocate. I need to forget. Even if it's only for a day. A few hours.

I think I understand how Ryker felt when he decided to drink rather than come to me for the truth.

Well, at least I don't have a car. I laugh to myself humorlessly. Unbending from my curled-up position, I suck in a deep breath and rise.

Escape. That's what I need. And that's exactly what I'm going to do. For one night, I want to escape this shitty existence that I'm living. Is it really that much to ask?

Chapter 63

Ryker

My new phone rings at two in the morning and I grab it immediately, hoping like hell it's Justine. I've been in a state of half sleep, waiting for her call and finding it less and less likely as the minutes ticked by.

"Hello?"

"Hey, Ryker. This is Corey Crow. You might not remember me . . ."

I flip through my memory. "Yeah, frat brother. You were a freshman when I graduated?" I think I've got it right.

"Yeah, exactly. I'm president of the house now. We've got a situation, and your name came up."

A sense of foreboding blankets the room. "What situation?"

"A couple of guys were out at the bar and they brought a chick back to the house. She's wasted, and I told them to put her in a cab, but she won't tell them where she needs to go. They said your name came up. Maybe she's a law student?"

Who the hell would give my name to a bunch of frat

brothers? Kristy?

"What does she look like?"

"Hold on. I'll text you a pic."

I wait until it comes through, my mind racing with possibilities.

The dark-haired girl with dark eyes is the last person I expected to see show up on the screen.

"Fuck. It's my girlfriend. Her name is Justine. I'm coming for her. Don't let her leave."

"She's your girlfriend? Dude, are you sure?"

Acid pools in my stomach. "What the hell happened?" My instincts rage. "If anyone touched her—"

"No, man, it's just . . . when your name came up, she didn't say anything about you dating."

Not surprising. "Just keep her there. I'll be there in fifteen. Don't let her leave."

"I'll do what I can, man."

I'm out of bed and grabbing up jeans and a hoodie as soon as he hangs up.

"What the fuck did you get yourself into, Justine?"

I'm done letting this shit between us fester. We're setting the record straight before the sun rises.

I pound on the door to Ian's condo for five minutes before he pulls it open, rubbing the sleep from his eyes. "What the fuck, man?"

"I need your keys."

His gaze sharpens on mine. "Are you drunk?"

"Sober as the day I was born. I gotta get Justine. She's at my old frat house, hammered, and I have no fucking clue why."

Ian's eyes go wide. "No shit. You need a hand?"

I shake my head. "No. Just your keys. Promise I'll bring

it back in one piece."

He nods and turns away from the door to disappear into the darkness behind him. When he returns, he tosses me a set of keys. "Fuck it up and you're buying me a new car."

"Deal."

I break every speed limit between my condo and campus, not caring about anything but getting to Justine.

What the fuck happened to her? These last few days have been a clusterfuck of epic proportions, but this isn't something I ever would have been able to predict. *Drunk at a frat party?* That's not like her.

When I pull up in front of the house I lived in for three years in college, I slam the car into park along the street. Music still blares, and every light shines bright.

I rip open the door, haul ass up the sidewalk to the front porch, and let myself in. I freeze as soon as I step foot inside.

Justine is dancing on top of the pool table, wearing the black skirt I assume she wore to work at the firm, with the top four buttons of her blue blouse undone. Her dark hair flies in every direction as she moves to the beat pumping from the sound system.

No. Fucking. Way.

I stalk across the floor and shove through the crowd of guys throwing dollar bills on the table. *Jesus. What the fuck?* My thoughts are as dark as the night I saw her walk into Déjà Vu. She reaches for another button on her blouse.

No fucking way.

Corey reaches out and slaps a hand on my shoulder, a frown on his face. "Sorry, man. You just said keep her here, but I couldn't stop her from doing this."

I shrug him off and push through the crowd to the edge of the pool table. I wrap my arm around her knees as she spins to face me. Her hair falls across her eyes, obscuring her vision, but I don't fucking care. I pull her off the table and settle her over my shoulder, careful to keep my hand on her ass so none of these frat-boy douche bags get a look at my girl.

She struggles against me, and I grip her tighter. "Justine, calm the fuck down. I'm taking you home."

The sound of my voice quiets her movements, but the rest of the room erupts into protests.

I look around at the drunk college kids, my rage approaching murderous levels. They must read it in my face because the shouts die off, and I turn and head for the door. Corey jogs to keep up with me, but I'm not slowing my stride for anyone.

"Sorry, man. At least she didn't leave."

"Thanks." I grit the word out between clenched teeth and push open the door.

Justine is the one with a hell of a lot of explaining to do, and if I'm anywhere close to right about how much she would have had to drink to get this hammered, she's going to have a monster-sized hangover tomorrow.

I lower her and pull open the passenger door before settling her into the seat. She bats at my hands as I fasten the seat belt, but I don't stop.

Don't speak. There's nothing I want to say to her here. I want her home, in my bed, where I can figure out how everything went so fucking sideways.

I close the door and round the hood to slide into the driver's seat. Justine's head hangs to one side and then flops toward me.

"They're dead," she mumbles.

"What the hell are you talking about?"

Her dark eyelashes flutter as her eyes open, and she pierces me with a pain-filled gaze. "My parents. They're dead and I hate them." Her eyelids squeeze shut as tears spill over and down her cheeks.

I'm shocked by her words. What I know about her parents—beyond the fact that her mom broke into her apartment—wouldn't fill a single page, but the fact that they're dead shocks the shit out of me.

"Jesus Christ, Justine. When? Why didn't you call me?"

"No one cares. I hate them. They hate me. You hate me. I hate me." Her babbling words make no sense, but the tears that continue to fall say everything I need to know.

I reach over and grab her hand. "It's going to be okay, baby. I promise."

"Just wanted to forget everything. I can't even do that right." Her voice is raw, and her words break my heart.

She passes out before we get back to my apartment, and I carry her from the car to my bed. I smooth her hair away from her face after I tuck her under the covers in one of my T-shirts.

"I don't hate you, Justine. I love you. So fucking much."

Chapter 64

Justine

Everything hurts and my stomach is staging a mutiny. Someone, kill me.

I'm hanging over the toilet, gripping the porcelain rim as capable hands pull my hair into a ponytail at the base of my skull. Once it's secure and I'm done heaving, a bottle presses against my lips.

"Drink, baby."

Ryker.

Cool water hits my tongue as he tips the bottle, and I swish and spit before taking a little more. The bottle disappears, and a cold washcloth presses against my forehead before gently moving down to my mouth to sweep the nasty residue from my lips.

I release my death grip on the toilet to keep the cloth there. Silently groaning against the fabric, I bow my head.

"What did I do?" I assume my mumble is inaudible until Ryker replies.

"That's a story for when you're feeling better. You think you're good for now? Want to go back to bed?"

The thought of moving an inch from where I'm slumped is more than I can handle. I shake my head.

"You want to sleep in the bathroom?"

I nod, carefully, so as not to wake my calming stomach.

"Okay, then come here." He slides his hands under my arms and pulls me back into the cradle of his legs.

"Towel—"

"I gotcha."

Ryker guides my face to his shoulder, and a soft towel cushions my cheek. Now at least I know I won't drool on him. He must grab another towel, a bigger one, because something thick and fluffy covers us both.

"Try to sleep, baby. I got you."

"No one has me."

"That's where you're wrong."

When I wake again, I'm no longer in the bathroom but tucked into bed. My head pounds, my tongue sticks to the roof of my mouth, and once it unsticks, the nastiness is enough to gag the strongest stomach.

I've had hangovers. Not a ton, but enough to know better.

What the hell did I do?

As I roll over, one arm flops like a dead fish . . . and lands on something solid and warm.

"How are you feeling?"

I blink twice because my memory is still a little faulty. *How did I get here?* I flip backward, attempting to grasp my last solid thought . . . and I come up with blackness. And pain. And regret. And sorrow.

My parents. Dead. Organ donation. The bar. Walking to the bus stop. Accepting a ride from some kids headed to campus. More booze. And then it all gets a little disjointed. *Loud music, laughing, yelling.* Running through every memory is a solid dose of self-loathing.

I managed to block out reality for a few hours . . . but it didn't last. And somehow I ended up with a concerned-looking Ryker studying my face and wrapping his body protectively around mine.

I don't deserve it.

"You hate me. You drove drunk into a guardrail because of me."

His concerned expression hardens into something more serious. "I don't hate you. Fuck, Justine, I'm in love with you. I could never hate you. And I drove drunk into a guardrail because I was a fucking idiot. That's on me. Not you. Everything that's fucked up is because of me—not you."

His words wash over me like some kind of healing wave, but they can't repair everything. I'm too broken for that easy of a fix.

"You can't love me."

"Fuck if I can't." His tone is unyielding. "And you're not pushing me away. You can try, but I'll push back every time. I'm finally starting to understand you, and the more I learn, the more sure I am that I'm not letting you go."

"But what about the money, your dad, our deal—"

He lays a finger over my lips for a beat. "I don't fucking care about any of that. I care about you." His blue eyes darken as he lowers his hand to grasp mine. "Tell me what happened to your parents."

Sharp knives of pain slice through me and I squeeze his

fingers, seeking some kind of connection. "They're dead. There was an accident with one of those fucking trains. They didn't make it."

Ryker sucks in a sharp breath. "Jesus, I'm so fucking sorry, Justine. I saw it on the news. I had no idea. How did you find out it was them? Emergency contact?" The sympathy he feels is almost tangible, and his thumb sweeps back and forth over the back of my hand.

I let the whole story spill out. What my mother said when I caught her breaking in. About fighting the insurance company, and the check I've never seen or heard about.

"We'll figure it out, babe." Ryker's grip tightens on my hand.

We. He says it so easily, but there's nothing easy about where we stand right now.

"Don't we need to figure us out first?"

He hauls me closer, pulling me across his body before cupping the side of my face and wiping away my lingering tears with the pad of his thumb. "Look, we both fucked up, and unless you're going to tell me that you don't love me, then there's nothing to figure out. We move on from here together."

This is the moment. The moment I could follow all of my past habits and push him away for good, or I can grab the best thing in my life and hope to hell it lasts.

My decision is an easy one.

"I'd be lying if I told you that."

"Then fucking tell me you love me. I want to hear it."

I meet his stare. "I love you, Ryker. So freaking much."

As soon as the words are out, I'm locked in the circle of his arms, my face pressing against his chest, his lips close to my ear.

"I fucking love you too. I'm not letting you go. Whatever happens, we're going to get through it. We're a hell of a team, Justine. There's nothing we can't do."

"I love you." I whisper the words again, getting more comfortable with the feel of them on my tongue. Getting more comfortable with the warmth that fills my chest when I say them. The self-loathing isn't gone, but its sharp edges are blunted.

Maybe he's right. Maybe we can do anything.

Chapter 65

Ryker

The rest of the week passes by in a blur. A minister said a blessing over the ashes of Justine's parents, even though she said she didn't need to hear it. Someday, I hope she'll be thankful she had the closure. We went to all our classes, and I took notes when Justine would space out, her fingers stilling on her keyboard.

She needed to get away, and because figuring out what Justine needs and giving it to her has become one of the most important purposes I've had in my life, I decide to take her away from everything.

She looks out the window of my dad's truck as we drive up into the hills, lost in her head. This weekend is about getting her out of her head and back to the land of the living. She's had it rough, and I want to give her easy. I want to give her peace.

I turn down an unmarked drive and Justine still says nothing. I wonder what she's going to say when she sees my family's summer cottage. To me, it's fancier than some, less fancy than others, but Justine has made it clear that my childhood and hers were light years apart.

When she drops her hand from the window and sits up straighter as the house comes into view, I try to see it through her eyes. The white clapboard house with a giant front porch sits at an angle on the lot, facing the river that flows by below. A large covered wooden deck sits at the edge of the bluff, marking the top of the stairs that lead down to the water.

I pull to a stop in front of the house.

"This is your cottage?" A tinge of awe colors her words.

"My great-grandfather built it, and it's been handed down to each generation. Someday, it'll get passed down to me."

So many of my best memories were made here, and I want to give those kinds of memories to Justine.

"Come on, let's get inside and get the place warmed up. I can impress you with my manly fire-building skills."

We both climb out of the truck, grab a few bags—our clothes and the groceries we picked up before we left—and I lead the way up to the front door and unlock it.

The tour of the inside doesn't take too long, but Justine stays quiet through most of it. It's that quiet I brought her here to fix. I want the real Justine back. The one full of life and fire. The one who didn't hesitate to tell me to go to hell. We've got two nights and two full days before we have to go back to the real world, and I'm hoping it's enough time for her to find that girl again.

We end our tour in the kitchen, and I pull two bottles out of the six-packs we brought in. Popping the tops on both, I hand the cider to her. "Do you want to put away the groceries, and I'll get the hot water and furnace going?"

She sips her cider and nods. "Yeah, divide and conquer.

Sounds good."

I lean in to press a quick kiss to her lips when she lowers the cider. "I'm glad we're here. We needed this. Just you and me."

Her smile isn't bright and brilliant yet, but it's still a smile nonetheless. "I'm glad we're here too. Now, go do manly things."

When I return to the kitchen twenty minutes later, I find it empty. The grocery bags are gone, and so is Justine.

With the winter shutters down over the windows, I can't see a damn thing out the front side of the house. From the side windows in the kitchen, the car is visible, but she's not out there either.

I head out of the kitchen, through the porch to the screen door, and down the front steps. A large gazebo-like roof covers the deck that sits at the top of the bluff before the stairs heading down to the river. The furniture has all been stored in the garage for the season, but the built-in benches are still there.

That's where I find Justine. Curled up, a blanket from the sofa inside wrapped around her shoulders, tears streaming down her face.

"Baby, what's wrong?"

She doesn't even notice my presence until I speak. Her head turns toward the river, and one hand comes up to swipe away the tears.

A crumple of plastic draws my attention. The blanket falls from her shoulder at her movement, and I catch a glimpse of a bag of marshmallows clutched to her chest.

"Sorry. I'm—"

"Shh." I don't let her finish. Instead, I sit behind her on the bench and lift her onto my lap before closing my arms around her, the blanket, and the marshmallows. "It's okay."

She turns sideways, curling into my body, and I squeeze her tighter. I don't ask for an explanation, but I know I'll get one if she wants to share.

"I didn't know you grabbed these at the store."

"You were getting orange juice, so I thought we could make s'mores. It's a little too cold out here for a campfire, but you can make just as good ones inside over the fire."

"Do you know that I've made s'mores once in my life? The only time I've ever been 'camping.'" She uses her fingers like quotation marks around the word *camping*.

"How old were you?"

She curls closer to my chest and I tighten my grip around her shoulders, as though my strength can be transferred to her.

"Seven."

"What happened?" I don't want to push, but I have a feeling she needs to get this out.

"I thought it was an adventure. We packed up the car with a tent and sleeping bags and everything, and headed out to the campground. My mom made my dad stop at a store to get hot dogs and marshmallows and all the stuff. Everything about that night seemed magical. My dad didn't have a swearing fit when he put up the tent. My mom didn't yell at me for sneaking chips out of the bag before we ate. My dad rounded up firewood and long sticks so we could cook over the fire, and I thought it was the coolest thing ever."

A tear slips down her face, and I wipe it away. I suspect

the part of the story I probably don't want to hear is coming next.

"And?"

"And then we were about to make s'mores. I've got my stick and my marshmallows ready, and the chocolate and graham crackers are out. I had my marshmallow up over the perfect spot because I wanted it to be golden brown and delicious . . . that's when they started arguing. My parents must have cracked open some booze or something. I remember my dad yelling that it was her fault this time. Couldn't she have been *nicer* to the landlord to buy more time? I don't know how I knew it, but I did. We were homeless. It wasn't a camping trip. S'mores weren't a treat. They were something to keep me occupied because we had nowhere else to go."

I can't imagine being seven years old and knowing you were homeless. Growing up with that kind of knowledge would change everything.

"How many times did you have to move as a kid?" I can't help but ask the question. I want to understand.

"Before I finally moved in with Gramps? Dozens. I lost track. We'd be one place for a few months before getting evicted or my parents packing up fast and moving us somewhere."

This is the part I still don't have a grip on. "What did your parents do?"

Justine is quiet for several moments. "They were scam artists. They ran cons. Petty theft. Worked odd jobs when there was nothing else available." She finally turns to meet my eyes. "They weren't good people. And I feel like I'm just like them."

I release my hold on her in favor of cupping her jaw

with both hands so I can keep her gaze on mine. "You are not fucking like them. *Nothing like them*."

"But—"

"No. Don't even think it. You're not like them."

She swallows. "All I wanted when I was growing up was to be normal. I wanted a normal family. A normal house. A normal existence. I wanted parents who tucked me into bed, read me stories, and told me they loved me. Why couldn't I have that? Like you did."

I press a kiss to her forehead before lowering my hands to wrap my arms around her once more and crush her to my chest. "Baby, no one's family is perfect. Even the ones who seem normal and tuck their kids into bed and read them stories. There's no such thing as normal. And for the record, you became an amazing woman in spite of everything. You're smart, strong, resilient, resourceful, and fucking mind-blowing. The fact that you're all those things should prove to you that you didn't need normal. They didn't do you any favors, but they gave you a gift—just look at how much you've accomplished. You're the most capable, intelligent, and incredible woman I've ever met. That's why I wouldn't give up asking you out. I knew you were everything I could ever want."

The tears that fall from her eyes now are happy ones. "I thought you just wanted a piece of ass." The words come out on a laugh.

I shake my head. "I told you, since that day you opened your mouth in Torts class, I knew you were a hell of a lot more than a great rack and perfect ass. I wasn't going to stop until you were mine. Now I'm the luckiest fucking guy in the world because you are."

She leans forward, her tears wetting my cheeks as she

presses her lips to mine before drawing back an inch. "Can we agree that we're both lucky?"

"Definitely." I smooth the hair back from her face as her stomach growls. "Now, it's time to feed my woman."

She nods. "That too."

I lift her up and carry her to the house, determined that this weekend will be the beginning of all good memories. She deserves it, and I'm going to work like hell to give it to her.

Chapter 66

Justine

My lips are sticky with melted marshmallow as I finish chewing the fabulous concoction that also includes melted chocolate and crunchy graham crackers. I never thought I would be able to laugh and make s'mores, but Ryker is helping me systematically replace all my sour memories with sweet ones.

And who knew the guy I thought could be crowned King of the Douche Bags once upon a time would turn out to be the best man I know. Gramps would approve.

Ryker has been giving and giving, and now it's my turn. I need to right the balance and give him back some portion of what he gives me.

"I love you." The words come easier to my lips every time, and his face lights up in the glow of the firelight when I say them.

"You don't know how fucking happy it makes me every time you say that. I love you. I want to show you just how good it can be."

"I already know how good it can be. You've been showing me."

I reach for the chocolate squares and graham crackers, and sweep the golden toasted marshmallow off the stick to make another delicious dessert. I hand it to Ryker and he wastes no time crunching into it.

"You want another?" I ask, reaching for the bag of marshmallows.

He shakes his head and I'm glad, because I know what I want next. While he finishes his s'more, I gather up the sticks and bags and boxes, and stow them in the kitchen. Ryker joins me in washing our sticky hands, and we both head back to the living room and settle on the floor in front of the fire.

His expression turns serious. "There's something else we need to talk—"

I shake my head. "No more talking tonight. I don't need more words. I just need you." I reach for the hem of my shirt and tug it over my head.

"Baby—"

"No. Really. I need you. Take your shirt off."

He hesitates for a moment before grabbing the back of his shirt and tugging the entire thing over his head in that solidly male move. I never tire of looking at him. His muscles are defined and sexy as hell. I get a very strong *I licked it, so it's mine* feeling whenever I see them.

I push him back on the rug, my fingers going to the button of his jeans before pulling down the tab of the zipper. Ryker lifts his ass as I tug them down off his hips. His cock springs free because once again, he's opted to go commando.

When I wrap my hand around his shaft, he stills, even though I know his heart rate is picking up. Normally he's the one who makes me yell his name and writhe against him, but tonight, it's my turn.

"Baby, what are you—"

"I think that's pretty obvious," I whisper as I lower my mouth and suck the head of his cock inside.

His groans, quiet words of encouragement, and the crackling of the fire are the only sounds I hear for long minutes. When I've teased him to the brink, and the salty taste of his pre-cum hits my tongue, he grips my hair and pulls my head back with a soft tug.

"I want to come inside you."

I can already feel the heat building between my thighs, and I want the same thing. When I nod, he pulls me forward, his fingers tugging down the waistband of my leggings until the heat of the fire hits my skin. I shimmy them the rest of the way off, and because I took a page out of his book, I'm bare beneath them.

"Fuck, baby." His hand cups me between my legs, and he groans at how slick and ready I am. "Always so wet for me. I love it. You couldn't be more perfect. I want you on my face. I want to eat you before I fuck you."

I look down at him, a smile tugging at the corner of my lips. "You mean before I ride you? Because this is my show."

His blue eyes blaze with heat. "Then you're going to ride my face first—until you scream."

When I move up toward his face, Ryker's hands grip my ass and guide me the rest of the way. "Fucking love your ass. Your pussy. Your brain. Your heart. Love you, baby. So much."

I open my mouth to reply, but my words fall away as Ryker steals my power of speech and catapults me into pleasure. His tongue, his lips, his teeth—he uses them all in an effort to make me scream. And he succeeds.

"*Ryker!*" His name bounces off the walls of the room before I collapse onto my elbows, hovering over him.

I'm only still for a second before he grips my hips and flips me over onto my back.

"I know you said you were going to ride me, but baby, I'm taking charge of this show." He reaches for his pants, retrieves a condom from the pocket, and has it on before I can come up with a single argument as to why I shouldn't let him take charge. Probably because my body is totally in favor of this plan.

Ryker slides a hand under my ass and tilts my hips upward until the head of his cock nudges against my entrance.

"Hard and fast. I'll give you slow and sweet later."

I nod. "As long as I'm getting you, I don't care."

His gaze never leaves mine as he presses forward, burying himself to the hilt in a single stroke.

Full. I'll never get over the feeling of fullness. I love every single second of the stretch as my body takes everything he has to give.

Ryker leans down to take my lips in a hard kiss before pulling back. "Hard and fast," he murmurs before delivering on his promise.

With every stroke, he owns me. My climax barrels down on me, and his name rings out from my lips again. He fucks into me harder and faster until he finally stills with his release.

I belong to him. I've found my place, and it's not a *where*. It's a *who*.

Whatever happens now, I'm stronger for having him in my life and experiencing this.

Chapter 67

Justine

My phone chimes over and over on the nightstand.
Shit. Alarm.

I'm not ready to get up. I'm not ready for this to be over. If I could have conjured the perfect weekend out of thin air, it wouldn't have been better than this one.

We cooked, we ate, we joked, we teased, we fucked, we made love, and more than anything—we laughed. Laughter hasn't been a constant in my life, but with Ryker around, it's now coming quicker and easier.

Neither of us wanted to let this weekend go, so when Ryker suggested we stay Sunday night and head back to school early the next morning for class, I didn't hesitate to agree.

But my alarm is signaling our return to reality.

I grab my phone, intending to hit the screen and the snooze button to make it shut up. But when I hear a voice instead of silence, I sit up straight, waking Ryker.

"Shit. What's—"

"Where the hell are you?"

The voice finally penetrates my sleep-muddled head. It wasn't my alarm. It was my ringtone for Merica.

"Where the hell are you?" she repeats.

I look down at the screen, my stomach dropping at the time. *Fuck,* it's already after eight.

"Shit! My alarm didn't go off!"

Ryker bolts up in bed next to me. "Fuck, we gotta go. We're missing class."

"Justine—" Merica's voice sounds like a muted yell as I hold the phone away from my head.

"We'll be there. I gotta go."

"Wait—"

But I hang up. I'm already in panic mode as I vault out of bed.

"We gotta go. I don't know what happened to my alarm."

Ryker grabs his phone off the nightstand. "Fuck, my phone's dead, so my alarm didn't go off. I'm so sorry, babe. I know how you feel about missing class."

"It's okay. I probably set my alarm for PM or some stupid crap like that. Let's just go. Maybe we can make the next class."

Ryker nods. "Pack our stuff. I'll shut down everything in the house and we'll be on the road."

"Sounds good." I lean over to press a kiss to his lips. "We're a good team."

Twenty minutes later, we're headed back to reality as my phone chimes with a text.

MERICA: *Call me before you get to campus. We need to talk.*

JUSTINE: *I'll be there as quick as I can. Talk soon.*

Ryker looks over at me as he pushes the truck harder and faster down the highway.

"Everything okay?"

"Merica wants me to call her, but I'll see her after class. I owe her for calling and waking us up."

"I'm sorry we're missing—"

I cut him off. "Don't be. It's not a big deal. Missing one class isn't going to kill us."

He reaches across the center console and squeezes my hand. "I love you, baby."

"Love you."

We hold hands as we haul ass toward campus.

I should have listened to Merica. I should have called her, shouldn't have hung up on her. If I'd done any of those things, I wouldn't have walked blind into the shitstorm that meets us at the doors of the law school.

When Ryker and I walk into the building, we're still holding hands, and I have one of those *everyone is staring at us* moments.

"Why is everyone looking at us like that?"

He wraps a hand around my hip and pulls me closer. "Because you're fucking gorgeous, and they're all amazed you finally gave me the time of day."

I shake my head because it's more than that. I can practically feel the buzz of gossip flying through the air.

"It's something else. Something bigger."

Ryker presses a kiss to my forehead. "Babe, don't worry so much about everything."

We step out of the elevator, and Ryker is proven wrong.

Everyone *is* watching us. A few look up from newspapers to us and then back down again.

"What the hell is going on?" It's not the student paper they're holding, but the local paper.

Merica rushes toward us. "I told you to call me!" She grabs me by my free hand and drags us both toward a corner. Merica shoves the paper toward Ryker.

"Did you know?"

He takes it from her and flips to the front. My stomach twists and cramps as I lean over his shoulder to read the headline: "Abuse of Power at Every Level."

There's a picture of Justice Grant and a woman I assume is Ryker's mother just below it.

"Fuck." Ryker whispers the curse. "I have to call my dad."

I yank the paper from his hand and read the article as fast as I can.

My eyes lift to Ryker's as I get to the part about his mother being in rehab because she caused an accident and left the scene, which resulted in a law student going to jail. The article says that Justice Grant knew about the accident but didn't report it.

All the pieces start falling into place.

Chad.

Ryker's mother.

The police report I read last week said it was a red car. Was it the same red car under a cover in the garage at the Grants' house? It has to be.

"What . . . ? Your mother . . ." My voice shakes when I start to speak. "Your mom is the one who hit Chad?"

I'm not sure if I expect him to dodge the question, but what I don't expect is stony silence. "I have to talk to my dad."

"You have to get the family story line straight before you can say anything?"

Ryker glares at Merica. "Give us a minute?"

She looks to the open door of the Law Review office behind us. "You've got two, and then I'm coming in. Make her cry and I'll kill you."

Ryker pulls me into the empty office and shuts the door.

"Why didn't you tell me?" My voice is still shaking and betrayal cuts deep within me. "I laid myself *bare* in front of you, and you never said a goddamn thing to let me know that you were hiding something too. Why?" I realize that my questions might be unfair, given the secrets I kept, but . . . "I thought we were done with hiding. I thought everything from here on out was supposed to be *real*. No lies. No secrets. Just *real*."

Ryker's face is an unreadable mask. "I didn't have a choice."

The words hit me like a blow. "Do you have any idea how shitty I felt every time I had the opportunity to come clean and I didn't? Do you know how badly I beat myself up over it? And the only thing you have to say right now is *I didn't have a choice*?"

"What else do you want me to say? That I would've been thrilled to tell you that my mother is a functional alcoholic who drove drunk and hit one of our classmates, and my dad wasn't about to let her go to jail, so he called on me to help clean up her mess?"

"That's why you didn't come? The morning I moved?"

He nods. "I couldn't tell you. Even if I wanted to tell you, my dad wouldn't have let me."

Preserving the family name was more important. It's

not a concept I understand, but apparently it made sense to him.

"Were you ever going to tell me?" I whisper the question because I need to know. I thought we were free and clear of all the bullshit, and that I was the only one living with guilt. And now, after I've shown him every part of me, right down to the ugly, awful memories, I find out that there's more going on than I realized.

He shakes his head. "You didn't need to carry this burden. You've had enough shit in your life. Why should this be your problem? It wasn't relevant to us."

"It wasn't relevant?" I try to keep my voice down, but it raises an octave anyway. "I've known Chad for more than half my life! You don't think that if your mom had turned herself in as the cause of the accident that maybe a judge wouldn't have been more lenient? One word from your dad, or a single offer to help him out with the character and fitness committee, and maybe he wouldn't have dropped out of school? But instead your family decides to keep its secrets and let someone else suffer for your mom's actions. Who does that?" Now that the words are spilling out, I can't stop the rest. "What else are you hiding, Ryker? What else don't you think I can handle knowing?"

He drops his gaze to the floor. "That I knew—"

Before he has a chance to say more, the door of the Law Review office flies open and Merica strides inside. "The dean is looking for you both. More shit hit the fan."

My stomach twists into even bigger knots. *What now?*

"We're not done with this conversation," Ryker says, his face pained, and stabs of guilt slice through me.

I don't even know what to think or feel anymore.

What a fucking disaster.

Chapter 68

Justine

I feel like I'm walking a gauntlet, headed toward a guillotine. How many more blows can keep coming?

The dean stares us both down from across his desk.

"Ms. Porter and Mr. Grant, we've received a report from a student claiming that you've violated the student code of conduct."

"What?" My shock is evident in my tone.

The dean crosses his arms over his chest. "Who is paying your tuition, Ms. Porter?"

I open my mouth to reply but Ryker beats me to it.

"How is that relevant? And what part of the student code of conduct are we accused of violating?"

The dean shifts his gaze from me to Ryker. "That's what we're trying to figure out. We've received a report that you are paying Ms. Porter's tuition in exchange for sexual favors."

No freaking way. One name flashes through my mind. *Kristy Horner.* That bitch.

"You've gotta be joking. That's ridiculous."

Ryker leans forward and meets the dean's stare. "I think we all know who made that accusation, and it's completely bullshit. My father paid Justine's tuition in exchange for her to help me study." He pauses as though gathering himself. His next words hit me like shotgun blasts. "I read the independent contractor agreement they entered into shortly after it was signed, and for the record, my father couldn't have picked a better tutor."

"I read the independent contractor agreement they entered into shortly after it was signed . . ."

He knew. He fucking knew. My brain reels with the information. All those times he pushed me to tell him how I paid for school . . . he already knew.

"Justine can confirm that she felt it would be more fair if they transitioned to a private loan agreement. My father can provide you with copies of both documents."

Ryker finally looks at me, and I can't imagine my face is anything but the picture of shock. *He knew.* And he let me believe that he didn't.

The dean's look of surprise probably rivals mine. "We'd need to see the agreements to confirm, but if what you're saying is the truth, then we have no problem here and the accusation would be wildly incorrect."

"Wildly incorrect? More like malicious and unfounded." Ryker leans forward in his seat. "Is there a provision of the student code of conduct that punishes students for falsely accusing others? Or perhaps in the employee code of conduct that prohibits the sharing of confidential information learned on the job? For instance, if someone's mother were to work in the registrar's office and they shared confidential information with a student."

The dean sits back and crosses his arms. "If you were to

level either of those accusations, they would be investigated seriously because both would indeed be violations of our policies."

"You want my official complaint now to begin your investigation?"

He shakes his head. "I think you've got more than enough to deal with today, Mr. Grant. Tomorrow is soon enough." Looking to me, he adds, "I apologize for dragging you into this, Ms. Porter."

I can't form words yet. My brain is still trying to comprehend that *Ryker knew*. Nodding at the dean, I rush for the door. I yank it open and find Merica standing outside.

"Get me out of here. Please. I need . . . I need to go."

Ryker comes barreling out of the dean's office, but Merica throws a protective arm around my shoulder.

"Justine, wait—"

The dean's voice interrupts from behind him. "Mr. Grant, there's one more issue we need to discuss. Alone."

I know Ryker wants to tell the dean to fuck off, but he can't. It's the miracle I need to escape.

Merica pulls me toward the elevator. "Let's go."

Ryker's blue gaze drills into me. "You can go, but know that I'm coming for you. I'll always come for you."

Chapter 69

Justine

A best friend is called *best* for a reason. Because when your entire life implodes and everything you thought you could count on turns to shit and falls apart, a best friend is there with wine, even if it's not quite noon, to help glue it back together.

Ryker knew.

There's not enough wine in the world to make me comprehend. I babbled the whole thing to Merica on the way home and she just listened, muttering the occasional *holy shit*.

I carried so much guilt for not coming clean, and all that time, he *knew*.

I'm in the shower, my wine on the shelf just outside but still within reach. The spray beats down at me as I replay the events of the morning over and over in my head.

"Jus! You're going to want to see this! I'm recording it for you. Hurry your ass up!"

I have no idea what Merica is yelling about, but I don't think she'd interrupt me at this point for anything that wasn't crazy important.

"What's going on?" I yell through the bathroom door.

"Press conference. Justice Grant. You need to see this."

I shut off the water and grab a towel to wrap around me before rushing into the living room.

"What?"

Merica rewinds whatever she recorded on TV and presses Pause before tossing me the remote. "I'm supposed to go to work, but you need to watch this. And then you need to figure out what the hell you're going to do about Ryker. Because . . . damn, girl, I don't have any advice for that one." She looks at me again with sympathy. "I can call in sick if you want me to. I feel like shit leaving you here."

I shake my head. "No, go. It's okay. I'll be okay. I just need some time alone to think." I wrap my best friend in a hug. "Thank you for everything."

"Anytime, babe. You know I've got your back. Always."

"Love you."

"Love you more."

I sit on the couch in stunned silence, retrieved wineglass clutched in hand, as I watch the press conference for the third time. Tears are streaming down my cheeks because I don't know how else to react.

The former Justice Grant is a strong, proud man, but he looks so humbled as he delivers his resignation from the state supreme court.

"As justices, we are held to the highest standard, and I have not lived up to that standard. Beneath these robes, I am only a man, and that man would do anything to protect his family. The choices I made are my own, and so must the consequences be. As of eight o'clock this morning, I have resigned my position on the court. My wife has also officially resigned her position at Grant Bentham Beckett. We understand the cycle of addiction and have all become victim to it. Today, we break the cycle. We end the lies, the shame, and the hiding. There is nothing we can do to take back our actions, but we will accept all responsibility for them."

His words hit me hard. *We end the lies, the shame, and the hiding.* Justice Grant isn't the only one who has been a victim of the cycle. Ryker has been brought up in this world where you hide the truth to protect others. You keep the shame secret. You tell no one for fear of upsetting the balance.

Maybe that's all he knows . . . how to hide the truth? Wasn't I doing the same thing?

God, what a fucked-up situation this is. Too many secrets to count.

How could I expect him to turn his mother in to the cops when I couldn't bring myself to turn mine in the night she broke into my apartment? And I hadn't seen my mother in years.

So really, how much can I fault him for protecting her? What son wouldn't?

I hit the button to rewind and replay the press conference again, but a knock on the door interrupts me. Wrapping my towel tighter around me, I set my still half-full wineglass on the table and go to the door.

A glance through the peephole reveals Ryker, with hair mussed like he's been jamming his fingers through it. I yank open the door, and he steps inside before pushing it shut behind him.

I wait in silence, because I truly have no idea what to say.

"I'm sorry, so fucking sorry, that I didn't tell you—about my mom and that I knew about your deal with my dad. I can't lose you over this. I can't lose you over anything. I won't let it happen." Ryker's blue eyes are tormented with emotion. "Just . . . give me a chance to get it all out before you say anything."

I swallow. "I'm so freaking tired of all these lies. If you want to tell me anything, it has to be the truth."

Chapter 70

Ryker

Two months earlier

As I waited for Justine to grab whatever she needed to head to class, my dad watched me carefully from the bar where he sipped his coffee.

"What?"

"Your mother would really like you to call her. She's making significant progress."

"And you need to do something for Chad France. He fucking dropped out of school, Dad. How is that fair? Mom's in cushy rehab and he's . . . gone."

"The board of trustees sent a letter when they received notice of his withdrawal stating that although there was no guarantee, the conviction could be explained to the character and fitness committee of the state bar, and that the school would help him in that process."

"And?" I still couldn't get over the raw deal Chad got.

"And he never replied. The second letter went unanswered as well. We can't help him if he doesn't want to help himself."

"How do you know he even got the letters?"

My father shook his head. "We don't, but if I keep pushing the issue, it's going to raise suspicion."

The whole situation left my stomach in a knot, but what the fuck could I do? Turn my mom in to the cops for leaving the scene of an accident while she was too drunk to drive? What kind of son would that make me?

But not saying anything made me feel like a shitty human being every fucking day. Why did she have to drive? Why didn't my dad admit she had a problem and force her into rehab before she could spin out of control?

"Fine. I'll call her. What's the number?"

My dad reached for his pocket. "Crap. I keep forgetting I left my phone on my desk at work. It's on the paperwork in the office too. Want me to grab it for you?"

"I can grab it. Finish your coffee. Where is it?"

"In the file cabinet. Second drawer. It's labeled Pine Crest Manor."

"Always so organized."

"Have to be or I'd lose everything."

My dad turned back to his coffee and paper, and I strode toward the office.

As I was going through the filing cabinet, I spotted the Pine Crest file. Right behind it was a folder labeled Porter, J.

What the hell?

Pulling it out, I flipped it open, expecting to maybe see notes from her externship when she worked for him last semester, but that wasn't what I found. Instead, it was a contract.

I skimmed the terms and my stomach twisted into a knot.

What the fuck?

My dad was paying Justine's tuition in exchange for tutoring services. I thought back to last night. How she told me she couldn't do this.

The words of the contract burned into my brain, I made a quick copy on the printer behind my father's desk and shoved the file back in the cabinet. Paper clutched in one hand, I leaned against the file cabinet and let the knowledge sink in.

What the hell am I going to do with this?

My mind twisted the information over and over until it hit me. It was so fucking simple.

Justine was desperate; I saw it firsthand when she walked into the Vu. What else would she have possibly considered if my dad hadn't made what I recognized as one of his magnanimous grand gestures?

I just wished to fuck he would have clued me in.

What did he think I'd say? *No, I want Justine to drop out.* Not a chance in hell. She wanted this more than anyone I'd ever met, and now I had the ability to make sure she could reach her goals, achieve her dreams . . . and spend time with her. Win her over. Make her mine.

This way, we'd both get what we wanted.

Folding up the paper, I stuffed it in my back pocket and headed out of the office. *I'm not going to fuck this up.*

Chapter 71

Ryker

Present Day

"You've known since that morning? Why didn't you say anything?"

"Because it didn't matter. You needed your tuition paid, and I didn't want you to have to drop out of school." Pausing, I reach out and wrap my hand around hers when she stiffens. "I know that makes me sound like a dick, but why the hell do you think I studied so fucking hard for the midterm to make sure my grades didn't slip? I was already halfway in love with you, and there was no way I was going to let you down. Your degree was way too important for me to fuck up."

"But the deal we made—"

"I wanted you, and I knew you wanted me. I figured that you were pushing me away because you didn't think you could have both me and the tuition money. I wanted you to have it all, so I did what I had to do."

"Then why did you go to the bar and get drunk when

you found out? And drive into that guardrail?"

I can't help but grit my teeth about that. *Fucking stupidest thing I've ever done.*

"Because Kristy threatened you. Threatened to expose all of it. I was fucking pissed—at her, at my dad for leaving you vulnerable to that kind of attack—and for a few minutes, I was pissed at you for not trusting me enough to tell me the truth so we could fight this together."

Chapter 72

Justine

"Why didn't you tell me then?"

I wait for Ryker to answer my question, my mind still trying to keep up with this new revelation.

"Because of everything that happened with your parents. I couldn't. But I wanted to tell you last night—"

And I distracted him by getting him naked . . .

I shake my head and reach for my wine to gulp it down. "Everything between us is built on a foundation of lies. How the hell can we recover from that? How do we even try to move forward?"

Ryker closes the distance between us and lifts his hand to cup my chin. "That's not true. The first time I kissed you, it had nothing to do with tuition, losing your scholarship, or any of that shit. That was as honest as it gets."

"You demanded it as payment! How does that count?"

He lowers his mouth to mine, stopping only an inch away. "Because you wanted that kiss as badly as I did. Tell me that wasn't the beginning of everything for us. That was our foundation."

"But we both—" I start to protest.

"We both fucked up. We both lied. We both kept secrets. Hid the truth. However the hell you want to describe it, neither of us is innocent here. Fuck, is anyone ever truly innocent? The real crime would be throwing away everything we have now." His blue eyes plead with me to agree.

He's right. Neither of us is innocent.

How can I hold it against him that he knew about the agreement but didn't tell me, when I didn't tell him about it to begin with? We're both at fault. We both share the blame. And at the end of the day, even knowing what I know now, I still love him.

"Tell me I didn't lose you, Justine."

I swallow because any feelings of betrayal I had have drained away. "You didn't lose me."

"Thank fuck." Ryker crushes his lips to mine and for long moments, nothing exists but this kiss.

When he finally pulls away, he stares down at me. "I swear to God, there's nothing else. No more secrets. I'm done hiding anything from you."

"Me too."

In my ear, he says, "But that means you need to know that my parents are both unemployed, my free ride to law school is gone now that my dad's no longer a trustee, and I'm going to have to take out student loans to cover the rest."

I pull back and can't help but laugh. "Sounds like we're not all that different, are we?"

"We've never been all that different, Justine. Ever." His lips find mine again, and anything else I have to say is lost to his kiss.

The rest of the world might be spinning out of crazy control, but this I understand. This, I will always understand.

Epilogue

Ryker

Eighteen months later

"Where are we going?"

I'm leading Justine down a sidewalk, but with the blindfold over her eyes, she can't see a damn thing. I turn her in the direction I want her to be facing, and pause. I really fucking hope she likes this.

I pull the blindfold away from her eyes and point across the street. "There. That's where we're going."

She blinks twice and confusion is clear on her features—until she sees the sign.

Porter Law Clinic

Justine's head jerks around toward me. "What is that? Did you do that?"

I nod. "Yeah. I did that."

She looks from me to the sign and then back to me again. "Are you serious?"

The surprise and excitement and disbelief on her face is everything I wanted to see. As a matter of fact, it's the same expression she had when the university's mail room tracked her down to let her know they'd been holding a letter for over a month that was sent to the dorm she lived in during our first year of law school—the last address her Gramps had for her.

The life insurance check wiped out everything she owed my father and enough to cover the rest of her tuition for the year. She graduated debt-free, summa cum laude, just like she and her gramps had dreamed about. I was proud as hell of her.

I was also proud when she got her job at Legal Aid after we both found out we passed the bar exam, and I started clerking at the court of appeals. But three months ago, budgets were slashed and Justine's position was cut. I expected her to be brokenhearted, but that wasn't the case. She finally admitted she'd been frustrated for months because of all the bureaucracy involved in her job, and she wasn't making the difference she'd hoped to make.

She told me about her new dream—to have her own firm. To help clients who didn't qualify for low-income assistance but couldn't afford to pay for big-firm help. She wanted no rules except for the ones she put in place herself.

So she started working out of our condo—the one she'd moved into with me shortly after my father's press conference. However, meeting clients at Unwired wasn't exactly the most glamorous option.

So I decided to make her dream a true reality.

"You want to see the inside?"

"Are you nuts? Of course I do." She presses both hands to her face and looks from the sign to me again. "I can't believe it's real. You did this. I can't believe . . . I don't know what to say."

I thread my fingers through hers and pull her across the quiet street to the front door of her new office. Fishing the keys from my pocket, I hand them to her. I even picked out the keychain specifically for her—it's a small Wonder Woman Pez dispenser.

Her laugh echoes down the street, and it's my favorite sound.

"Really?"

"You think that Wonder Woman costume was forgettable? No way in hell."

Her hand shakes as she pushes the key into the lock and turns it. The glass door opens, and we step inside the small waiting area.

"If you hate the furniture, they'll let us swap it out for something different." I picked simple chrome-and-black chairs with a matching receptionist's desk.

She's practically bouncing with excitement when she unlocks the door to the interior office and peeks into the two small conference rooms and two offices. The biggest office has two desks facing each other.

Justine looks at me in confusion.

"I thought you might want a partner in crime."

Her eyes widen. "Are you serious?"

I nod. "There's no one I'd rather work with, baby."

"But you don't want to work at a firm." She's only half right.

"I didn't want to work at a big firm, but you sold me on making a difference. Let's do it together."

"Are you serious?"

"Absolutely."

Justine throws herself at me and I lift her up in my arms.

"I love you so much. Thank you for this."

"I'd do anything for you."

When I finally set her down, she goes through the office, opening every door and drawer. Her squeals of excitement reassure me that I made the right decision.

Now, I just can't wait to see what she says when she finds the bride Pez dispenser with the ring box . . .

The End

Click here (http://www.meghanmarch.com/#!newsletter/c1uhp) to sign up for my newsletter, and never miss another announcement about upcoming projects, new releases, sales, exclusive excerpts, and giveaways.

I'd love to hear what you thought about Justine and Ryker's story. If you have a few moments to leave a review on the retailer's site where you purchased the book, I'd be incredibly grateful. Send me a link at meghanmarchbooks@gmail.com, and I'll thank you with a personal note.

Also by Meghan March

BENEATH Series:
BENEATH THIS MASK
BENEATH THIS INK
BENEATH THESE CHAINS
BENEATH THESE SCARS
BENEATH THESE LIES

FLASH BANG Series:
FLASH BANG
HARD CHARGER

DIRTY BILLIONAIRE TRILOGY:
DIRTY BILLIONAIRE
DIRTY PLEASURES
DIRTY TOGETHER

DIRTY GIRL DUET:
DIRTY GIRL
DIRTY LOVE

Acknowledgments

Wow. This one was a doozy. Note to self for next time: don't try to write a book immediately after a one-week road trip that spans more than three thousand miles and three countries (with two dogs). If not for the collective help of my fabulous team, this book might never have seen the light of day.

Special thanks go out to:

Pam Berehulke and Angela Marshall Smith, for your patience in helping me make this story shine.

Angela Smith, Jamie Lynn, and Natasha Gentile, for your insight and kind words.

Danielle Sanchez, for every amazing thing you do, which goes far beyond PR.

Emma Hart, for creating this drool-worthy cover and overall just being freaking awesome.

My Runaway Readers, for being the best cheerleaders on the interwebz. I truly can't thank you enough for your endless support.

My crew of fabulous bloggers, for tirelessly spreading the word about books simply for the love of books.

My family, for supporting even my biggest dreams.

JDW, for so many things I can't even put into words, but most especially for helping me live out my crazy dreams. My life wouldn't be what it is today without you. I love you.

Every reader who picks up this book, for taking a chance on me and allowing me to write you stories every day. I have the best job imaginable, and I'll endeavor never to take it for granted.

Author's Note

I'd love to hear from you. Connect with me at:

Website: www.meghanmarch.com

Facebook: www.facebook.com/MeghanMarchAuthor

Twitter: www.twitter.com/meghan_march

Instagram: www.instagram.com/meghanmarch

About the Author

Meghan March has been known to wear camo face paint and tromp around in the woods wearing mud-covered boots, all while sporting a perfect manicure. She's also impulsive, easily entertained, and absolutely unapologetic about the fact that she loves to read and write smut.

Her past lives include slinging auto parts, selling lingerie, making custom jewelry, and practicing corporate law. Writing books about dirty-talking alpha males and the strong, sassy women who bring them to their knees is by far the most fabulous job she's ever had.

She loves hearing from her readers at meghanmarchbooks@gmail.com.

CPSIA information can be obtained
at www.ICGtesting.com
Printed in the USA
BVHW070709260620
582048BV00002B/9